god face

Devian Nikei

Other Nikei Novels by Devian Nikei

Safety in Lovers
Just in Case

Devian Nikei

god face

By

Devian Nikei

ISBN-10: 0692566929
ISBN-13: 978-0692566923
BISAC: Fiction/Romance/New Adult

Interior design by Devian Nikei
Printed in the U.S.A.

A publication of Nikei Novels Publishing-Charlotte

To order copies and other merchandise or for more information, contact:

www.deviancebydevian.com
email: nikeinovels@deviancebydevian.com

This is book is dedicated to my nephew, Thomas and posthumously to my sister, Connie

Foreword

I am quite certain that this life is not the beginning or the end of our
being...

Today I experienced a most overwhelming sensation of déjà vu. I was
positive that I had been in a certain place doing a particular activity before.
I even had a memory of the situation and had done things very differently
in the other instance, than what I was doing at the time. So I began to
romanticize the idea that maybe there were these other versions... alternate
endings, if you will, of our lives. Possibly, they were even playing out
simultaneously somewhere in another dimension. Perhaps this Devian
chose to stay with a certain guy, or take another job, or abandon some
project, maybe move to another country; but another Devian made a
different choice and was somewhere else completely in this other life.
Maybe that Devian was rich and happily married. Maybe another Devian
was homeless or drug-addicted. The possibilities could be limitless.

I can remember being a young girl and having these books which gave
you a choice at the end of each chapter. There would be a question such as,
do you open the door... or do you walk away? Then it would say, if you
opened the door, turn the page... but if you walked away, go to page 59,
etc.

I thought those books were so great. Based on the choices you made
while reading, you could control the storyline. Sometimes you would get
the same ending no matter what you did. But sometimes you could get a
whole other ending, as you skipped around from page to page reading the
story that you were creating with your decisions. I was thinking back to my
memory of those books, when I started writing this one. I started thinking
that free will must be something like those books. There are certain factors
you cannot control; such as your race, your parents, when and where you
are born or die, your gender, etc. In that respect, some aspects of your story
are already predetermined. But then however, there are all these choices
and decisions that lie in our hands, which shape our destiny from day to
day.

I was in a place of wondering if simple- possibly minute- decisions that I made could have had resounding effects on my life and current situation. I thought about the day I met my ex-husband in the cafeteria. Something in my soul told me to just walk on by- just keep going, but I didn't want to be rude (I was young)... and so goes the story. During the bad times of our marriage, I would always go back to that day... always back to that unheeded warning. Not to the day we wed, nor the day our first child was born... nor the day we bought our house... always just that one day... in the cafeteria. It always stuck out in my mind as the one day that put my life on a certain trajectory. I always wondered who and where I would be if I had just ignored his advances and walked right on by that day.

I think mostly all people can pinpoint that *one day-*

A missed opportunity... an epic fail... the wrong place at the wrong time. Whatever it was, you're positive in your mind that if you could go back to that one day, your life would be different. This book is about that one day. It's about a second chance at that one day... to do it right or at least the way you think is right... Would it make a difference? Would the outcome be better... or worse?

The issue I have found is that while we are busy with the work of perfecting our own lives, we are seemingly unaware of how those decisions and changes would affect other people's lives. What if every action or inaction is a pebble dropped in a pond with rippling waves of reverberating effects? Even if we are just here today and gone tomorrow, isn't there some irrevocable and undeniable imprint? Some eternal evidence of our existence. Because I knew this book was different from all my others, and therefore probably the first and last of its kind, I really wanted to fill it with the full gambit of my research. I wanted to span the human experience (or the human experiment, if you will) with the farthest most wide-reaching systems that I have encountered and experienced.

Some people have remarked that my stories and novels seem abrasive or far-fetched at times. There is definitely an element of imagination, embellishment and fancy woven into my tales. However, I have not now nor will I ever be dishonest in my perspective as a writer. I have to be true enough to myself and my audience to authenticate my stories with real, ugly, unyielding, uncomfortable, and oftentimes disheartening- **truth**. Many of these lines come from my observances and experiences of real life. At least, real life as I have seen and known it. These novels are my progeny- **my** legacy and I understand that is an indelible fact. With each line I write, I make a permanent imprint on the fabric of not just my own life, but the lives of my readers as well. I want to share all that I am, from exactly wherever I am. Whether my experience is atypical or universal- it is... honest. This is my race with destiny.

The problem with trying to change destiny is that as you manipulate certain factors, you cannot account for how those changes will affect a new situation. I present to you a story about that vast, relentless vanity which is trying to deify humanity.

In this book, I will attempt to show the faces that we never fully see, not even in the clean, polished mirror of the soul. The face which for all of the hours spent looking in glass; for all of the photographs; for all of the covering up- cannot be easily detected; the face we sometimes don't even recognize. Who are we really when no one is watching but God? Some might say that a person is two-faced. We all have a duplicitous nature in that there are things we keep hidden deep inside of us, in the dark of anonymity. This novel, god face, is about seeing past race, color, nationality, socioeconomic, political, religious and any other divisive factors, to see all people as an extension of the same life force.

Enjoy,

Devian Nikei ☆

"...For warnings from the future to the past must be taken in the past. Today may change Tomorrow, but once Today is gone, Tomorrow can only look back in sorrow that the warnings were ignored."

- Rod Serling,
Creator of "The Twilight Zone" circa 1964

Prelude

Evening is the best time.

The early evening is my favorite time of the day. It is the time in my home when the family comes together. Mother pulls a huge, roasted hen from the oven. The warmth of the heat wafting from the mouth of the oven makes its way over to me, offering a cozy hug, as I watch her from the kitchen doorway. Visible steam, so fragrant with spices, hovers in the air just above the deep pan. It swirls and sways in an alluringly seductive dance, a ghostly imp teasing and taunting me with the promise of succulent, flavorful poultry.

I am not old enough to help my mother. She calls me Under-foot. If I step even one toe into the kitchen while she is cooking, she will run me out like a stray cat. She has a sixth sense about these things. She knows– even without looking, that I am standing here... and that is fine. But the second my heel touches the linoleum, she will instantly order me away– also without the acknowledgment of a glance.

So- for that cause, I will remain silent and motionless, waiting in eager anticipation at the doorway, but safe from her scolding. I watch my mother- graceful and elegant. She doesn't know how beautiful I think she is. The glow of her smooth brown complexion captivates me as her slender arms, the color of milk chocolate candy bars, strain under the weight of the roasting pan. Mother is strong- invincible even, like an African goddess, as she heaves the enticing bird up onto the stovetop.

Then... as if its aroma had a voice with which to beckon, or better yet– some supernatural power to transport my father home, he appears beside me at the doorway of the kitchen. I peer up at him, with eyes full of adulation. Father stands, in his soiled, navy-blue work uniform, as magnificent to me as a Mandinka warrior back from the victory of battle. His shoulders are slighted bowed from his labor, but nonetheless powerful, as he leans against the doorframe. His sooty hand is heavy, as he offers his masculine gesture of affection in the form of a pat on my head. He remains like me, silent and motionless at the edge of the kitchen. Like me, mother will unleash her discipline on him, if he steps foot into the kitchen. But unlike me, it is because he is dirty.

Like me, he is in socks. His work boots, heavy with the weight of grime, sit beside the front door, outside on the porch. He, like me, only came to admire her– just a glimpse of her angelic frame before he is off to prepare himself for dinner. He, like me, is spellbound at the presentation of her. Pristine and unblemished in her bright, yellow dress, protected by a pink checkered apron. Her hair neatly arranged, and constantly rearranged into a French bun. Our very own beautiful, Black June Cleaver. We know what we have in her and she knows what she has in us.

We are her men. Strong and Black like the coal that surrounds a perfect, gleaming diamond. The Black man she married, taken as a gift from God's hand, and the Black man she produced like a treasure, a rare Black pearl in the world. For all the greatness that her hands have wrought, we both stand in awe of her.

"Your bath is waiting upstairs," she says without the acknowledgement of a glance. "Hurry up before it gets cold," she states warmly, offering her feminine gesture of affection in the form of her internal smile at my father's presence.

Their love language is nonverbal, demonstrated through compromise and sacrifice. My father shuffles away hurriedly. His weariness barely visible amid the anxiousness to become presentable for his mate. He knows the reward for his tireless efforts– the feel of her soft, fragrant skin against his. His yearning for her touch... a passion so intense that it conveys itself with groans deep within his soul that mere words cannot express.

A longing so desperate that it begs for release, when my father- fresh and still moist from his bath, reaches for my mother's waist, then pulls her tightly to him. Although it shouldn't, his lust embarrasses her. Under the heat of his touch, she melts, transforming from his wife back into the teen-aged girl that he fell in love with years ago. She giggles against his cheek, as she turns to hug his neck.

"You are mine," he whispers in her ear, squeezing the plump flesh of her full hips so tightly that she tenses. "Give me what I want."

He wraps his huge hands around her head and kisses her long, then pecks tiny anxious kisses on her lips, like a thirsty man lapping cool water from his hands. She accepts him and returns his kisses because his breath is minty. Their dark lips swim together jumping and diving like beautiful, Black dolphins in an ocean of desire. Her hands slip from his neck and journey along his broad, muscular shoulders as she loses herself in his seduction.

"Well," Mother says finding her way out of the fog. "You can have your fill of me... after you fill your stomach," she states coyly, pointing towards the dining room, containing a table covered with heaping bowls.

His sexual appetite still not abated by her reference to food, my father treats himself to the entree of her neck instead, caressing the soft skin with gentle, sucking lips. My father's hands grope desperately at her body, like a blind man hoping to find his way home in its darkness. My mother clears her throat abruptly.

"Courtney honey..."

My appetite could not be ignored either. The biscuits summon me from their plate, as I wait at the dining room table for my parents. My stomach grumbles, but rather than take the risk of reaching for one and drawing back a nub, I choose instead to seek them out. I stand once again at the doorway, peering with large, round innocent eyes into the light of the kitchen from the darkness without.

"We have company," she sighs lowly, resigning from their passionate exchange.

We take our seats for supper. Father, in his pressed shirt and slacks, sits at the head of the table. He takes our hands and bows his head. Likewise, we follow his example. He says the grace, humbly thanking the Lord Jesus for the meal which sits before us, for the lovely Black hands that prepared it, and for all of our many blessings.

"Amen," in unison.

Father carves. Mother serves. Each plate is neatly arranged with chicken, whipped potatoes smothered in yellow gravy, and a side of cabbage mixed with collard greens, just the way my father likes them. When Mother passes out the biscuits, Father is the only one to receive a double portion. He holds a thick, fluffy biscuit, using it to shovel the food onto his fork, as he eats from both hands.

With no food left on our plates, Mother awards, to Father and I, a piece of carrot cake with cream cheese frosting for the seemingly insignificant accomplishment of a full belly. Our decadent reward is devoured down to moist crumbs, which are carefully collected against the back of the fork, and then enjoyed as well.

Nighttime is different.

We are not all together at night. My parents are in their bedroom and I, tucked into my bed down the hall, sleep soundly.

Well- maybe not so soundly tonight.

Tonight, I am awakened by a sound not unfamiliar, although occasional- the sound of my parents pleasuring each other. I used to think the shrieks that escaped my parents closed door were bad, possibly the rage from a fight, but they assured me that was not the case. Actually, the muffled thumps were quite the contrary. So it doesn't disturb me anymore. Now, I smile to myself instead. As I hear my mother laugh, I am happy to know that my parents enjoy each other's company so much.

Although I am separate from them, I feel the love of their affection, even in my room. I feel like the warm, gooey marshmallow center of a S'more in the blaze of my parent's passion for each other. I am comforted, as I return to slumber in the luxury of my own soft, twin bed.

All is calm.

All is bright.

I am six years old.

And this is the end.

I remember the very day that I became colored.

**- Zora Neale Hurston,
<u>How It Feels to Be Colored Me</u>**

CHAPTER ONE

"Courtney Ulysses Turnage Jr."

Miss Calhoun, his sixth-grade history teacher, insists on using his full name. This is to humiliate him in front of his peers. They always laugh at the presentation of his middle name.

"Yes ma'am," C.J. mumbles, more upset at being interrupted from his meditation than embarrassed in front of the class. C.J. has no friends. They have all gone on to Junior High School.

"Do you ever consider what you will be when you grow up?" Miss Calhoun slides her thick glasses up on her nose. Her eyes are as dark as onyx stones. Her skin is as shiny and black as a newly tarred road after a summer rain. "Do you ever think about your future, Mr. Turnage?"

Miss Calhoun plops her large, round behind down on the edge of her long, steel desk. She and Courtney Jr. both, are as Black as midnight in a sky absent of the moon and stars. Their blackness is darkness, so devoid of light, that one cannot find their hand in front of their own face in it. The blackness, which covers them is more than the complexion of their skin– it is an ignorance that cloaks the mind in darkness.

Courtney Jr. is beautiful... like the smooth surface of an undisturbed cup of pure, black coffee. His eyes, dark pools, reflect all of the comeliness in the world- everything that is exquisite. He is full of unlocked, untapped potential. The strength and magnificence of a Kushite pyramid deceptively disguised in the frame of a young, impoverished Black child.

C.J. is, in the opinion of many, the antithesis of beauty and therefore by definition, the very embodiment of it. Beauty is that which commands our full regard, that which makes our hearts still in reverence. If Courtney were not beautiful, then why would people who do not know him, even exert themselves so much as to hate him?

People never have, and never will, spend their precious energy trying to eradicate or subjugate that which does not command their undivided attention. Despite all the efforts on the part of so many, both White and Black, to correct the problem of Blackness, there never has been nor ever will be a skin bleaching cream or colorist propaganda that can stamp out that manner of Blackness. For that reason, the Blackness will always be feared.

C.J. doesn't know it, but the world is his oyster; even though he is little more to it than dirt. He is a Black grain of sand, an irritation to the oyster, which forces it to protect itself by creating a Black pearl inside of its walls– That Black pearl, a rare treasure to the world, is more valuable than the oyster will ever be– and thus, that is the source of the hatred... *jealousy.*

Miss Calhoun is not beautiful.

One could call her hideous– a word that could only partially describe her Blackness. Her blackness is not the sole product of skin pigmentation. It is the bleakness that grabs a spirit by the neck and wrestles it to the ground in defeat, smashing its face down into the black dust of despair. Casting over said spirit- a long, dark shadow that will never be illuminated by the light of love, or even the hope of the light of love.

Miss Calhoun's Blackness hides itself under a dense, elaborate drape of self-hatred so expansive that one cannot reach the end of it. This self-hatred is as deep and bottomless as a black abyss, and Miss Calhoun has dropped many a Black child into it, so that she can have company. Miss Calhoun only perpetuates the same oppression she has experienced, the abuse that shaped her own life.

How did she become such a monster?

To understand that– you would have to walk a mile in her skin. But how could one describe what it means to be clothed in Black skin?... To wear it like an outdated suit that cannot be removed when the fashion changes.

Well, to start, you could turn off the lights in a room until you are covered in darkness, until you can no longer see anything at all. Then you will begin to encounter just a fragment of the Blackness. When in the pervasive darkness of that room, other people can look directly at you but never see you as a person, never see anything more than the blackness which cloaks and covers you. It is then that you begin to experience the Blackness, to observe its vacuous barrenness.

This Blackness cannot be explained in terms that everyone can understand. Only those like Courtney and Miss Calhoun, who have been harnessed with and become accustomed to the desolation of Black skin, can empathize with it.

C.J. has transcended, but Miss Calhoun has plummeted to her demise, into the despair of self-hatred– and a hatred of all things Black. The Blackness has stolen her very soul. She had to sell it away to afford the cost of living in skin as Black as hers.

Miss Calhoun has come to identify herself within the catalog of vile, Black idioms such as– the Black cat, the Black sheep, the Black kettle, the Black ball, the Black skillet, the Black Spade, the Black market, the Black list, the Black mail, the Black book, and the Black pot (which also called the kettle Black).

Add to that list the Black man, the Black woman, and the Black child; then the inventory is complete. Now all of the Blackness is accounted for and ascribed its respective baseness.

Miss Calhoun has never in her life been told that she is pretty. The very measure of every woman's worth. She has been made to feel useless, as if she should never have been born, as if the Blackness is a hole where her life should have been. All she has is discipline. All she has ever known is insult. These are the principles on which Miss Calhoun's education was founded. And now, it is all she has to offer her people. This is what she will teach every Black child that she instructs about the world. This is her definition of– Education.

The world hates us. It fears us even... because we are monsters.

A drop of liquid activator from her jheri curl drips down the side of her face. Miss Calhoun promptly wipes it away with a tissue. Despite all of her efforts to conform to the European standards of beauty, she failed even to attain acceptance amongst her own race. Placed into an impossible competition against the *Red Bone* with *good hair*, what else could she do but give up. Miss Calhoun is not good for much anymore. She is broken beyond repair. Broken, from a child, in the place where fairies, leprechauns and unicorns should live. Long before she could come to believe in Santa Claus, the virtues of belief, faith, hope... and even love– were snatched from her into the vast void of her Blackness. The Blackness, which covers the surface of her skin, has now penetrated into the deepest tissues of her heart, severing her from all that is good.

All Black women have bad attitudes...

The wound– the anger has festered over, rotting her from the inside out, making her acrid to everyone she encounters. She does not want to be... does not even mean to be so- intolerable. She still desires to be loved just like everybody else does, no matter how unattainable it may be for her. But the rage of bitterness, like vinegar has pickled her, souring her demeanor into an incurable, possibly terminal condition called Blackness.

"That is true," Miss Calhoun thinks to herself and then hates herself, embarrassed for embodying the stereotype.

"Yes ma'am, I do think about my future," C.J. answers dismally, letting his mind wander into the dense Blackness that his foreseeable destiny.

"Well then... What do you see yourself doing when you grow up?" she asks with mild irritation.

Courtney Jr. conducts a lengthy deliberation, as if he has never pondered the question before, as if he must choose from a long list of possibilities. But C.J. is not making selections. He knows the answer. He has always known the answer, but never vocalized it before. "I wanna' be a astronaut," he answers with the satisfaction of a visually-impaired, elderly woman who has finally threaded her needle. The light bulb comes on within him and pierces the darkness. He sees clearly, but his inner glow hurts Miss Calhoun's eyes. She must break him... like she is broken. She must stamp out his light, before he has the chance to hope or she has the chance to see her own reflection clearly in the mirror of his childlike heart.

"Now that doesn't seem very rational, Mr. Turnage," she replies mockingly. The other children in the classroom begin to snicker into their palms, knowing that Miss Calhoun is about to tear Courtney apart for the class to observe... again.

"Since NASA began sending men into space in 1968 until this very day in 1986, there have only been two Black-American astronauts to go into space and one of them died in flight. I know you can't possibly think you have what it takes to be the third."

"No ma'am," C.J. answers with a tiny smile. "I hope to be at least the twentieth Black astronaut by that time." His internal contentment beams on his face. It cuts Miss Calhoun to her heart. C.J.'s confidence confounds her. *Doesn't he know who he is?* How can he have the audacity to think that he can afford a commodity as expensive as... *hope*? Courtney Jr. is not only Black, but add to his list of social handicaps poverty and you have quite a destitute situation. Miss Calhoun wonders where could he have attained his name brand hope?

That kind of hope is almost always reserved for the White, and often the *high-yellah*, occasionally the *dirty-red*, but it almost never manages to trickle down the color scheme of hues to their shade of Black. Their Blackness almost always swallows hope whole and spits out the bones.

C.J. folds his arms on his desk and lowers his chin into his elbow, preparing for lift off. He will leave the atmosphere of the classroom and go back to hovering somewhere high overhead in his imagination.

"Get your head up off that desk," Miss Calhoun snips, tapping the edge with her meter stick. She glares at him with visible disdain. Repulsion drips from her twisted lips like saliva. "What does your father do, Mr. Turnage?"

"My daddy is dead," C.J. hisses lowly, brooding with a rare defensiveness. He usually disregards Miss Calhoun's ridicule and allows her weekly lynching of his character without much resistance, but the subject of his father is the landmine that just may end her rebuke of him once and for all... one way or another.

Miss Calhoun senses the invisible boundary and decides to retreat a bit, leaving her toes at the very edge of the line without crossing it. "What did he do for a living, while he was still living?" she inquires with considerable reservation.

C.J. eyes Miss Calhoun maliciously, as he wrings his mind for an appropriate response. He has never been a disrespectful child, so he feels inclined and somewhat obligated to answer her question.

"My father was a mechanical engineer," he replies boldly, with a tinge of haughtiness.

The truth–

Courtney Sr. was a mechanic, but C.J. heard somewhere that you could add the word engineer to just about any profession and make it sound distinguished. For example, custodial engineer sounds better than janitor and structural engineer is an improvement over construction worker. C.J. smiled internally at his cleverness.

"Well, Mr. Turnage," Miss Calhoun sighs, both surprised by his pedigree and disappointed at the lack of ammunition for her point. "Given your current grades and your obvious contempt for education, maybe you should consider a more reasonable occupation. Perhaps a skilled trade like auto mechanics or brick masonry would be more suitable for your... *talents*," she offers with a broad smile, genuinely pleased at the pockets of quiet laughter that burst like tiny bubbles throughout the classroom.

Miss Calhoun found the nerve, the one that C.J. kept hidden from her, so she couldn't get her rocks off at his expense. She realizes as she watches the young boy begin to fume that she has secured a tiny victory in the war against Blackness. She managed to snag yet another Black child and toss him down into the deep, dark ditch of ruin, before he can know anything other than the icy chill of disappointment.

"I say these things to light a fire under your hiney, Mr. Turnage."

C.J. is sure that Miss Calhoun would much rather set him on fire than to set one without the hope that it would consume him.

"Every one of you sitting here in this class," Miss Calhoun continues on diplomatically, satisfied with the oozing wound she has punctured in C.J.'s heart. "… should be aware that history is not a dead subject. It is more than mere, meaningless words on a page. History is as alive as you and me… constantly changing and evolving, even as we change and evolve."

It was then that the idea first surfaced in the dark, murky waters of C.J.'s mind. The concept floated to the top like a dead man's bloated body. It could not be denied contemplation.

Could history really be like a live person? Did the past have a will or plans for the future, just like people do? Could the past have hope… a real hope for the future independent of what actually happens in the future?

"Those who don't know their history are doomed to repeat it…"

Courtney Jr. thought back to his English class. He liked literature– poetry especially. The words of a poem by Langston Hughes began to come to him. Foggy and hazy at first, but clearer as he concentrated.

What happens to a dream deferred?

C.J. began to meditate on that idea.

What does happen to that dream? Does it just charge on, like an empty, runaway freight car, continuing on to its destination without an occupant? What about life in general? Could it be that we all have various futures, like alternate universes? Maybe destiny is a large house with many fully furnished rooms that do not disappear even after we choose one. What happens to all those unfulfilled plans and hopes? Do they get heaped up into a refuse pile to be burned? But how can that be… when they (the hopes and the dreams) continue to live on in our hearts and haunt us in our sleep?

"... cannot be erased, Mr. Turnage?"

Maybe we can just leave this room and choose another one. What if I could go back and change one minor event, thereby rerouting and rewriting my own history? Could it even be possible that somewhere I am living a life completely unlike this one? The life I would have had if my father never died...

"... what is done in the past can never be changed."

Maybe

"Mr. Turnage?"

Just... maybe

A beam of brightly colored hope bursts from C.J.'s chest, so luminous that no one in the class could deny its painful glare. They almost had to squint just to tolerate his radiant smile.

"Did you hear me, Mr. Turnage?" Miss Calhoun yelps sharply with great annoyance at the boy, who lacks the luxury of being able to ignore her. A child who, by all respects, should worship at her feet- clamoring for the opportunity to receive this education.

Education

The only thing that could possibly make C.J. of some use to the world one day, even in his state of irrevocable Blackness.

"Yes ma'am," Courtney Jr. responds courteously, with euphoria in his eyes as the smile fades from his face like the sun setting down into the horizon.

"Well I hope you have been paying attention because history is a very important subject. Without this history class, you will be doomed to repeat... the sixth grade *again*. I hope you understand me, Mr. Turnage."

C.J.'s commute home, usually a race as swift as his legs can carry him, was slowed to more of a saunter, drifting haphazardly along like a dead leaf blown by a late autumn breeze. This afternoon was much too chilly for his leisurely stroll, seeing as C.J.'s shabby jacket was very lightweight for the frigid conditions. But Courtney didn't care about the icy nip in the air. He was being warmed internally by the mirth from memories of his father. They burned within him like a furnace, producing a faint, glowing smile on his shivering lips.

C.J. didn't have to worry, as many children do, that his mother would get on to him about being improperly dressed for the weather. Camille didn't care what he put on, or even where he wore it for that matter. C.J. assumed that his mother would still be asleep when he arrived at their low-income duplex in Dalton Village. She usually doesn't wake until late in the afternoon. Just a little nap, to revive her for drunken binges that last from evening into the early morning.

The evenings are different for C.J. now. No longer the happy days, when he ate meals at the dinner table with his family. All tradition died with his father. His mother became a hollowed out stump, a shadow of her former splendor, unable to give or receive love. C.J. watches each day as she deteriorates into a state of self-loathing, waiting... and waiting, just... waiting for the chariot that took her husband and her very soul away to come back and claim her body in the sweet surrender of death.

Pass me not, oh, gentle Savior

Death–

That is her daily prayer– her fantasy. The most blissful hope that she has left. She dreams of it daily. Her death– the slow poisoning that her son has the unfortunate torture of witnessing. She hates herself for being a coward, for not having the strength to just get it over with, to end the perpetual misery for herself and her child. If she were more brave, she would just pull a trigger and splatter her brains across her bedroom wall, leaving a smoking, Black hole where her life used to be.

"Camille," C.J. calls to his mother. "Camie..."

He doesn't call her Mother anymore, because she is not... his mother... anymore. He presses lightly on her shoulder, but she doesn't stir. She lays, wrapped tightly in a blanket like a swaddled baby, on the tired, tattered sofa that willingly exposes its underlying springs and wood frame like the hookers at the corner of their street.

Hear my humble cry

"Camille," C.J. growls with more assertion, his voice gruff with agitation, as he shakes his mother's shoulders roughly.

While the others Thou are calling

Camille swims against the current of the waves. She fights hard until her arms are weary from exhaustion. Then the sudden acquiescence washes over her, the realization that she will not escape the will of the ocean. She lays back and lets the surges crash down onto her body. The waves beat forcefully against her. She surrenders, as each swell crests high above her head, then swallows her up, pressing her beneath the surface. She drifts down, swirling in a death spiral to the bottom.

Dear Lord, do not pass me by

"Camille!"

She hears her name and knows that she must be dead because it is Courtney who calls out. His voice travels through the dark water, a vibration that can be perceived more as a feeling– or emotion, than an audible sound. "Camille," Courtney bellows urgently. She looks for him but cannot find him in the darkness of the ocean. His large, strong hand, like salvation, reaches down into the water and wraps tightly around her wrist. With a mighty tug, he yanks her back up toward the surface. The water is so heavy on her body that she can offer no assistance. She drifts listlessly as she is drawn from the darkness into the light.

The Light

She squeezes her lids closed, as blinding rays of sun pierce her eyes. She opens them slowly, blinking heavily. Her vision is blurred at first, but then Courtney appears before her face... in a halo of light. It is him– her one and only love, staring down at her. She reaches out to touch his face. His eyes are full of furious rage.

"Damn Ma," C.J. heaves the words at her like a ten-pound medicine ball, as he flinches away from her touch. "You scared the shit out of me."

Camille blinks, dispersing the vision of her husband and her son comes into view. He stands, arms crossed over his chest, in front of the window between the curtains he just opened. He is almost a mirror image of his father. At only thirteen years old, he is already 5'11', towering over his mother. You almost couldn't tell him from his father at that age, if it weren't for his eyes.

His eyes

Which burn incessantly, day and night, with anger. A rage that will not be satisfied with any of the momentary joys that should be experienced by a child. The bright light of anticipation which dances in the eyes of young children, enticing like sweet powdered sugar sprinkled over doughnuts, has long gone out in C.J.'s. There is only an empty Blackness, so cold in his stare, that it is sometimes frightening to his mother. In that way, Junior differs from Courtney Sr. His eyes were always kind, soft and moist, like he was almost always on the verge of tears. Especially when he laughed, his tender eyes glowed like romantic candles against the backdrop of his smoldering dark skin.

Camille swoons at the memory of her dead husband.

"Don't do that shit again, Camille," C.J. erupts at her, with the authority of a fully-grown man. "I thought you were-"

"Dead," she interrupts cheerfully, excited by the image of it.

"No-" he answers angrily. "Sick. I thought something was wrong with you. I was about to call the ambulance."

"I didn't mean to scare you, C.J." His mother beckons to him with her arms in the gesture of a hug. Her voice softens with a rare sympathy in its tone. "Come here."

C.J. eyes his mother suspiciously, figuring that she must be in the musing stage of drunk, which precedes sloppy drunk on its way to belligerent drunk. But he obliges her because this would be the first time she has offered to hug him in months. So he bows his head down level with hers.

Whap

She smacks his face so unexpectedly hard that he tumbles to the floor, hitting his shoulder on the dusty, scuffed hardwood boards. "I'm still your fucking mother," she barks at him, pointing her finger down in his face. Camille instantly feels guilty, in the place where the mother in her used to live. She pushes it down. At this point, she has so many things to be ashamed of that she dares not allow the floodgate to open. She throws back the blanket and sits up on the sofa. She reaches for her pack of cigarettes.

"If you done forgot who you talking to, then I'm the one to remind you," she huffs in frustration when she finds the package empty. She looks around the coffee table, shoving magazines on the floor in the frenzy of her search. The roaches scatter quickly from their disturbed resting place.

Camille doesn't even flinch when one runs over her fingers. She simply flicks it away, undeterred in her lioness-like hunt for a cancer stick.

"Shit," she finally relents and abandons the mission. She sits back against the creaking coils of the once beige, now brown sofa. "Damn," she groans lowly to herself, licking her lips and scratching her head of nappy, disheveled hair. She rubs her hands together, dispersing the grease on her fingertips. She sulks listlessly, then sits up suddenly. She reaches down into her bra. The strap slip from beneath her three-day worn purple tank top and over her shoulder. Delight brightens her face when her hand emerges with a soggy, half-smoked cigarette. She retrieves her lighter from the ashtray on the end table and sticks the drooping cigarette into her mouth. Her eyes roll back, as she pulls on a long drag; sucking desperately like an infant at its mother's nipple. Her pleasure is fleeting when her eyes return to C.J., who has spent the entire time shimmering to a boil in the corner of the living room.

"You lookin' froggy, C.J.," his mother says, her eyes squinted with hostility equal to his own. "If you got some thought about laying a hand on me, then you can just get your Black ass out of my fucking house." The smoke hovers around her face. She watches him with the darkly-rimmed, yellow eyes of an owl.

Courtney doesn't break the stare. He sits curled up in a ball, staring out from under his hands at her. His jaw clenches. The heat in his face is unbearable, both from the slap as well as his intense fury at his mother. He wishes that he, like a dragon, could breathe fire; relieve the pressure in his head by unleashing on her all of his unbridled wrath, so as to envelope her with flames.

His mother tires from the game of Chicken. "You got something you want to get off your chest?" She dares with little more than a smoking filter between her fingers.

The temperature rises in his bubbling pot of anger. Violent images of his hands around Camille's throat flash across his mind. He imagines strangling her, shaking her limp body like a rag doll.

"Boy, you wanna' say something?" She hollers. Her left eye twitches with the intensity of her command.

"No," he growls under his breath. The anger is a tight, painful knot in his chest. His breaths sting when he exhales. His eyes begin to tear up from the agony of holding back the beast that wrestles within him, clawing and ripping at his chest.

"No... **What**?" She asks with raised eyebrows. Camille is mocking him now. His rage revives and makes one final escape attempt.

"No ma'am," C.J. blares out, then presses his lips closed, releasing just enough pressure to dissuade a meltdown. The tears slip from his eyes. He is humiliated but more because he is an orphan than the words of this imposter who poses daily as his mother.

"That's what I thought you meant," she says, gnawing on the words and then spitting them at his feet like chewing tobacco.

"Camille," the familiar baritone voice calls through her screen door. That is Jerome. He is one of three men who can be called upon to sponsor his mother with monetary sums in exchange for certain services rendered.

"Come on in, Jerome," she yells back. She situates her bra straps back up on her shoulders and smoothes (as best she can) the stray halo of hair at the front of her head back into her ponytail. She stands up from the sofa with only saggy underwear to cover her bottom half. C.J. is sickened by the sight of his mother so scantily dressed. Zebra-striped stretch marks decorate the cream corn-like appearance of her cellulite thighs. He turns his head and tries to scrubs the image from his mind before it sets in like a stubborn stain.

"Hey there, sugar," Camille coos with feigned coyness. "You caught me off guard. I ain't know you was coming through today."

Jerome is what many women consider attractive. He is light-skinned with hair that lays down in soft, shiny waves on his head. He wears his navy Members Only Jacket and matching shell-toe Adidas with fat laces when he comes to the ghetto. On another day, Jerome would look like new money in a business suit because he works with White people over at the Observer, but he dresses down– more casual for the hood, so the dope fiends don't rob him. Jerome is young, Black and successful. He lives in the high-class Negro luxury of Clanton Park in a big, brick house. He has a wife and two well-kept girlfriends; however, none of the aforementioned company includes Camille. Camille is a sidepiece who is not even distinguished enough to have a title. If these were the end credits of "The Jerome Lifetime Movie", it would read:

Smoking Woman #2- Camille Turnage.

Still the cast of female characters grows, and despite the fact that any one of the project chicks would be happy to be his Welfare Mother #3 or Woman Chewing Gum #1, Jerome only darkens the doorstep of 1553-B– at least here in Dalton Village anyway.

"What's up, babe?" He walks up to her assertively and grabs a hearty handful of her butt cheek.

To C.J., Jerome looks like the devil himself with jewelry dangling from his neck and wrists. Something is just too smooth about him. From the way he dresses to the way he talks, Jerome is just slimy. Wouldn't matter to Camille anyway. Jerome could look like the sole of a shoe. She doesn't have any affection for him. She is cordial enough to keep him coming around, so she can have money for her light bill, wine and cigarettes, but she can feel nothing for any man– Jerome included.

That is his fascination with her. No way would a man like Jerome go slumming with the likes of Camille, no matter how good her pussy was. She is more than a few years his senior, but he hit it once and kept coming back for the challenge of her. *How could she resist him and keep it so uncomplicated?* He finds her *don't-give-a-damn* attitude astounding. Jerome never met a woman that he couldn't have, a woman whose mind he couldn't wrap around his finger. He was a glutton for Camille's punishment and probably would have given her much more than what she asked in exchange for it. He jumps willingly into the freezing cold lake of her seduction over and over again, just for the thrill of it. Like those White people who go ice diving in sub-zero temperatures "just to feel *alive*"- as they describe it. What Jerome could never grasp about Camille... what all his years of pussy hunting couldn't teach him- was that the icy chill that runs up his back when he lays between her thighs and gazes into her lifeless eyes is the same attraction that a necrophiliac feels towards a corpse. To have someone who will never judge or complain, just a willing recipient. C.J. never understood how a dead, passionless woman like Camille could make a man feel so alive that he would pay for the experience. Whatever it was about Camille, Jerome was addicted to her and she was the pusher, ready to supply his nasty habit.

"Oh, I'm sorry. I didn't see you over there in the corner, Little Man." He steps over to C.J. and offers him a low five with the same hand he just retrieved from his mother's unbathed butt. C.J. is reluctant to touch his hand, but smacks it quickly, so as not to disrespect his mother's *company*. "Why are you down on the floor like that? You a'ight, Little Man?"

C.J. hates it when Jerome calls him- Little Man (#4- no doubt), not because he knows that Jerome has long forgotten his name, but because he is way taller and bigger than him, even at only thirteen years old. Young Man is more appropriate than Little Man in C.J.'s mind.

"Yeah, I'm good." C.J. answers hoarsely, still holding the dap hand away from his body. He stands up from the floor to go and wash his hand before it falls off.

"C.J. was just about to go to the stowe for me when you came," Camille says, glaring at C.J. with *get-the-hell-out-of-here* eyes. "They say it could snow, so get them food stamps out of my purse and go get us some eggs, milk and bread from the co'ner stowe."

The embarrassment of pulling out the blue stamps was too much for C.J. It was bad enough that he had to go shopping with her, but to be the one who counts out that multi-colored monopoly money, while the clerk looks at you like trash on a park bench, was enough to make him pack his bags and go down to Social Services himself.

"Ma, I got a lot of homework to do. I can't go to-"

"Boy, get your ass to that stowe. We ain't got shit for your big, Black ass to eat in here, so go on-" Her neck whips back and forth like a charmed cobra, as she threatens with tightened lips.

Who is this loud, obnoxious woman? C.J. thinks, snatching the stack of food vouchers from her pocketbook. He marches angrily towards the door.

"Hey, Little Man," Jerome says with a grin that makes C.J. want to punch him in the face. "Get something for yourself too." He pulls a thick wad from his warm-up pants pocket and rolls off a twenty-dollar bill for C.J.

C.J. would not have gone to the store while his mother sexed Jerome, but sheer desperate hunger drove him to it. When he went to pay at the counter, he was almost inclined to just use the twenty and save himself the embarrassment, but as levelheaded as C.J. is, he thought the better of it. He knew they needed other things at the house that food stamps couldn't buy and decided not to spend the money.

Winter was coming, so it was dark by the time C.J. began his walk back home. He trekked along, holding the brown paper bags against his chest to shield against the brisk wind that sliced through his jacket and down to his bones like icy, Samurai swords. His thin jacket left him feeling as defenseless against the blasts as if he were naked. He hurried along as fast as his numb toes, which peeked through the edge of his high tops could, carry him.

C.J. probably would have seen them coming, if he hadn't buried his head behind the shopping bags to protect his ashy, chapped lips from the sting of the cold. He hit the ground before he knew what hit him. The teenagers pushed him down, smashing the eggs against his chest. He covered his face with his arms while they kicked him mercilessly until they were sure he could not rise.

"Check his pockets, Smoke," one guy calls to the other.

"He ain't got shit but stamps," the other kid replies, as though he too is embarrassed for C.J. "Oh wait-" He digs in C.J.'s back pocket and his hand closes around the twenty-dollar bill. "I got something." The boy waves the money.

"Broke ass motherfucker," the first thief sends another sharp kick into C.J.'s defenseless ribs before he takes off running down the street behind his partner-in-crime.

"Help," C.J. cries out painfully, grabbing his ribs. He rolls and writhes on the pavement right outside of 1553-C. He sees from the corner of his swollen eye that Shaqualisha Meeks peaked out of her blinds, but she quickly turns off her porch light, once her curiosity has been satisfied. The lights inside of all the duplexes between the 1551 and 1553 block, go out almost simultaneously.

When C.J. is certain that help will not come, he gathers himself by the light of a street lamp. His bones ache from the cold, as much as from injury. There is little food he can salvage after the attack, but even if there was anything left that wasn't busted open on the sidewalk, he wouldn't be able to carry it. He is sure, as he sucks in short, painful breaths which stab like a long knife, that his ribs are broken.

He staggers up the steps to their duplex. "Momma," he whispers on what breath he can collect.

"Boy," she begins, rattling off the complaints that have been brewing in his absence. "Don't tell me you been gone all this time and you ain't bring back no damn food." She steps into the hallway with her hands on her hips. Her expression wilts when she sets eyes on her son's bloodied face.

"C.J.," she runs to her son and tries to catch his collapsing body, as he falls forward through the doorway. She strains under his weight, but they both topple to the floor. She cradles his head against her chest, rocking hysterically. She presses her hand against the deep gash on his cheek and blood rushes into her hand. She cries out, stricken by the sight of her wounded child. She is whisked away, in her mind, to that night six years ago. The night her husband, Courtney, was killed.

The night of the phone call. The night that she rushed to the morgue, hoping against hope, that it was all just a big mistake. The night that she flung her arms around Courtney and pulled at his lifeless body, begging that he take her with him. She even woke the next morning hoping that it was all a dream, but when she rolled over to find that Courtney wasn't there for the first time in ten years, she was sure that it was real and he was dead, because only death could have kept him from their bed.

She begins to wail and moan over her son, her tears falling down into his face.

"Don't cry, Ma," he winces with the words and blood leaks from the corner of his mouth. "I'ma be fine."

god face

Anger, used, does not destroy. Hatred does.

- Audre Lorde
"Eye to Eye," Sister Outsider (1984)

CHAPTER TWO

"Hey man," he says, extending his dirty right hand. "Could you spare some change? I haven't eaten in days."

My house is only a few blocks away from the grocery store. On warm Carolina evenings like these, I prefer to make the trip on foot. Camille needed some eggs to finish her cake, so I told her I would go. She insisted that I stay, knowing how tired I am from working at the garage. She said it could wait and that she would go back tomorrow, but I decided to go. It's good exercise for me. I'm not getting any younger and my schedule is more hectic than ever, so this is the way I stay sexy for Camille and energetic for C.J.

We live in a decent neighborhood, not far from many conveniences, but that has its disadvantages as well. Usually I can breeze right past this corner without being hassled, but occasionally there's that one. I do my best to keep my eyes down and not make any eye contact with the man.

"Look Mister, I'd greatly appreciate anything you could give me," he whispers almost as if in prayer, while I tap my foot waiting for the pedestrian signal to change.

"Well, I don't really have any cash on me," I lie and begin to walk away. I would have crossed the street and never given the man a second thought, if something hadn't caught my attention.

It was his shoes.

I always look at a man's shoes. People say that the clothes make the man, but I say the shoes make the man. A man's shoes can tell you so much more about that man than anything he will ever say to you. A man's shoes will tell you if that man works, what kind of work he does and if he takes pride in his work. For me, that is the measure of a man–

His work ethic

I have seen poorly dressed men beg for money from me while wearing new, unblemished name brand shoes and I have had professional men in fancy, high-priced suits, throw sales pitches to me while wearing shabby, unkempt shoes. That beggar and that salesman are one in the same in my eyes because their shoes would say that both are men without pride. But this broken, homeless man who approached me at the corner wore the shoes of a proud, hardworking man and I realized that instantly, because they were the same shoes I had given him.

"Jackson," I whisper, reaching out to tap his shoulder. The man turns back towards me. Even with the dirt and sweat covering his face, I still recognize him. "Jackson Burgess."

His eyes look up, hunting for some recognition of my face. He rifles through his mind, trying to find a match. "Uh... uh... Calvin, right?"

"No. It's me. Courtney."

"Oh yeah, yeah. I meant Courtney. How you doing, man?"

"I'm good, Jack. I'm real good," I reply, nodding my head.

Jackson Burgess used to attend my church. I worked on his cars several times. He was a real decent, hard-working, White man. I didn't know him well and I wouldn't call us friends, but any time we saw each other out, we would exchange a few words, even went to get a cup of coffee a time or two. The bottom fell out for Jackson when he lost his job. Not much later, he lost his house, then his wife took their two children and moved back to Philadelphia with her parents. I had heard Jackson's testimony once in the Men's ministry at church, so I knew that he had struggled with drug addiction as a teenager, but watching his fall from grace was more disheartening than I could have ever imagined.

I hadn't seen Jackson for about two years after he lost his job. He stopped coming to church and both of his vehicles were repossessed, so I didn't see him at the garage anymore either. It was almost a year ago, in September 1979, before I saw him again. He was on the corner of Trade

28

and Tryon. He discreetly asked me for some change, but when I recognized him, I took him to get some food.

It broke my heart to see him that way and hear what had happened to him over the years. I knew what kind of man he was. The kind of White man I had respect for because he wasn't waiting around for anyone to give him anything. He worked hard for what he had, but in one fell swoop, everything he accomplished went up in flames.

After that day, I began to minister to Jackson. I made him my own special project. I would bring him a little food in the evenings on my way home from work. No burgers and fries; I would have Camille pack up extra food in my lunch, and then bring Jackson sandwiches and meals from home. Late in November when the cold of winter began to come on strong, I urged Jackson to go into a Rehab Center and dry out for the New Year.

"I don't know, Courtney." Jackson shook his head as he chewed on the turkey club sandwich that I gave him. "I just don't know if I'm ready for that." His eyes darted back and forth with paranoid frenzy.

"Look, I won't be coming out here anymore now that it's getting colder," I reasoned with him. "Even birds fly south for the winter. You're going to have to fend for yourself, man. You need to do this now."

The look in Jackson's green eyes pierced me to the core. I thought I had been helping him out of the kindness of my heart. He was my charity case, my good deed for each day. But as I watched the grief on his sweat-stained face, I realized that we were not so different.

Camille is my only love. I met her when I was seventeen. We were virgins when we first laid down together. I knew from the start- from the very first moment I experienced her body that I wanted to live inside of her forever. I didn't go away to college, against my father's wishes, because I wanted to stay with Camille. I got my auto mechanics certification and worked a whole year to buy her a ring and get us a place. We married and moved into an apartment when I turned twenty. I wanted to wait for children until we had a house. I saw a beauty in Camille that I didn't know a woman could possess. She was such a hustler. Camille was an excellent money manager, stretching a dollar to screaming. She worked right *alongside of me; sewing for the women at the church, cleaning houses, babysitting, styling hair, whatever she could do to contribute to the House Fund.*

Be it change she saved by switching laundry detergent or money from selling items at the flea market, a day didn't go by that she didn't put something into that large pickle jar on the dresser. By the time our lease was up the next year, we were closing on our brand new, beautifully spacious three-bedroom, split-level brick house in Hidden Valley.

When she came to me the following year and told me that Junior was on the way, I vowed to her from that day forth that her only job would be Mother to our child. And she was just as good at Mother as she was at Wife and every other thing I had ever seen her do. Camille is every woman to me. In twelve years, I have never desired any other female besides her. She has given me a son and we have a wonderful life together– the life we always dreamed we would have when we were kids.

I would die for her and I would die without her. I couldn't imagine what could bring a man as low as Jackson was, but as I thought about losing my wife or my son, or even just losing my means to provide for them, I came just a little closer to understanding.

Jackson was a man abandoned; a man stuck right between a rock and a very hard place. This is a place that all men experience on some level and rationalize the exact same way. Either Jackson would run from his demons or fight them. I prayed daily that he would fight... not just for him, but also for me. I needed to see him fight, to know that there could still be life on the other side of loss.

"Alright Courtney," Jackson resigned with a sigh. His eyes showed defeat, although I knew he had just won a huge victory. He wrapped his fatigue jacket tightly around his shoulders and stood to his feet. "I'll go to Rehab," he whispered with the shame of a sinful confession.

I walked with Jackson down to the Drug Rehabilitation Center on Elizabeth Avenue. I gave him a big hug when he signed himself into the program.

"I know this is just the beginning for you, Jackson," I said with a smile. "You're going to get a job and get your life back," I continued

confidently. "So, I brought you something that you will need where you are going." I reached into my workbag and pulled out a box. "I say the shoes make the man, and these shoes represent the man I see in you." I handed him the box containing expensive leather Oxfords.

A faint smile appeared on Jackson's stubbly face. "Thanks, man. I really appreciate this," he said, looking down at his tattered, gaping canvas shoes. A puzzled look appeared on his face when he opened the box. "These are eleven and a half." He replaced the top. "I wear an eleven." Disappointment supplanted his excitement.

I shrugged at his comment. "I guess that just gives you a little room to grow." I smiled and jabbed at his shoulder. We hugged once more before I left. He stared at me through the glass door with sad, scared green eyes, as I started on my way home.

Now less than a year later, I see the same sad, scared green eyes; his blonde hair so slick with filth that it appears brown. A matted beard covers his face like overgrown weeds. His eyes are yellow and his pupils are almost fully dilated. He looks worse than ever. He looks... like a dead man walking.

"How are you doing?" I ask out of habit.

"Obviously, I've seen better days," he says, scratching his head. "But what's complaining gonna' do?"

An awkward, uncomfortable silence stretches between us as a deeper darkness falls on the corner where we stand.

"Look I was on my way to the grocery store," I say, starting to stride and hoping that he will follow. I know Camille will worry if I'm gone too long. "I'd be more than happy to pick you up a few things while I'm there." Jackson walks beside me with heavy labored steps like he is walking through high grass.

I guess that half-size did make a difference.

"Where you staying these days?" I ask making small talk, but prying as well.

"You know. Here and there. Anywhere... Everywhere," he replies, making a big exaggerated motion with his hands.

"What happened with the Rehab program?" I huff on labored breaths, realizing I am more out of shape than I thought.

"I guess I just wasn't ready," Jackson sighs his frustration. His brows furrow with disappointment. "But," his eyebrows rise. "You'd be proud of me. I quit drinking. I gave up the booze all on my own. I just don't want it no more."

"That is good and I am proud of you. All anybody can ask for is progress." I pat his back, looking genuinely impressed with him.

He offers me a bashful, brown and yellow grin through his chapped lips. "Now if I could just kick these bad boys." He lifts a pack of cigarettes from his fatigue jacket pocket and puts one between his lips, then searches his pants for a light.

I look at him with a little envy in my gaze when he sparks his lighter. "You don't mind if I bum a smoke, do you, Jack?"

A glimmer of surprise appears on his face, as he cocks his head to one side. "I didn't figure you for a smoker," he says, offering me a sly smile.

"Trust me. I'm not," I say lowly, taking the cigarette Jackson pulls from the pack. "But every once in a while, I like a little fiber glass in my lungs. I keep it to an occasional minimum because Camille would kill me if she found out I took even one puff off a cigarette."

"I know what you mean." Jackson laughs a little. "I kept chewing gum and cologne in the dash of my Jaguar. Asheema was like a bloodhound. She could smell the smoke on me from a mile away." Jackson's eyes glaze over with a faraway look. The memory of his wife takes him away on its wings.

I am hesitant to interrupt, until I see the pain of the image begin to crush him under the weight of its beauty. His eyes start to moisten, so as we round the corner to the shopping center, I say, "Hey Jackson. What do you need out of the grocery store?"

"Yeah, about that," Jackson presses against my shoulder to stop me. He puts out his cigarette on the arm of his jacket. I can tell that he is searching for words when the anxiety seizes him. His fidgeting unnerves

me, as a panicked expression appears on his face. "It would probably be better, if you could just give me the money." He runs his fingers through his hair, and then wrings his hands.

I offer a concerned glance towards Jackson. He searches around with his eyes, up and down the dark street, as if he is looking for someone. When his gaze returns to me, he wilts like a child caught in his father's discerning stare.

"All I'm saying is if you're going to spend the money anyway," Jackson squirms as if someone just set fire ants loose in his pants. Then suddenly, his mind consents to allow him one minute of clarity with which to present his best argument. He straightens his back and squares his shoulders, still standing only as tall as my shoulder, but as tall as he can. "I need some things that they don't carry in the grocery store."

"Oh yeah." I narrow my eyes suspiciously. "Like what?"

"Aww man, you know– **stuff**." He scratches his head like a dog with fleas.

"Stuff like what?" I inquire more aggressively, throwing down the cigarette and stamping it out, before crossing my arms across my chest.

"Umm," Jackson cuts his eyes to the left and bites down on his bottom lip. "I'm embarrassed to say this, but since you force me." Jackson shrugs his shoulders. "Man, I need some clean underwear and ointment for a rash that broke out on my feet, since I don't have no socks."

I'm instantly angry with myself for my mistrust. I almost want to cry when I think of how hard it must be for any man to put down his pride and resort to begging for something so basic but necessary. I can tell that the admission has taken a lot more out of him than just energy, as his shoulders begin to slump back down.

"You know that we have never done things that way, Jackson." I state courteously, trying to retain as much of his dignity as possible. "I tell you what... I can't give you any money, but once I get what I came for, you can come home with me and I'll drive you out to get whatever else you need."

"No!" Jackson bellows, balling his fists with an anger that I didn't know he could produce. He catches himself, covering his mouth like he just expelled a disgusting belch. "I mean– you don't have to go through all that trouble. Besides, I'm real tired. If you just give me some money. I can catch the bus tomorrow and go get it myself."

"Can't do that, Jackson," I sigh quietly. "Either take what I'm offering or have a nice night." I turn away from him and begin to cross the street. Before I can step off the curb, Jackson grabs my shoulder so tightly that the strength of his grip startles me. I pull his hand away easily, letting him know that he should not consider a physical altercation with me.

"Look Courtney man. I need this money," he cries out, offering his palms to me in surrender. His shoulders shake with his sobs. When I would have turned away from Jackson a second time, a tall, young White kid with menacing dark brown eyes closes the gap on me before I can take a step.

"Nigger, you're wasting our fucking time."

The kid is probably nineteen, maybe twenty, but he is as wild and dangerous as they come. When he speaks, I notice one of his front teeth is missing. His brown hair is shaved close to his head. His large, round eyes are focused with a **go-ahead-and-make-my-day** glare. He shrugs his shoulders and buries his hands in the pockets of his jean jacket. "My friend asked you nicely, porch monkey. So now, give him your money," the boy speaks so politely, matter-of-factly even, that it is almost hard to take his insults personally.

Jackson intercedes quickly when he sees me roll my shoulders, realizing that his companion's insolence will soon cause a very bad scene. He steps between us, but faces me.

"Hey Shelton. This is my friend, Courtney. He's cool man. He's gone help us out. Ain't that right, Courtney?" Jackson nods his head towards me with urgency in his tone, as he cuts his eyes discreetly back at Shelton who stands behind him.

"Actually," I say calmly. "I'm not giving you shit."

Jackson begins to shake his head warily. He waves his hands, begging me with tiny gestures to reconsider. I smile and dismiss him with a swipe of my hand.

"Fuck you... and fuck you. Both of y'all can kiss my ass."

"Hey," the kid whines, pulling a gun up over Jackson's shoulder, so quickly that I would not have noticed it perched there, if I had not heard the sound of him cocking the hammer back. "Now what kind of way is that for a nigger to talk? Where's your respect?"

Jackson looks nervous when he glances at the revolver on his right shoulder, as if the gun was on him instead of me. "Just give him the money," Jackson whimpers. His face is pale and solemn with genuine remorse. Large tears sit on the rim of his eyes.

"Alright," I resign, holding up my hands in a hesitant surrender. I reach into my back pocket for my wallet. I only came for eggs so all I have is a twenty-dollar bill. As I open the bill folder, I am distracted by Jackson's screams.

Bang!

When I look up from my wallet, Jackson and Shelton are struggling over the smoking gun. I couldn't have stopped it, but I would have seen what was coming if I hadn't dropped my eyes.

I hit the ground before I know what hit me.

If we were made in his image, then call us by our names. Most intellects do not believe in God, but they fear us just the same.

- Erykah Badu, "On and On"

CHAPTER THREE

"Hey Ma," is what C.J. would have said, if forming the word *hey* didn't smack him in the face with such an intense, stinging pain that even the *H* failed to initialize.

"Don't try to talk baby," Camille says gently, gazing into his eyes with sympathy. "Your jaw is in pretty bad shape, but at least it's not broken," she smiles. "The doctors ran x-rays and confirmed that none of your bones have been broken." When C.J. sees the tears well up in her eyes, he can't help but sob too.

"I'm sorry, Momma," he manages to mumble through a wince.

"Don't apologize, C.J.," her voice quivers, as she wipes her nose on the back of her hand. "I'm the one who should be apologizing... for so many things." She drops down into the chair at his bedside. "Damn, damn, damn," she says pounding her fist against her palm.

"Ma," C.J. grumbles faintly. "You gotta' stop this." He struggles to look at her with one eye almost completely swollen shut. "You can't keep beating yourself up."

Large tears begin to roll down her cheeks. She shakes her head before burying it deep inside of her hands. She rocks back and forth in the chair.

"Daddy is dead, and he ain't coming back." The words, spoken so softly from her son, break Camille down. She begins to bawl and moan. C.J. places his hand on her shoulder. "It's time to let the guilt go and forgive yourself. It wasn't your fault."

"It was my fault," she answers as soberly as if she were never crying. Her moist, reddened eyes are full of unwavering conviction. "It was all *my* fault. I forgot the eggs. I shouldn't have let him go back out that night."

"Ain't no guarantee that Daddy would still be with us, even if he had stayed home that night," Courtney's voice is thin and frail, as he pleads with his mother. "Maybe it would have been a car accident, or a heart attack or anything. Sometimes things happen for a reason. Sometimes things happen just the way they are supposed to happen whether we think so or not."

"Are you saying that your Daddy was supposed to die?" Camille fumes, her eyes narrow with anger.

"No. Of course not. I miss him every day," C.J. says dropping his eyes. "Sometimes I wish it was me that died instead of him because it's too hard living here without him."

Camille nods slowly. Her eyes reflect the empathy that she shares with her son. They never talk about Courtney's death. They never talk about their feelings. Camille didn't know that C.J. felt the same pain she did.

"I pray for that," she admits shamefully. "Every day I hope for my death, so that I can be with him. The hope of death is the only thing that I live for now."

C.J. studies his mother carefully. She trembles with a frightened nervousness that makes him want to hold her, offer her all the security that he can. For all of the features that he has in common with his father, he cannot fill his shoes. C.J. cannot replace his father, in the black void where his life used to be.

Fatherlessness- that is the Blackness for both mother and child.

"Momma?" C.J. calls lowly, bringing her attention back from the brink of despair. "Do you ever want to live for me? Do you realize that I still need you?"

C.J. spoke with the calm serenity of adult insight. Camille was surprised by the maturity of his inquiry.

He is his father's son.

"I think you deserve the truth C.J., so I won't patronize you," she licks her lips and lowers her eyes. "I have become someone that I don't recognize. Every morning I wake up, my soul is so dark with shame and guilt that I can't even see my own reflection in the mirror. I have done things in front of you that let me know you would be better off without me.

I'm living a lie. I'm not the wife, the mother or the woman that I always thought I was."

"No Ma. This life is the lie." C.J. wags his finger disapprovingly. "We were never meant to live this way. This wasn't what our life was supposed to be."

Camille and Courtney both fall silent, pondering the possibilities. They both search and seek in the quietness for the life they should have had.

"Courtney, honey." His mother takes his hand. "You don't understand the burden that I live with. It is unbearable. No one should be asked to endure this torture."

She glances around the emergency room triage unit. Her eyes trace the tiles in the ceiling, and then the designs on the floor. "The last time I came to this hospital was to identify your father's body." The pain of the memory pricks Camille's heart and her face begins to burn, as she holds back yet more tears. "I always wanted to remember him alive– to remember his smile… his touch-"

She closes her eyes and rubs her hand across her cheek. "I would drive to the garage some days and just wait outside, hoping to get a glimpse of him. There were nights when I would put his navy uniform in the bed beside me, hoping that the scent of him would induce a lovely vision. And I would dream some nights. I would dream that I saw him, but when I woke, what I dreamt was as lost to me as Courtney was. When I am awake, all I can remember is the corpse stretched out on a steel slab like a wax museum exhibit. All I see when I think of Courtney is the cold, dead body that your father used to live in. I touched his skin– his beautiful, Black skin that use to burn with a warmth like the summer sun, but it was icy and lifeless. You can't imagine what it means to see the arms that held you and made you feel safe– the strong Black arms that built your home and rocked your child lay stilled with no hope of ever rising again." Camille stands and goes over to the counter to get some tissues, both for her and C.J.

"Every day for a while, I kept thinking that he would just come home. That the door would open and he would come waltzing in with an arm full of gifts like he just came back from a long trip." Camille smiles with a faraway look in her eyes. "But then," her smile fades as quickly as it appeared. "When we lost the house, I knew that Courtney could never find us, even if he did come back. None of this would have happened if it had not been for me. That night plays over and over in my head, and if I could do one thing over in my whole entire life, if I could just get that one do-over, I would make your father stay at home that night, even if it meant me going back for the eggs myself instead of him." She groans, pressing her hands against her chest.

Her tone rises to near hysteria. "They killed your Daddy over twenty dollars! One twenty-dollar bill was all Courtney's life was worth to the bastard who killed him. We put every dime we had into building up our house. Your father was only twenty-nine. Life insurance was the last thing we figured we'd have to worry about." Camille shakes her head in disbelief. "Twenty dollars was enough to purchase his life. And now– all because I couldn't keep you safe, because I couldn't even be a fucking decent mother and keep you out of the ghetto, I almost lost you over the same thing. History just repeating itself all over again."

Camille collapsed against C.J.'s chest. It took all the strength he had not to scream out from the sharp pain in his ribs. Instead, he wrapped his arms tightly around his mother, squeezing her like a stress ball until the pain dissipated. C.J. wants to be the rock for her and prove that, in him, his father has left a life raft to which she can cling in her raging sea of despair.

"I don't think about you because you don't need me," Camille breathes into his chest. "You don't deserve to have a mother like me and I don't deserve to live after what I have allowed myself to become, and after all I have done to you."

"Camille," C.J. whispers softly, trying to sound as much like his father as he can. "I don't know why daddy died and I don't know why all these bad things keep happening to us. But what I do know is that we are still alive and we are going to live until we die. For whatever reason that hasn't happened yet and we don't know when it will, so I think that we owe Dad's memory more than this. We are all that is left of him, so I think we owe it to him to let people know what a wonderful man he was in the way we live our lives." C.J. takes Camille's face between his hands. "Momma, we can do this together. If you're willing to try, then I'ma do my best to be everything you need me to be."

She nods slightly, offering him a small grin. She rubs his face with her hand, watching him with adoration.

"You right, sugar. I'm gone be better, baby."

"We gone be better. You and me both, together– Okay?"

She smiles brightly. "Alright, my Big Man."

"Hence, both the horse and the nigger must be broken...KEEP THE BODY, TAKE THE MIND!... Therefore, if you break the FEMALE mother, she will BREAK the offspring in its early years of development; and when the offspring is old enough to work, she will deliver it up to you, for her normal female protective tendencies will have been lost in the original breaking process..."

Willie Lynch Speech (1712)

Chapter Four

That is the problem with addicts, C.J. learned.

Lies are like wishes and prayers to an addict. They speak those things that be not, as though they were; just reciting the words without any belief or conviction that their hopes will be accomplished. Still, with the same confidence that a child can convince you the monster under their bed is real, addicts can mesmerize you with falsehoods as authentic and persuasive as truth. They guide you unsuspectingly along, dropping breadcrumb lies to mark the dark, winding path of exasperation on which they lead you. Breadcrumb lies, which will be devoured by the vultures of selfishness only seconds after they are left. Bite-sized morsels that you discover (all too late) have conveniently disappeared without a trace, when you try to find your way back out of the labyrinth of self-pity. By then, you cannot be delivered from your fate. Waiting at the end of the trail is the Wicked Witch of Realization. The irony is that she will pick the same knife you used for offering sacrifices to the *addict-of-your-affection* to then, slaughter you in the end as well.

He who has offered sacrifices to the god of addiction will, in turn, be offered as a sacrifice on the altar thereof. Amen.

Camille tried-

Like a bird with a broken wing, to fly. She tried– like a toddler taking its first wobbly steps, to walk. But like a mangy, three-legged dog, which hobbles and begs daily for its discharge from misery, she soon tired to a hopeless crawl. Then, when crawling wearied her, she laid down to wallow in the blackness of anguish and sank into a pit of faithlessness that swallowed her up like quicksand.

43

Hence, both the horse and the nigger must be broken...

In the months which followed C.J.'s release from the hospital, Camille seemed to have a fire lit under her. She began to take better care of herself and C.J., making sure he dressed warmly and ate a decent breakfast. She had meals cooked for him when he came home from school, almost like old times. She began to leave out early and put in applications for employment. C.J. was glad to see his mother again. She would get up early to do her hair and look presentable during the day. Camille never had many friends in the projects, but the few women she did associate with started to distance themselves from her when they observed that her get-up-and-go had returned.

She thank she too good now. She thank she all that.

They didn't have to tell Camille what they thought. Their eyes, staring at her from the front porch lounge chairs, said it all.

"I 'on't know why you be walkin' up and down the street in them fancy outfits e'ry day and wasting yo' money on bus fare to go puttin' in all 'dem applications," Dejinericka Hopkins in 1553-A said, glaring judiciously at Camille in her pink cashmere skirt suit. Ricka continues to gnaw on her gum with an upturned lip. "Dey gone take one look at yo' address and know what 'chu all about. Can't no 'spensive suit change that shit. I 'on't know why you keep tryin'. 'Dey ain't gone never hire you." Ricka crosses her arms across her chest, looking as satisfied with herself as if she had just given out the most impressively insightful advice that has ever been conceived.

KEEP THE BODY, TAKE THE MIND!

Camille composes herself, wanting to speak as dignified as she is dressed when she offers her response to the Pink Hair Roller guru of the 1553 block.

"Well, Dejinericka. Nothing beats a failure but a try. You're right though. There is a strong possibility that I may not get this job, but there is a definite certainty that I won't get a job, if I don't even apply for it." Camille folds the thick stack of classifieds under her arm and climbs the steps to her door. "Jobs don't just fall out of trees, but that doesn't mean you can't climb up and shake one down."

That was in the beginning.

C.J. was proud of his mother. She got up every morning to look for jobs as if job hunting was her job. She was encouraged and energetic, at first. But C.J. could see the disappointment begin to mount on her back like a large, black anvil, as the months went by. C.J. should have seen the relapse coming. Daily, he could see the light dimming in Camille's eyes. Each time, she would return home from a long day of having doors slammed in her face, only to check the answering machine and retrieve a handful of voice messages from bill collectors. She would empty her mailbox and receive letter after letter stating- *Thanks*, *but no* thanks.

One evening, C.J. came home from school to find his mother crumpled into a little ball on the kitchen floor, like a used tissue ready for disposal. She had a letter, withdrawing an offer of employment for a housekeeping job at a motel, crinkled up in her hand. Camille had spent her entire TANF check on a decent coat and some shoes for C.J., banking that the job would come through. He watched his mother wilt and writhe with frustration for a few minutes before she noticed him in the doorway. She hid the letter and smiled, pressing away her tears with her fingertips, then offered him a dinner plate of fried chicken legs, baked beans and cornbread as if nothing happened.

C.J. had to hand it to his mother though. She put up a valiant effort and fought almost to the death to salvage their lives from the gutter. She gave a championship performance, but after a whole year, an entire thirteen-month span of endless, illusive job hunting; she was called back for only three interviews, one of which was cancelled– never to be rescheduled.

Camille was only offered one position, only to have it rescinded before her first day of employment.

Therefore, if you break the FEMALE mother...

You can't ask a person to endure but so much rejection. Every denial, every refusal sent the message to Camille that she was worthless. It seemed to her that employers would rather train a silverback gorilla with cymbals to fill a position than hire a welfare mother with very little job experience. The pain of all that rejection began to bleed into other areas of her life. Camille began to drink and smoke again. She began to hang out on the stoop with Ricka in the morning instead of taking the bus downtown to the Employment Security Commission.

Days blended together, dragging on into months that crept along like caterpillars, then sprouted large, black moth wings and flew away with years of their lives. By C.J.'s seventeenth birthday, things in their apartment had gone from bad to worse, and then even *worser* than ever.

Courtney dropped out of school after being told that he'd have to repeat the tenth grade because he failed Chemistry. He couldn't endure any more embarrassment than what he had to witness at home with his mother. He got a job at a local burger joint around the corner from his projects and went to class to get his GED at night. He probably wouldn't be able to get his GED either, but at least, it gave him an excuse to spend all the time he could away from the projects. C.J. knew that he didn't want to end up in jail or dead so he didn't want to hang out with the neighborhood hoodlums on the corner. He didn't quite have enough reckless abandon about him to really fit in with them anyway. Furthermore, Camille was increasingly becoming a burden on him. She took almost every dime of every paycheck he made, claiming that this or that bill was due. Her blood thirst for his income was only half of the problem though. His every waking thought was of her safety and well-being. He was beginning to fear that her wishes would come true and he would come home to find her deceased.

... She will BREAK the offspring in its early years of development

Her drinking was spiraling out of control. C.J. didn't know what to do. She was a danger to herself. He had come home on several occasions and found her on the floor in a puddle of some body fluid, be it urine, blood or vomit. One day, Camille's masochism came to a head, when C.J. found her unconscious and slumped over the toilet in the bathroom with tubing tied around her arm. C.J. failed to resuscitate her after a couple of attempts. He was finally able to revive her after throwing her into the shower, and dousing her with cold water. Once she was lucid enough to understand his words, C.J. told his mother that he was leaving.

"I won't watch you kill yourself. I won't live with nightmares of seeing your dead body like your memories of dad's," C.J. declared, slicing the air with his hand. His chest heaved with labored breaths.

"Okay, C.J." Camille begged while pulling on his jeans. "I'll change. I promise I'll stop drinking." Her eyes were wide with desperation. "Please don't leave me alone. I need you."

"No Camille. I'm not falling for it no more. You're on your own." C.J. charged into his room.

Camille struggled to her feet and stumbled behind him, as best as she could with the numbness in her legs. She sloshed down the hallway, her night gown heavy and damp. "Please, baby- don't go. The streets ain't got nothing for you. Stay with Momma. I mean it. I'll get help. I'll go to therapy, if you want me to."

C.J. stopped throwing clothes into his backpack and stared into his mother's eyes. She bit down on her lip to hold back tears. C.J. wanted so badly to believe her that he was willing to grasp on to any fragile straw that she offered. He knew she was right. The streets didn't have anything to offer him, other than more heart and head ache. If he left 1553-B that night, despite all his efforts to save whatever money his mother didn't siphon from him, he only had enough to afford a shady motel room for maybe one week. Still, C.J. couldn't let his mother know that his ultimatum was frivolous.

C.J., now fully grown at 6'2" with smooth, dark-chocolate skin and short, neatly-cut hair that coiled into tight, but shiny ringlets, melted his mother's heart because he was the spitting image of his father in every way. C.J. had Courtney's thick, dark lips, strong jaw line and slanted, cat-like eyes. Almost as if the handsome seventeen-year-old Black stallion she met when she was sixteen, had stepped out of her memory and into C.J.'s bedroom. She blinked back tears when she realized that for the first time in a long time, she could remember her husband alive. Her son had resurrected a vision of Courtney in her mind again. She clasped her hands over her mouth and wept bitterly, as she fell against the wall and slid to the floor.

"Okay Momma," C.J. relented, not knowing what caused his mother's collapse. He dropped down, kneeling beside her. He collected her in his arms and whispered in her ear. "I'll stay here with you, **if** you promise to get some help this time."

She buried her face in the warmth of his muscular chest, clinging to his gleaming, pressed white T-shirt. He hugged her so tightly in his arms that she sighed heavily.

"Thank you. I love you, Courtney," she breathed, speaking both to him and his father– who gave her the Black gift of C.J. "I will get the help... if you promise to stay."

... When the offspring is old enough to work, she will deliver it up to you

Stay- C.J. did... but help is not what his mother got- at least not in any clinical or professional capacity. She probably would have done better, or at least pretended to in order to lull C.J. back into a false sense of security. Addicts have to be careful not to lay flames to any bridges, so she would have laid off the booze at least until C.J. left for work for a few months just to appease him–

That is, if it hadn't been for the reoccurring role of a certain Mr. Somebody named Jerome- *enter stage left.*

By the time C.J. was counting down the days to his eighteenth birthday, in December 1991, Jerome was hitting an all-time low and dragging what was left of Camille down with him.

48

Jerome *"Romeo"* Pettigrew came to move in with Camille earlier that fall. His wife, Sharon found out about his girlfriend on the East side of town and kicked him out of his house. She would have probably taken him back if she, being childless at Jerome's request, had not discovered that he had two children by his East-side girlfriend. Sharon filed for divorce and was awarded a considerable amount in monthly spousal support. When Jerome's pockets slimmed down, the East-side girlfriend got a whim that her meal ticket had been cashed in. So, she ganged up with the West-side girlfriend and they decided to cash out on Jerome too, by taking him to Child Support for all three of his children.

That was a big hit for a man who was used to making as much money as Jerome. He couldn't live on his own and afford to live as he was accustomed, so Camille was the obvious choice since wine and cigarettes were all she would charge for his room and board.

Jerome settled in quickly as the man of the house, and even quicker as the Big Man on the block. Of course after he paid out three ways, Jerome couldn't stay as fresh as he wanted on what was left of his salary, so he soon turned a recreational habit into a lucrative enterprise. Now sure– Jerome was more of a high-priced, white lines cocaine type of guy, but once the ghetto dope boys taught him how to cook crack, he didn't see any reason not to invest in the local market. This new drug was booming. Niggahs in the ghetto were banking big loot by selling crack rock to junkies. It was the best thing since sliced bread because even the brokest, homeless mofo could afford at least a five-dollar crumb.

Jerome wasn't all idiot, he fortified himself against his Day of Reckoning and managed to tuck away a small, gold-digger proof stash of cash. Jerome took his hidden stack of rainy-day money and used it to start a full-scale thunderstorm in Dalton Village. Soon Jerome was pushing a Beamer and everyone in the neighborhood was standing outside of 1553-B like it was a government assistance line.

C.J. spent most of his time away from the projects, so he didn't quite know– at first– what was going on, but he knew that he didn't want any part of it. C.J. knew it wouldn't be long before he bumped heads with

Jerome, who strutted his bird frame around the apartment in boxer shorts like he owned the entire neighborhood.

And evidently he did- because a host of crackhead zombies leaned and swayed outside of the apartment at all times of the night; little more than listless, dark shadows of their former selves. Melancholy, nocturnal creatures waiting for the sun to come up and dissolve them, until the sun descends in the sky and they can reappear again.

... For her normal female protective tendencies will have been lost in the original breaking process.

It was then that C.J. realized he had to escape. He didn't know where he was going or how he would get there, but he knew he had to leave. It was time. The last recognizable characteristics of his mother had all but disappeared, as she was swallowed up in her co-dependent, parasitic relationship with Jerome.

Cause you're a sky, cause you're a sky full of
stars
I want to die in your arms
Cause you get lighter the more it gets dark
I'm going to give you my heart

- Coldplay, "Sky Full of Stars"

Chapter Five

I didn't know just how close my salvation was.

Moving in across the street and two blocks down- to be exact. I can remember the day I first saw her the way one remembers their baptism or their first kiss.

I was standing at the corner of my block, ready to cross the street once the light changed. I was on my way to work and not paying too much attention to anything in my surroundings. Still, her presence drew my eyes like a moth to a flame. She caught my attention– and not just mine alone, but almost everyone in the projects, as she bent to lift a cardboard box from the trunk of her tiny, blue Toyota Celica. I can't be certain, but it seemed as though time slowed and a 70's R&B love song began to play. I observed the eyes cutting at her, peaking through blinds and curtains, stalking her as she walked. Her smooth, slender thighs taking the steps up to 1559-B.

Then like a huge cloud rolls in suddenly and blots out the very existence of the sun, she disappeared into her building pulling all the light of day inside the duplex with her. She left the entire street cloaked in a dull, ashen grayness. A dimness that never seemed quite so dark until she blinded us with her light. We all were left, watching the flashing spots before our eyes, the way you do when someone suddenly turns out the lights.

Once her door closed firmly shut, I realized I hadn't taken a breath for a very long time and began to gasp desperately for air. I had never seen anything like her before.

She was beautiful.

Ajae Joslynn Burgess

The irony right? Her first and middle initials are the same as her first name. Perfect symmetry– just like her lips and her hips.

She was a sunray in the darkness. In a sea of Blackness, she stood before me like a beacon of light. All the other girls in the projects were Tracy Chapman "Fast Car" but Ajae was Mariah Carey "Vision of Love". I remember that day, like I remember the last supper with my father. The introduction of her into my life took away my past and gave me a hope for a future so bright, it was as golden as her skin.

Ajae, as I came to find out through the project grapevine, moved to Charlotte from Philadelphia. I should have known she was from Philly by the way she dressed. She was so hood chic with her giant, door-knocker earrings and cropped hoodie jackets. Ajae was, by all accounts, bi-racial; but to the untrained eye, she could pass for being as White as the pure, driven snow. She was at least as White as any person could be and still claim any Black lineage. Yet there she was, smack dab in the middle of the ghetto, moving around amongst us like a fallen angel.

She wore her hair slicked back into tight buns with gelled baby-hair framing her forehead. She looked like the other ghetto girls with her black lip liner and nose ring, but she was not like them, not in the slightest– despite all her efforts to blend seamlessly into the Blackness. And they (the project chicks) made a swift point of letting her know that although she was a welfare mother of two, she was not welcome in the only place where she should be. Even in the place where we all came to fall at our lowest; even Rock Bottom would not embrace her.

They were afraid of her, because she was different. Even in her destitute condition of poverty, she was still White– at least on some level and therefore a threat to them and their Blackness. Because in their minds, she could transcend the Blackness by virtue of her Whiteness anytime she chose. That fact made her an unwanted interloper. The other females isolated Ajae like a contagion and refused to bring her into their sanctum.

But me–

I fell in love with her. Watching her daily while she sat alone on her stoop. I came to know her every feature and how each looked in the changing light of the day. In the early morning her hair glowed with a redness that became more blonde at midday, and finally light auburn at dusk. Her eyes, however were always green... beautiful, radiant green. Tiny freckles speckled her cheeks, enticing me, like cinnamon-sugar on a soft pretzel.

I would imagine my hands, strong and Black, against her pale, White skin. The thought of touching her milky flesh was enough to send a shuddering chill of exhilaration up my spine.

Beauty– by definition, was Ajae. Everything I hated about myself... the things that made others laugh, mock and ridicule, she didn't possess even a trace of. She was the light and in her there was no Blackness– at least none that could be seen anyway.

Her lips were thin, and her nostrils small. Her hair was straight and her eyes were something, anything and everything other than the Blackness that I saw in my own. I would skip work some evenings to get my eyeful of her, just watch her- listless and unaware of my spying eyes, as she smoked dejectedly on a cigarette.

Yawn, stretch... twist... puff. I observed and memorized her figure, her movements and her expressions. Then I would steal away, creeping into my mother's apartment, once Ajae's head was turned. I would slip out of my clothes and under the covers within the privacy of my room.

There– in my bed, I would make love to her. I would give her pleasure like she had never known. As I gripped the thick, throbbing meat of my erection, stroking it fiercely, I would sit on the edge of my bed and image her on top of me moaning, "C.J. ... C.J.," with the ecstasy of my love. Her cool, green eyes watching me. Her creamy, White thighs straddling my Black lap. The fantasy of it would burst me like a bubble, leaving me covered in sweat and gasping for breath.

"C.J.!" my mother blares, standing in my doorway, with her hands resting on her hips.

"Damn, Camille," I huff in frustration, quickly tucking my manhood into my boxers, before she can see what I'm doing. "Knock next time."

"What the hell ever, C.J. If you want more privacy, then get your own place and move the hell outta mines."

I ball up my fists, trying my best to pour all of my anger into them, like emotional coffee mugs. "What do you want?" I finally whisper once the rage has drained.

"Go get me a pack of cigarettes from the co'ner stowe," she drawls between gum chews, dropping a five-dollar bill on the foot of my bed.

"You know damn well that I can't buy you no cigarettes for three more days," I say to her, more as a reminder that I have a birthday coming up because I know she has forgotten.

She offers a coy smile, then pinches my cheek. "You know they ain't gone card yo' big, Black ass. Just bring me a pack of Newports, a'ight?" I nod slightly and she disappears from my doorway.

Once I get freshened up and re-dressed, I step out into a dusk afternoon that is darker and colder than I anticipated. It almost never snows in Charlotte, but this bitch can get as cold as penguin's balls while still looking like a summer day outside. I throw the hood of my navy, Karl Kani jacket over my head, and begin to trek briskly down the street.

I want to be back before dark, but not because I'm scared or anything. I'm no longer afraid at night in the projects, I'm easily one the biggest men here, but all the same– niggahs is crazy, so I don't want to regulate if I don't have to.

I cross the street, then stop for a minute to brush some soot from the tip of my black, suede-leather Timberland boot. I don't have a lot of money, so I try my best to take care of what fly threads I can get my hands on. I may not have the most expensive clothes, but I'll bet anyone mine are the cleanest and best pressed.

That quality about me goes a long way with the females. I notice the way they check my nails for dirt (which they never find) when they take my hand. My hands ain't soft- that's for pretty boys and homos, but they are clean.

I admire them– the clean, neat nails of my left hand, as I push the door handle to enter the convenience store at the corner.

"Pack of Newports," I command nonchalantly in a deep, gruff voice.

The tall, Indian store clerk eyes me for a second, then asks "Mediums or lights?" with little regard.

Camille likes the lights, but if I say that he'll know they're not for me and that could raise more suspicion.

"Mediums good, man," I say with a confident nod.

"We're all out of mediums," the clerk states shortly with a smirk. "All we have are lights."

I fight the urge to ask why he didn't just say that from the start, but say instead, as if my arm is being twisted, "Damn man. I guess I'll take the lights then... since that's all you got."

When he gives me the pack, I tap it against the side of my hand before leaving out of the door. I don't know what that does, I've just always seen smokers do it, so I follow suit. Once I turn the corner, I drop the pack into my jacket pocket, zip up tightly and start striding quickly back down the street.

I probably would have seen it coming if I hadn't buried my face into the neck of my jacket to protect my lips from the cold.

"Damn, Black. You need to watch where the hell you going," she fumes.

At first, I didn't know what hit me. I had to look down before I saw her, but as soon as our eyes met, I knew what hit me.

Cupid's arrow–dead in the chest, straight through my heart.

Ajae didn't see me either. Her face was obscured by several large, brown paper bags. One of which, fell to the ground in our collision.

"I'm sorry, Baby girl," I apologize quickly, kneeling to get the bag before its contents can spill on the ground. "Let me help you with this," I say softly, collecting a few more bags from her until she holds only one while I gather the other four into my arms.

"Nah, son. I got it. I don't need no help." Her brows furrow into a frown above her eyes, as she reaches to retrieve her bags from me. I swing the bags out of her reach and block her hand with my forearm.

"Nope," I reply mockingly. "It's the least I can do after running into you like that." I start walking up the street towards her block. "Come on. I got you."

She follows slowly... hesitantly behind me, until we reach her front steps.

"I can take it from here," she states directly, letting me know to stay put. She takes one of my bags and goes into her door. She returns quickly for the remaining three and then heaves those inside with the rest. A few minutes later, when she realizes that I'm not leaving, she reappears on the steps.

"I appreciate your help-"

"C.J." I interrupt, eager to exist in her world by making my name known.

"Okay," she says with a quick roll of her disinterested eyes. "Thank you, C.J." She turns swiftly to go back inside of her apartment.

"Wait, Shorty," I call after her. "I didn't get **your** name."

She takes me in for a moment, glancing me up and down... down then up again. I'm not sure if her expression is offense or distrust, but either way I know it ain't good.

"Ajae," she finally sighs with reluctant resignation.

"Cool... Ajae and C.J. We already got something in common," I offer laughingly, flashing my pearly-white smile.

"Look little boy," she blurts out sharply, her patience with me wearing thin. "I'm glad you helped me out, but I'm sure you need to get back home before the streetlights come on."

'Whoa! She's a feisty female,' I say to myself standing on her steps, as stunned as if she had slapped me clean in the face. I almost wanted to run away with my tail tucked between my legs, but the G in me wouldn't let me go out like that.

"Aye yo, I ain't no little boy," I reply calmly. "Let me come inside and I'll show you just how grown I am."

Ajae's eyes narrow with a newfound interest. I see her eyes light up, as she bites down on her lip.

"How old are you, kid?" she asks with a shy, half-smile.

LIE!

"Umm," I stammer searching for a feasible number. "I'll be eighteen on Saturday."

DAMN! My nerves got to me and I told the truth without meaning to.

"Are you a virgin?" She asks directly.
"Oh hell, no....Watcha' mouth. I got experience."

If... you count that one time I fingered Tomichella Smiley, then busted a nut on her thigh and the four and a half minutes that I was inside of Zinfandel Morris before her mother came home and I was forced, half-naked, out of her bedroom window.

"Lots of experience." I assure her with a determined nod.

A tiny giggle escapes her lips, so she covers them with a gloved hand. Once she is sure that her laughter has subsided, she says lowly, "Tell you what... Come back and see me in three days. I'll have a birthday present for you." She winks at me.

My manhood stiffens to throbbing in a matter of seconds. I'm almost lightheaded by the speed of my arousal. I got her on my line, so I can't be satisfied to just go home. I have to at least try to reel her in before I can give up.

"*I'll* tell **you** what..." I offer casually, licking my lips. She watches them– my lips– as I speak and I can tell that she is formulating plans for them. I place my foot up on the step and lean towards her, taking her hand in mine. "Instead of waiting three days for me to become a man... why don't you take me inside of your apartment and make me one tonight?"

Before she can offer a protest, I place my hands her on creamy cheeks that have turned bright red, either from the cold weather or the heat of the fire that I am trying to build. I plant the best kiss I can on her lips. Her soft, pink lips. I suck on them, almost swallowing her mouth whole.

Then, to my surprise– she responds. I feel her hand slip around my waist, and then a panic seizes me, almost stopping my heart. The moment *that I had dreamt of... prayed and waited for, had arrived. I almost couldn't believe it. So many emotions raced through my mind that I couldn't fully enjoy the rapture of her body against mine.*

Her hand slides from my back and down over my erection. At first, I am excited, then I realize, as her hand continues to search along my leg, that I am being inspected.

"What you doing, Shorty?" I pull back from our kiss and look into her bright, green eyes.

"Just checking your equipment, Black." She offers a smile so seductive that I have a strange, sudden urge to bite her. "You can't build a house without the right tools."

"Well do I pass inspection?" I ask sarcastically, already knowing that my tool is impressive.

"That depends on if you know what to do with that big hammer you got," she pushes away from my chest as if she might leave me unsatisfied. I pull her aggressively back towards me; strong enough to prevent her escape, but not so much as to be forceful. I want her to want me.

"Trust me. I got a license to operate this equipment," I whisper on her lips before I peck them.

"How strong is your back?"

A puzzled look comes over my face. "I don't know what you mean."

"I need to know if you can hold me up against a wall and make my body quiver like we in a earthquake."

"Daaaamn!" I hiss, staring at her in astonishment. Any slack in my dick is gone and it stands at perfect attention to salute her.

"Well, Black," she dares with a raised eyebrow. "You think you can handle that?"

"Hell yeah," I breathe almost to myself, while I follow her into 1559-B...

god face

"It isn't a matter of black is beautiful as much as it is white is not all that's beautiful."

- Bill Cosby

CHAPTER SIX

"Happy Birthday, C.J.," Ajae whispers in his ear, waking him with the warmth of a kiss on his cheek. "I got a present for you," she says lowly, watching him with eager eyes.

"I got a present for you too," he grumbles, placing her hand on his morning wood.

"I'm being serious," she replies with conviction, still stroking his manhood. "Close your eyes."

C.J. squints his eyes a bit, watching her through the tiny slits in his lids. Ajae searches his face and finds the little bit of white peeking from beneath his eyelids. "Stop cheating, C.J." She pops his shoulder with the back of her hand.

"A'ight," C.J. sighs, blowing out a long breath and pressing his eyes shut. He crosses his arms across his broad, hairless chest, while he waits for her to return to the bed.

"Okay." She sits a black-leather box on his toned stomach. "Now, open your eyes," she says anxiously, displaying a smile that, to C.J., is better than any gift she can give him.

"What is this?" he asks suspiciously, turning the box over in his hands.

"Just open it and see," she replies, between the fingers that cover her excited grin.

C.J. opens the box to find a sterling silver, big-face Rolex wristwatch gleaming inside its case.

"Whoa," he breathes with astonishment, surveying the small diamonds which surround the face of the watch, but not touching it. C.J. closes the box before his eyes can bulge out of his head. "This is too much, Ajae. We've only known each other a couple of days. I wouldn't feel right taking something like this from you."

"A man as fine as you are should be rocking some serious bling. That's not a privilege, sweetheart. It's damn near the law." She smiles, then leans over to kiss him.

"What I mean–" C.J. starts, pressing against her shoulder to prevent her kiss. "This is too expensive. How can you afford something like this?"

"Oh, I didn't buy it," Ajae blurts out quickly, her expression scrunching.

"I don't mean to be unappreciative, but I don't want one of your ex's watches."

"Ain't no man never wore that watch before. It's new and it's yours." She grins with a satisfaction that lets C.J. know it's about more than the watch. "I got it just for you."
This is the first time in a very long time that a woman has looked at him with- *pride*.

"That still doesn't answer my question." The concern in C.J.'s heart shows on his face.

"Let's just say it fell off a truck," Ajae replies slyly, tapping her chin. "It doesn't matter where it came from. It only matters how it looks on you." Ajae takes the watch out of the box and loosens the clasp. She slides it over his wrist. "See, perfect!" she exclaims with childlike giddiness. "You look like a Boss, son."

C.J. turns the watch over on his wrist, marveling at the weight of it, as it sparkles in the light of the morning sun. He still looks disturbed by its presence on his wrist and studies it closely.

"What's wrong, Black?" Ajae asks with more concern than the situation should warrant.

"Nothing," C.J. lies, with a hesitant uneasiness. Then, realizing that she will not accept that answer, he says- "Well... I just ain't cool wit' wearing this around the projects. You know how scandalous these niggahs 'round here can be." C.J. begins to take off the watch.

"No, baby," she whispers, grabbing his hand. "Ain't nobody gone fuck wit' you 'round here. You just need to know who you are," she states ever so smoothly, as subtle and convincing as the devil himself. Ajae reaches into the bottom drawer of her nightstand and pulls out a Ruger semi-automatic handgun. "If a niggah step to you, then take his ass out."

As Ajae hands the gun to C.J., he tries to remain as calm and manly as he can in front of her, but internally he is doing the mental equivalent of pissing on himself. He can't believe the woman he beholds, so full of beautiful light, possesses so much blackness in her soul.

"Hey, Shorty," C.J. grunts, pushing himself to a seated position before reaching across her nude body to place the gun on the nightstand. "If you want me to stay here with you, I feel like I need to get to know you a little better 'cuz frankly— you tripping me out right now."

C.J. feels compelled to be honest with her. The revelation of the fact that he has spent the last two nights sleeping in a bed beside her, unaware that only inches away she kept a firearm, was enough to scare him straight. That news had a sobering effect on his mind and even her large, round breasts staring at him could no longer induce their intoxicating brain fog. C.J. longs to know her story. He needs to understand how someone graced with so much radiance can turn away into such bleak darkness.

"I'm not trying to put you off, but this is where we live. We got to protect ourselves. The hoodlums and crackheads got guns and they don't plan on using them for no self-righteous purposes, so don't you go getting all self-righteous on me."

"Nah, baby. It ain't nothing like that," C.J. wheezes instantly, trying to smooth over the offense. "I just want to know who you are... For instance, how old are you?" C.J. places his elbow on his thigh and rests his chin in his palm.

Ajae smiles at his boyishness. C.J. is so tall and commanding that sometimes she forgets just how young he is. But for her, that is a lot of his charm. She gets to experience so many of his firsts with him, it's almost like being able to reclaim some of her lost childhood. With C.J., she can just be a kid again. The thought of it makes her sigh.

"I'm twenty-seven," she replies with considerable hesitation, refusing to meet C.J.'s eyes. "Am I older than you thought?"

"Yes," C.J. states with simple honesty. "But that doesn't matter. I know I wasn't what you thought being with a teenager would be like."

"Now, that's true," Ajae laughs delightfully, pointing her finger at him with a wink. "You definitely hold your own, young man."

"Where are you from?" C.J. continues his line of questioning.

"Actually, I was born and mostly raised in Charlotte," she nods. "I only spent about five years in Philly."

"Wow," C.J. says with a mild astonishment. "Your accent is so thick, I would've thought you lived there all your life."

"Yeah, well..." Ajae drawls, allowing the Southern, sing-song quality to seep into her voice. "I picked up the accent and decided to hang on to it when I came back. You would be surprised how much more respect you get from Southerners when they think you're from up north. It's like they think Northerners are more savvy or something, but the truth is— all ghettos are the same no matter what part of the country they're in. Everybody's just scraping to get by and trying to survive."

"So then you posing?" C.J. inquires lightly, not wanting to offend.

"Not really," Ajae shakes her head. "I am actually from Philly... Just not originally, that's all."

"So I guess you gone keep peddling that story right along with the one about you being Black."

Ajae's expression becomes solemn. Her green eyes dim with a glazed coldness. "Why would you say that I'm not Black?" she questions him with a professor's tone.

"You honestly want me to answer that?" He raises his eyebrows.

"Yes, I'm very curious to know why you think that."

"You have pink nipples. Only white people have pink nipples. Everybody else, Blacks, Indians, Spanish, Chinese- they all got brown nips. It's like–scientific," C.J. expounds matter-of-factly.

"Oh, I see. I guess nothing I say could trump your nipple theory," Ajae whispers with resigned consolation. "So if I told you that my mother's name is Asheema and that to get any Blacker than her you would have to be blue, would you believe me?"

"I-... I," C.J. stammers nervously over his words. He never conceived that her claim to Blackness could be true.

Ajae interrupts his stuttering, "My mother is Black... She is as Black as you are and she is beautiful to me, just like you are. I always envied her in that way. She always knew exactly who she was and marrying a White man never changed anything about her Blackness." Ajae lowers her eyes. "I didn't have that luxury. I always felt like I was trapped between two worlds, never able to gain access to either one. Black people rejected me because I looked so White, and White people shunned me because I didn't talk and act like them." Ajae gestures with her hands; first with one and then with the other to demonstrate the hopelessness of her situation.

"For a long time, it didn't matter. My mother and father surrounded me with so much love. They never let me believe there was anything wrong with me. They represented, to me, the best of what it was to be both Black and White. I figured I had it good. That is until my mother divorced my father and moved us in with her family in Philly." Ajae lets out a deep breath and rubs her forehead.

"What happened then?" C.J. asks with genuine interest, squeezing her hand for encouragement.

"To be quite honest, my mother's family treated me like trash. My younger brother was very brown-skinned like my mother so they embraced him, but they always treated me like a White Sidney Poitier in a Black rendition of 'Guess Who's Coming to Dinner'. I never felt comfortable in my grandmother's home. My aunts always watched me with a sly suspicion like they expected me to turn into a vampire and kill everybody. But my cousins-" Ajae slices the air with her hand. "They were the worst. They were so cruel to me; calling me names and pulling my hair. They would push me down in the dirt and kick me. I never understood why they hated me so much, after all we were flesh and blood, but I guess my skin color made me as alien to them as E.T. They acted like I wasn't human... like I didn't have feelings."

"They were just jealous of you. They wished that they could be you. Who wouldn't?" C.J. offers with obstinate assurance.

"Yeah well, you try telling that to a teenager who is already dealing with self-esteem issues." She shrugs her shoulders, letting them fall like heavy potato sacks. "When my Black family rejected me, I tried making White friends at my high school. That worked out well for a while. I was doing a good job of passing for White. I found a way to blend in with them so well that they didn't know what I truly was. As far as they were concerned, I was as White as them, but that is where the problem came in."

Ajae stands up and slips into the pink silk nightgown that laid on the floor beside her bed. She takes her pack of Newports from the clutter on her dresser and sparks up a cigarette.

"One day after cheerleading practice, I was hanging out with a couple of White kids when a Black boy comes walking past holding the hand of a White girl." Ajae blows out a smoke ring, then continues her story, using her cigarette like a pointer. "So this senior named Shelton says, 'You know what I call a nigger walking with a White girl? ... Firewood!'... Then he laughs about the shit like he's Steve Martin or something." Ajae is visibly shaken by the memory.

Her face looks stricken. She drops down on the foot of the bed. "I couldn't believe that someone would say something like that. It caught me completely off guard."

"What did you do?" C.J. is wide-eyed like a young boy captivated by a story of Cowboys and Indians.

"I punched him dead in the mouth. I knocked out one of his front teeth. I attacked him like a wild animal. It took several of our friends to break us up. Me and Shelton both got expelled from school after that fight, but it didn't much matter to me no way. I couldn't have gone back, even if I wanted to. When my mother came down to the school and the secret got out that I wasn't White, my so-called *friends* wouldn't so much as look at me again."

C.J. gently rubs her shoulder, trying as best as he can to console her. "So then," C.J. changes the subject. "What brought you back to Charlotte?"

"My mother's family was very big on *Education*. They said I couldn't make it in the world without one. When I refused to go back to high school or even get my GED, they made it a point to let me know that those were the conditions of my room and board. So at seventeen, I went off in search of my father. I was twelve when we left Charlotte, so all I ever knew of my father was his unconditional love for me. I figured if I could find him, everything would be alright. He'd help me get back on my feet," Ajae says with facetious enthusiasm.

"I guess I don't have to ask whether he helped you out or not," C.J. retorts sarcastically, wringing his hands with a sudden, unexpected nervousness.

"A person can't give you what they don't have, C.J. By the time, I found my father he was a shell of the man from my memories. I almost wished that I had never seen him that way, so I could just remember him as a clean-shaven, mild-mannered gentleman. When I finally located my father at a homeless shelter, he was a complete basehead, vacant in almost every way– barely even human. I tried putting him into Rehab and Mental Health, but I think seeing me- his first-born, made it worse. He killed himself, just blew his own brains out about a year later."

"Oh, I'm so sorry," C.J. says, with eyes full of condolence.

"Nah, I'm cool about it. Everybody has to make their own decisions. Based off what I saw, maybe he was better off dead."

Ajae lets her head fall to one side while she savors a long drag off of her cigarette. "It was so long ago now, it kind of feels like a dream... Like my father is still somewhere walking around, you know?"

"Actually, I do," C.J. says, licking his thick lips, as he meditates. "I feel the same way about my dad. In my mind, I know he's dead but somewhere in my heart, it's like he's still alive and I might see him again one day. Still, it's hard because when my father died, a piece of me died too."

Ajae and C.J. both pause to reflect on the concept. A brief moment of silence passes between them to honor the dearly departed.

"Not that I'm complaining," C.J. smiles, threading his fingers between hers. "But why did you stay?"

"Why does every woman stay?" Ajae's reluctance displays in her eyes. "I stayed because of a man. I got pregnant."

C.J.'s eyes dart around her barely furnished bedroom with pink bed sheets hung up to the windows. He realizes for the first time in the two days and two nights he spent with Ajae that he has not seen any trace or sign of children. The question burns in his mind, but Ajae continues her story before he can pose it.

"I was doing pretty good for a little while. My babies' daddy was taking care of me, so I didn't have to worry about nothing... That is until-" Ajae's voice trails off and she stares over at the window, as if distracted.

"Until what?" C.J. urges, turning her face back to his.

"Until, he got married and gave us his ass to kiss." Ajae squirms with a discomfort that she cannot contain, then throws up her hands in frustration. "I just feel like I'm telling you too much of my business. I don't want you judging me."

"Trust me," C.J. assures, placing her hands in his lap. "I'm not going to judge you. I may be young, but I've already done a lot of things that I'm not proud of. I'm your man now. So if you can't tell me everything, then who can you tell?"

"Oh so, you *my man* now?" Ajae squeaks, showing her delight at the statement.

"Damn, right, Shorty. Hey yo, I fucks with you for real." C.J. declares with intensity. He pulls her chin closer to his and kisses her lips. "Now tell me about your kids."

"I got a little boy named Jackson, after my daddy, and I got a baby girl named Ashana, for my momma."

Ajae reaches down into her pocketbook and lifts out a Polaroid of two butterscotch-colored children with large brown eyes and big, sandy-blonde curls. She hands it to C.J. and he studies them. They look so happy, smiling and embracing each other, like a photograph that comes inside of a new picture frame.

"They some beautiful kids. What's they ages?"

"Jacks is five and Ash is three."

"Cool… So when I get to meet 'em?" C.J. inquires cautiously.

"Well, they in foster care right now, but I get to go and see them every other weekend. My social worker took them from me over some bullshit, but I should be getting them back right after I finish this drug treatment program."

C.J. raises one eyebrow, careful not to seem judgmental.

"I'm not a junkie, C.J. I'm a mule." She presses her cigarette down into the ashtray on her nightstand. "I didn't have no prior record, so when the cops busted me, I told them I was a user instead of a dealer. It always works out better that way. They said they'd drop everything, if I went through this program for addicts. I lost my apartment while I was in Rehab and had to get this place once they transitioned me to outpatient."

Ajae lays down beside C.J. in the bed. "I think this is a good thing though. Now I got time to get my dough back up, so I don't have to bring my kids up in this dump. They coming home in like two more months so that should give me time enough to situate a decent living arrangement for us."

"When you say '*us*'… you mean, you and them?"

"I mean, me… and *you*… and them… **Us**." Ajae wraps her arm around C.J.'s waist and snuggles up close to him, pressing her cheek against his warm chest. "You welcome to rock wit' me as long as you want to."

"Believe me Shorty. You got me coming along for the ride, but I got one condition," C.J. says, holding up his pointer finger.

"Whatever you want… I'll do it, Black," Ajae whispers vulnerably, straddling his narrow waist. C.J. feels himself slipping back into the deceptively comfortable web of her seduction.

"Take your hair down for me." C.J. caresses her thighs, watching her hands move with slow hesitation up to her head.

Ajae stopped wearing her hair down many years ago. She got tired of people asking her if she was mixed- (like a dog or a drink) or reaching their fingers into it to search for extensions, so she just tucked the distraction away and tried to disappear along with it. She only takes her hair down once a day to comb it, then puts it right back in the smallest, tightest bun she can manage. Usually, Ajae just rocks an assortment of colorful head scarves– today being no exception.

Ajae unwraps the green scarf and pulls out all the pins and bands. Her wavy hair tumbles down, dripping over her shoulders like dark, golden honey.

"Gorgeous," C.J. sighs in amazement, as he lifts his hand to touch it. He stops abruptly, his hand hovering just an inch away from her head. He is apprehensive- like a child petting a wild, exotic animal. But when he feels the smooth, silky strands under his fingertips, his manhood stirs instantly.

He has never felt anything so smooth and gentle before. Running his fingers through her hair, C.J. imagines that this is what angels' wings must feel like. Her hair slips between his fingers, not like the coarse, nappy boar's bristles that the Black girls try to pass off as hair. He pulls her face to his and kisses her longingly, needing to be one with her, to experience the soft innocence of her Whiteness from the inside out. This is the closest he can ever get to knowing what it is to live in White skin– the delicate silkiness of it under his hands as he lifts the gown over her head. It– her skin– feels different and more supple to him than the thick, oily skin of the Black girls.

C.J. rolls over on top of Ajae. He parts her thighs and then hugs them tightly to her sides. He presses his long, thick manhood as deep inside as her Venus will allow. Ajae moans her pleasure, as C.J. fills her love to overflowing. She pulls him to her chest, embracing him tightly and running her hands over his lean, muscular back. They have been sexing like rabbits for days, but this morning the urgency of love has been satiated by the intimacy they just shared in their conversation.

C.J. makes slow, passionate love to Ajae, sucking on her lips as he kisses them. He works the middle, focused in deep concentration like a smith forging precious metals. He inhales the pleasant fragrance of her hair– like sweet bananas, but unlike the stale smell of curling irons and two-week old styling gel in the hair of the Black girls. The contrast instantly arouses C.J. to the point of popping like a water balloon tossed on hot pavement. C.J. feels the pressure of Ajae's warm, moist walls, clenching down on his organ in contractions.

"Yeah," she sighs. "That's right. Just like that, baby."

Ajae is more than his lover–

She is... his mother.

He feels the pulsing in her vagina and is exhilarated by the image of her giving birth to him, covering him in a new White life and delivering him to a world that might finally embrace him. Ajae is White– and therefore right. The solution to all the wrongness C.J. has felt in his life; the cure for his terminal case of Blackness. She is not, nor can she be the reflection of him– that is to say his Blackness, and for that reason he loves her. He can love her so completely, because it is as natural as his indoctrinated hatred for himself. He stares down into her serene, green eyes and is transformed. She completes him, the restitution of everything that the Blackness has stolen from him.

"Put your hands down here," she whispers, guiding his large hands to her buttocks.

His accomplishment, his award–

She is... his teacher.

"Don't stop... Go harder."

His validation, his reason to be–

She is... his father.

She is everyone and everything that he will ever need. Even in the midst of his darkness, her light still shines brightly, illuminating all things lost.

She is... The Great White Hope for his future.

"If a nation values anything more than freedom, it will lose its freedom: and the irony of it is that if it is comfort or money that it values more, it will lose that, too."

- W. Somerset Maugham

CHAPTER SEVEN

The first two weeks with Ajae went well for C.J.

Ajae took excellent care of him. He was astounded daily, by what a hustler she was. She brought home lots of cash each day from one venture or another. C.J. was glad that she was honest with him and didn't hide anything. He learned that she was a stripper, a thief, a drug dealer and a con-artist. There wasn't too much she wouldn't do for money, except mess around on C.J. with other guys. He accepted her and continued to love her because she was kind and respectful to him; treating him like an African king. Her vehement dedication to him bordered on that of a worshipper for her god. Ajae's love was overwhelming to C.J. and he often found himself in awe of her generosity. There wasn't anything she would not do for- or to him, if it made him happy.

Ajae upgraded C.J.'s style and introduced him to a new way of life. His haircut stayed sharp and fresh. His gear was tight. C.J. donned huge diamond solitaires in both of his ears. She made sure he stayed laced from head to ankle in COOGI, FUBU, Cross Colors, Starter jackets and fitted caps– all the most famous name brands and latest fashions. His feet were an entirely different affair. His ever-increasing array of rare footwear became the star of the show. Ajae kept him in fly multi-colored Tims, Air Jordans, Duckhead and Air Force Fives. He had silver and gold jewelry to go with any ensemble she put together, but more than anything he put on, it was Ajae that looked the best on him.

He encouraged her to wear her hair down and take off the dark makeup. Ajae started rocking big blonde, baby-doll curls and light lavender and turquoise eye shadows with pink lipsticks. She became so beautifully feminine. No longer the *Around-The-Way Girl*, she looked more like a European fashion model. C.J. beamed with pride whenever they would walk, hand-in-hand at the mall, up and down the aisles of the stores.

He could see the look in the eyes of people, both Black and White, astonished at how he landed such a fine, White girl. They were impressed with him. The store clerks, the brothers, even the police showed him more respect. The homeboys would check Ajae out, in her skin tight DKNY denim jacket and jeans, then shoot C.J. an approving nod, as if to say in the unspoken man language, "You doing it big, homey. Shorty phat as hell."

The Black females cut their eyes at them, but C.J. knew that was just because they were jealous. Being with Ajae had finally made him– visible. Her light shined on him and all of a sudden, it was like C.J. was the most attractive man on the planet. All the project chicks, who never gave him the time of day, came out of the woodworks, lining up to try and jock him. Some of them were bold, even going so far as to offer to suck his dick. An offer that he always declined because Ajae was the undisputed champion of that craft.

As a matter of fact, there wasn't a female alive who could fuck with Ajae, on any level, as far as C.J. was concerned. He toted her on his arm, up and down the block, like a blinged out diamond bracelet.

"C.J." Ajae appears in the doorway of the bedroom.

"What's up, Shorty?" he asks casually, looking up from his video game. He puts the Nintendo joystick down and steps over to her, wrapping his arms around her waist.

"I'm pregnant," she replies flatly, revealing the plastic strip she held behind her back.

"Whoa," C.J. bellows, releasing his hold like her body suddenly became scalding hot.

"I know you not gone start tripping now," she fusses with a whip of her neck.

"No, um..." C.J. searches around with his eyes, hunting for the right words. He looks as nervous as if Ajae had a loaded gun to his head. "If this is my baby, then isn't it a little too soon for you to know you pregnant?"

"*If* this is your *baby*?" Ajae mocks him with narrowed eyes. "What are you trying to say, C.J.? I'm not a slut. I don't get down like that."

"I'm not saying that you do. All I'm saying is that it may've been somebody before me."

"Oh so now you gone try me like that," Ajae says, pointing her finger in his face. "Like I just let every niggah hit me raw."

"You said that– not me," C.J. mumbles, pressing his hands to his chest.

"You know what?" Ajae hisses at him. "Fuck you, C.J. I don't have to explain my whereabouts and give you detailed accounts like I'm some fucking criminal being interrogated by the cops. I took care of you like you was one of my kids. I don't need you to raise our baby. Get the hell out of my apartment." She points towards the front door.

"Oh no, no, no, Shorty. I'm not going nowhere." C.J. hugs her tightly to his chest, pinning her hands behind her back. "I love you. You got me for life Boo, so I hope you don't think I would skip out like that over something like this."

Ajae struggles against his unyielding restraint. "Let me go," she grunts angrily. "You can go right on ahead and leave. You damn sho' ain't the first and you probably won't be the last neither."

"Look, I don't care whose baby this is. You're mine now. I accept you and everything that comes along with being in your life."

"So you still don't believe that this is your baby?" She asks calmly, glaring at him with cold eyes.

C.J. remains silent for a minute while he thinks. His doubt is as big as an elephant in the room.

"I believe *you,* since you say it is. You ain't lied to me yet, so I don't have no reason not to trust you."

A slow, hesitant smile appears on both of their faces. C.J. kisses her and releases her hands. She hugs his slender waist, pressing her cheek against his broad chest. C.J. makes his best effort not to let his apprehension show in front of Ajae. He tries to mask his emotions and kisses her once again.

"I love you, Shorty," he declares, caressing her chin. "I'ma be there for you and this baby. Believe that."

"I do," she responds quietly, peering up into his dark, slanted eyes.

C.J. tucks the Ruger at the small of his back and picks up his hoodie, then starts for the door. "I'm going out to pick up some things from the store. You need me to bring you something back?"

"Nothing but you, Black," she says coyly with a grin. "I don't need nothing but you."

"A'ight. Be back in a minute." He presses his fingers to his lips and brushes them on Ajae's cheek, then disappears out the door.

Even though he doesn't need to, C.J. pulls on his jacket while he trots down the front steps. There is still a cool chill in the night air, but his blood is boiling. He takes long, angry steps down the street to the corner, as he tries to clear his mind.

"Hey, C.J." Epiphany Jennings appears on the steps of 1555. She startles C.J. a bit. He didn't see her sitting there on the stoop. She blended into the darkness, almost as Black as the night itself. Only her eyes and gleaming, white teeth, displayed in a smile, revealed her location.

"What up, Shorty?" C.J. says, without glancing in her direction.

"Just hadn't seen you in a while and I wanted to speak."

Epiphany used to crush on C.J. back in tenth grade when he went to her high school. She even offered to tutor him in Chemistry, the class they had together, but he declined. Epiphany with her smooth, chocolate complexion and large afro puff, failed to solicit any attention from the boys at her school because she wasn't known for giving it up. But giving it up is what she was just about ready to do. She waited though because she never wanted to give it to any other boy but C.J. What she didn't know is that for all of her Black beauty, her passion for C.J. was lost on account of her Blackness. Ajae had diminished C.J.'s attraction for teenage girls, but even if he were to sex a girl his own age, Epiphany was way too far down on the complexion color chart to even register his attention.

"So what you getting into tonight?" Epiphany asks, allowing her knees to spread apart with the question.

"Look– I'm in a bit of a hurry," C.J. replies dismissively, looking down at his diamond-faced watch. "I'll catch up with you later, Monie."

Instead of turning left to go to the convenience store, C.J. crossed the street and continued straight. Even though she was only a few buildings down, C.J. hadn't seen his mother even once since he moved in with Ajae. He still had the pack of Newports his mother requested over two weeks ago in his pocket. Before C.J. could climb the first step, he heard a familiar voice in the distance.

"You wanna' party, darling?" she slurs, leaning over into the driver side window of a red Geo Metro. C.J. would not have recognized the woman with the long, almost plastic looking blonde wig, if she didn't sound just like his mother.

Couldn't be, C.J. thinks to himself, as he begins to walk down to the next corner. When he gets a little closer, he starts to relax. The woman is clearly too old and skinny to be his mother. C.J. turns to go back to Camille's apartment.

"Hey, C.J. baby!" Camille calls out from across the street. She comes trotting over to him in a silver mini-skirt and tall, red pumps, slinging the blonde hair over her shoulder. "How you doing, Sugar?" She asks, licking her lips anxiously.

C.J. is horrified. He looks down on the woman with disbelief, still trying to keep the image of his mother separate from this night stalker standing before him.

"Don't stand there gawking at ya' momma like that. Give me a hug." She throws her arms around his waist. C.J. almost jumps out of his skin, but resists the urge to push her away. Instead he takes his mother's gaunt face between his hands. He looks deeply into her eyes, searching for some recognition, but doesn't find any. Even her eyes are empty, their chestnut brown turned a dark, void sea of blackness.

"What's wrong with you?" C.J. breathes in disgust.

"What you talking 'bout boy?" Camille waves him off with a flip of her hand, then shoves it into the pocket of her black sweatshirt. "I'm doing fine– no thanks to you. I send you out for a pack of cigarettes weeks ago and you don't even come back, or call, or nothing. You coulda' been dead for all I know. Hell, *I* coulda' been dead for all *you* know."

"You right, Mama," C.J. says compassionately. "I shouldn't have done that, but what the hell are you doing out here?"

"Well, you know they cut my check off now that you eighteen." She purses her lips and glares at him with disapproving eyes. "But you don't look like you missed a meal since you been gone. You got some money for ya' Mama." She holds out her hand.

C.J. places the pack of cigarettes in her palm. She smiles as though he placed a hundred-dollar bill in it.

"What's Jerome doing? He ain't taking care of you?"

Camille grunts with furrowed brows, as she pulls the wrapping off the pack. "He doing what he do," she drawls passively. "I don't get in his business."

"Well, if he's living with you, then taking care of you is his business." C.J. grabs his mother's elbow tightly and drags her back to 1553-B.

She struggles against C.J. grip. "Just leave it alone, baby. Don't worry about me," she insists. "I'm fine. Really, I'm fine."

C.J. pulls back the screen door and steps across the threshold of the open front door. He walks down the dark entryway to the living room where red light is spilling from the doorway. C.J. is dismayed when he enters to find Jerome standing in the center of the room with his jeans around his ankles. He holds up the bottom of his black wife beater while some young crack hoe kneels at his feet, sucking and slobbering hungrily on his penis, as if it is her first meal in days. His homeboys, chilling on the couches and drinking forties with topless females, cheer and yell when he begins to piss all over her face.

"What the fuck?" C.J. bellows from the doorway.

"Oh hey there, Little Man," Jerome greets him cordially, shaking his dick like he is finishing up at a urinal. He pulls up his jeans and tosses a plastic bag at the soggy girl before crossing over to C.J. He extends his palm for a handshake- the same hand that just previously held his genitalia.

"Nah man." C.J. takes a step backward to avoid the hand. "This ain't no social visit. I got some business to handle with you."

"Oh well, why didn't you say so?" Jerome presents a devious smile. "I been waiting on you to get hip, Little Man, so I could put you on to some real shit."

Jerome calling him *Little Man* again, almost sends C.J. over the edge. He calms himself, then glances back at his mother who stands by the front doorway, shaking and trembling absently, as if by some other force than the cold weather.

"I know you ain't put my momma out there to trick," C.J. hisses through clenched teeth.

"No son, I didn't. Camille put herself out there." Jerome looks past C.J. at Camille and then back to C.J again. "Your mother developed a nasty little habit. I told her to stay away from my stash, but Camille's got an appetite for destruction like you wouldn't believe. She didn't stop until she got herself in debt with me. I told her she has until next week to pay me back or else." Jerome shrugs his shoulders. "Everything she did after that has been her own decision," he states diplomatically.

"You must be out yo' fucking skull, if you think I'm gone let you crack out my momma, and then threaten her all while you living up in her house."

"Now ain't that the pot calling the kettle Black," Jerome replies laughingly, cocking his head to the side. "From what I understand, you living off one of my dope girls down the block and looks like she been keeping you up real good."

C.J.'s eyes widen with rage. His breathing intensifies.

"Let me tell you something," Jerome whispers, throwing his arm around C.J.'s shoulders. "That Ajae is a hustler man. Don't let her snow you. She makes me a lot of money in this drug game– but before all that, she was the best piece of pussy I ever put niggahs on to. She used to have them lining up around the block just for a taste of her lemon meringue pie." Jerome stands back and crosses his arms with a look of nostalgia in his eyes. "But I don't have to tell you about that do I, *Little Man*?"

More than Jerome's insult of his mother and his female, it was probably the third *Little Man* that sent C.J. careening past the point of no return– never to return. He punched Jerome in the mouth, sending him flying into the closet door.

"You gone let a ran-through piece of pussy fuck up your mind," Jerome blurts, wiping blood from his mouth. He charges C.J. grabbing him around the waist and tackling him to the floor.

Camille screams for help while they tussle, but none of the men in the living room will get involved. They stand on their feet as spectators instead. Jerome doesn't keep the upper hand for long. C.J. grabs Jerome's black wife beater and throws him against the wall like a rag doll. C.J. jumps to his feet, armed with undeterred rage. He lifts Jerome from the floor, holding his ripped shirt in one hand, while he smashes him in the face with fists pulled far back past his shoulder and launched into his jaw.

C.J. pummels Jerome until his jaw breaks, then lets him slump to the floor, realizing in that moment, that he may have likewise broken his own hand. C.J. stands over Jerome, wagging his hand to dissipate the pain. C.J. looks down at the wounds on his knuckles and is instantly enraged again. He begins to kick Jerome in the ribs.

"Who's the fucking Little Man now, bitch!" he yells, between kicks. Before he has time to realize what he's doing, C.J. finds himself standing over Jerome with the Ruger in hand, racked and aimed at his chest.

"Don't do it, C.J." His mother calls empathetically to him. "Jerome ain't worth it." Camille takes a step toward him. All of the muscles in his outstretched arm are tensed. C.J.'s face is constrained in a malevolent scowl. Camille doesn't dare touch him, but instead allows her voice to perch on his shoulder like a tiny guardian angel. "Don't do it. Put the gun down, baby."

C.J. huffs out labored breaths, his chest heaving in pain– a stinging pain so intense that his eyes water. His heart races and he can't think straight.

"Put it down," Camille urges more insistently.

If a niggah step to you... then take his ass out, Ajae's voice took up residence on the unoccupied shoulder.

C.J. squints his eye to aim. He slowly squeezes the trigger and fires a shot... into the wall, mere inches away from Jerome's right ear. Not a miss, but a test. C.J. wants to see if he has the heart to kill a man. Jerome presses his eyes closed and trembles. He cautiously puts his hands up in surrender to C.J. Blood and drool drip from Jerome's mouth and he begins to cry. He probably would have wet himself if he hadn't already emptied his bladder in the face of the crack hoe.

Ashes...

"C.J." His mother begins with clarity in her eyes that he hasn't seen since he was six. "You are your father's only son. Don't do this to him and his memory. Don't do this to yourself. If you pull that trigger, then you will be a coward– not a man."

C.J.'s resolve begins to dissolve. Images of his father teaching him how to fish rush into his head and he is instantly ashamed of himself. Then C.J.'s thinks about Ajae and seeing his child born; the vision of it pulls the gun down all on its own. C.J. lowers the weapon, as if forced by a will other than his own. His shoulders slump dejectedly. The gun feels heavier in his hand than it ever has.

To Ashes...

"Thank God," Camille sighs, wrapping her son in her arms. She lays her hand on the back of his head and presses his face into her collar, reducing him down to her little boy. "I love you C.J. You did the right thing." She kisses his cheek and rubs his arm.

C.J. begins to sob and for that reason, he could not hear– the rack of the slide. His mother holds him close to her bosom and for that reason she could not see– the flash of light from the muzzle of Jerome's gun.

Unsuspecting and innocent, embracing each other with love.

They all fall down...

83

Take this kiss upon the brow!
And, in parting from you now,
Thus much let me avow --
You are not wrong, who deem
That my days have been a dream;
Yet if hope has flown away
In a night, or in a day,
In a vision, or in none,
Is it therefore the less gone?
All that we see or seem
Is but a dream within a dream...

**- Excerpt from <u>A Dream Within A Dream</u>
By Edgar Allan Poe (1850)**

CHAPTER EIGHT

"If you gone pull a gun on somebody, Niggah, you best be ready to use it."

Pow, Pow, Pow

C.J. startles awake, his heart racing wildly. The loud gunshots from the Black gangster movie frightened and roused him out of slumber.

Or was it?

C.J. looks around the unfamiliar bedroom. It is nicely decorated with modest cherry wood furniture and fancy hunter green drapes over the windows. Although the room looks completely foreign to C.J., he searches his mind and cannot produce an image of how it should be. He reaches over to the nightstand for the television remote and turns the set off. He listens carefully, sure that he heard something... or someone else.

"C.J.!" Camille belts out. Her voice finds his ears, but it is faint as if she called to him through water. C.J. is still groggy and disorientated, but he manages to get to his feet and shuffle out into the hallway. C.J. shakes his head. He is dizzy and short of breath. He can't quite identify the source of his anxiety, but he knows that something is *very* wrong. C.J. stretches his back and rubs his smooth baldhead, doing his best to gather his bearings. Before he can get a grasp on reality, he glances up to find that he is on the second level of his childhood home, staring down the stairs at his mother in a turquoise knee-length, A-line dress with a pink-checkered apron over it. Her shiny, salt-and-pepper hair is pulled back into a neat, pristine bun.

"I know you're still not feeling well since your fall, but do you think you can come down here and help me out for just a second."

C.J. blinks hard and stares blankly at his mother. He holds his breath. He would have been sure that his heart stopped, if he couldn't hear it beating loudly in his ears.

"Did you hear me, C.J.?" She inquires with frustration. "I said I need your help."

This has to be a dream, C.J. thinks to himself.

C.J. holds on tightly to the banister and slowly double-steps his way down the stairs towards her. He reaches out his fingers to touch her face. The warmth of her smooth, brown skin alarms him. She is real and that is shocking to him. Yet again, he searches his mind for an answer to the conundrum, but cannot find one. After all, she is supposed to be real– *right*? She is his mother and, by the smell of things, she is working on their dinner, as she has at this same time of the day, every evening for three decades.

"Stop playing around, C.J.," she says forcefully, swatting his hand away from her face. "Your daddy will be home any minute now and I still haven't finished the cake because I can't lift that heavy bird out of the oven. With all these grown folks living up in this house, you'd think I could get more help around here..." Her voice trails off, as she goes marching through the dining room and back into the kitchen.

C.J. blows out the breath that he's been holding in. He looks around the foyer of the house in Hidden Valley and can't shake the feeling that he shouldn't be there.

But why?

C.J. couldn't put his finger on the bizarre terror that gripped him when he looked across the dining room at his mother, standing in front of the open oven door beckoning for him to come.

"This bird gone be dry as the desert, if you don't come on and get it out now."

C.J. pushes the uncomfortable feeling down into the pit of his stomach and trots over to the kitchen. He stops involuntarily at the edge of the carpet, before the linoleum flooring starts. He stands there frozen in place, wide-eyed and stunned like a deer in headlights.

"Come on, C.J." Camille bellows in aggravation.

C.J. delicately tiptoes across the kitchen, as if his socked feet will break the floor. His mother glares at him disapprovingly with puckered lips, as she hands him the oven mitts. C.J. pulls the bird out of the oven and places it on top of the stove for her.

"Thank you, baby," she says, promptly nudging him out of the way with her forearm. She makes quick work of putting her two cake pans into the oven and adjusting the temperature knobs. "The arthritis in this shoulder is getting worse. I just couldn't carry the load by myself. Good thing I got two good, strong Black men and one on the way to help me manage." She glances up at him with love and pats his cheek.

"You ain't pregnant are you, Momma?" C.J. asks, perplexed by her last comment.

"Oh heavens no. I tied my tubes after I had your sister," she offers dismissively. "I'm talking about *your* baby."

C.J. is taken aback. He puts his hand against the refrigerator to steady himself.

"I know y'all think this is another little girl, but Epiphany is carrying that baby too low. I know a little boy when I see one." Camille whips the air with her wooden spoon.

"What baby?" C.J. stammers, his eyebrows furrowing with genuine concerned confusion. "Who is Epiphany?"

"Epiphany is your wife," his mother replies with a tone that is equally as concerned.

"My what?"

"Your wife."

"Who?" C.J. blares, his tone rising in agitation.

"Epiphany!"

"Who is Epiphany?" C.J. catches himself shouting in his mother's face. She presses her palm to his forehead, then checks his cheeks and neck.

"Sugar, I know that fall got you all disoriented. The doctors told us to expect some complications, but I need you to just take it easy. Alright?" She squeezes his hand, and gazes into his eyes. "Why don't you go on back upstairs and lay down a little while longer. Epiphany has to pick up Najah from dance. Once your father gets home, he still needs to take his bath and put on his dinner clothes, so you've got plenty of time to rest before the meal."

C.J.'s mind races, but his thoughts dead-end on back roads of memories that he cannot forget or remember. C.J. resigns from the conversation with his mother and starts out of the kitchen. Since he cannot pinpoint the problem, C.J. decides to just clear his mind and enjoy the silence. As he steps into the foyer and begins to climb the stairs, the front door swings open.

A female who looks as much like Camille as C.J. looks like Courtney comes waltzing casually into the house. She is gorgeous, with creamy bronze skin and a comma-like dimple in her left cheek. She wears a flannel headband on her long, black hair that is pulled up into a ponytail.

"What's up, C.J.? You feeling any better?" Samantha asks with her dark, slanted eyes steady on him.

"I don't know," C.J. sighs dejectedly.

"Well... if you play this thing right, Ma won't keep making you come down for her *family dinners*. She's so anal. She's about to work my **nerves**; making me come for dinner every night. When I'm home from school, I want to see my friends and hang out, not be cooped up in the house every day with y'all. You'd think that with you and your family living here, she would have enough people around the table without forcing me to show up." She slides out of her navy pea coat and opens the closet to hang it up. "I just want you to know I only came because it's your birthday... otherwise I would've gone to the movies with my new boo, *Omavi*."

"It's my birthday!" C.J. huffs in astonishment, glancing out the window to see snow on the ground. "How old am I?" C.J. asks, touching his chest and stomach, as if his body has suddenly become alien to him.

"You're twenty-nine for like three more hours or whatever." Samantha watches him with suspicious eyes. "Are you sure you're going to be alright, Big Brother? I know you actually bumped your head, but right now you acting like you done *really* bumped your head."

"What day is it today?"

"It's Monday."

"No I mean the date. What is today's date?"

"I told you– It's December 28th... It's your birthday."

"I know, but what year is this?" C.J. grips her shoulders, staring at her with the eyes of a crazy man.

"It is the year of our Lord, two thousand and three," she states sarcastically with a British accent, as she eyes C.J. nervously. "Are you in a time warp, C.J.?"

Before he can answer, the door swings open a second time and Courtney stands at the doorway. He takes off his boots, placing them outside on the mat before crossing the threshold into the foyer.

The sight of Courtney almost brings C.J. to his knees. He runs to his father and falls on him, hugging him tightly around his neck. C.J. begins to kiss his face and lips in a way most inappropriate for a father and son.

"What the hell is your problem, C.J.?" Courtney growls angrily. His work bag drops to the floor. "Son, can't you see my hands are full?" He pushes C.J. aside with his forearm and stares at him in bewilderment.

"I'm sorry, Dad," he heaves heavily, out of breath from excitement. C.J. dabs the tears from his eyes with the back of his hand. "I'm just so glad to see you. I missed you so much."

Courtney looks from C.J. to Samantha, who shrugs her shoulders and then walks towards the kitchen.

"I just saw you this morning before I went to work. I checked on you before I left, remember?" Courtney says, picking up his work bag.

C.J. shakes his head. It seems as though he couldn't recall seeing his father for a very long time. He is compelled by an overwhelming urge to hug his father again...

But why?

C.J. and Courtney have never been very physically affectionate towards each other, so he didn't know why he longed to embrace his father and never let him go. Something felt different about today. C.J. searches his mind yet once more and cannot find anything out of place. His mother was in the kitchen, poking her carrot cake layers with toothpicks. His father arrived home right on time, not a minute too early. Sam was back from Fayetteville State University on winter break, and itching to be fast– as usual.

Nope– not even one thing out of place.

"Do me a favor?" Courtney says, tapping C.J.'s chest to get his attention. "Next time you get to missing me too much. Just come see me at the garage like your mother does instead of jumping on me like that when I walk through the door. You don't want to give your old man a heart attack, do you?" He pats C.J. heavy on the shoulder and then heads off to the kitchen to get an eyeful of his wife, before going upstairs to bathe.

C.J. pauses at the foot of the staircase and muses momentarily, as he watches his family positioned in their various places around the dining room. Samantha helps Camille put the dishes on the table while she shoos Courtney away.

C.J. smiles, then shuffles slowly back up the stairs and down the hallway to the room that has always been his. As he enters it and steps over a couple pairs of high heels, he realizes that he has come to share this room with a female. C.J. drops down on the edge of the disheveled bed. His head is still spinning from all that he has just witnessed. However, the pressure that closes in on his head like a vice grip refusing to let him go, is the discomfort of not knowing why he is so uncomfortable. Why is he so disturbed by being in the house he has spent more years inside than outside of?

C.J. lays back against the large, fluffy decorative pillows on the bed. He throws his feet up and crosses his arms over his chest. He closes his eyes, trying desperately to relax and clear his mind. The throbbing in his head, along with several unsolved mysteries will not let him rest.

He begins to search around the room with his eyes, hunting for a picture of this supposed wife of his. C.J. is sure that he should know what she looks like. After all they have been together since high school. They met in Chemistry class during their tenth grade year. Epiphany was his science tutor before she became his girlfriend. Thanks to her, C.J. got an A in the class and his first piece of ass. Still, C.J. rifled through a myriad of vivid memories with her and could not recall one glimpse of what she actually looked like.

C.J. laid in deep meditation, stretched out across the bed. He didn't even know he had fallen asleep until he was awakened.

"Hey honey." Her voice is soothing to his ears, with the familiarity that a husband and wife of so many years should share. "I didn't want to wake you, but dinner is ready." Epiphany sits down next to him on the bed. C.J. is awake, but he opens his eyes slowly to observe his wife again... but as if for the first time.

She is beautiful to him. Just as she should be. He surveys her face, feeling a foreign intimacy with her surfacing in his heart. Her smooth, dark skin is the color of mahogany. Her long, auburn Nubian locks are twisted into a decorative style that resembles a large crown. C.J. places his hand behind her neck and pulls her lips to his.

The kiss feels right and complete to him. He looks into her large, black eyes and loves her with an instant, but perennial affinity. He sees, not just in the mirror of her eyes, but also in her face, in her keen intellect and in her strong, toned body the reflection of himself. She is his queen- the consummate compliment to all that he is. He favors her. C.J. places his hand to her cheek and they blend almost seamlessly into one another. He observes the solidarity of their skin tones and is instantly satisfied, knowing that there is no other creature designed who can bring perfect balance and harmony to who he is as a man.

C.J. presses his forehead to hers. As if by telepathy, they communicate without words. In each other, they find sympathy and empathy, unduplicated anywhere else in the world. Epiphany understands him in the silence because she is him. They are one and the same. In their Blackness, she has shared with him his failures and defeats, his challenges and struggles, his obstacles and stumbling blocks. Irrevocably bonded through the adversity that Blackness has wrought for them both, she has also celebrated with him his triumphs and successes, his achievements and his evolution, his transcendence and his excellence. Because of the Blackness they cannot be separated–Black man and Black woman, from each other and still thrive. Apart from each other they would cease to exist. That is to say,

The beginning of him

She is... his mother

The best of him

She is... his sister

All of him

She is... his daughter

Epiphany is the combination and culmination of all the Black women that C.J. loves and who love him. For that reason, he loves her with his whole heart– out of respect for himself, respect for her who birthed him, and respect for the daughter he must raise and inspire to love herself. Epiphany- his wife, is deserving of an even greater love and honor, than he has ever bestowed on any of them because out of them all, she is the only one who will always and completely be his.

"I heard you had a rough day," she says empathetically.

C.J. nods. "Mostly because I missed you," he breathes. "I'm so glad to see you." He kisses her again, then allows his hand to come to rest on her swollen belly.

"Really?" She gawks at him, half-suspicious and half-astonished.

"Yeah. I needed you to help me sort this whole thing out."

"Camille told me that you were pretty confused today." She reaches over to the small pharmacy on their night stand. Epiphany lifts one of several light brown bottles. "Did you forget to take your medication?"

A confused expression appears on C.J.'s face. "What medication?"

"C.J.– I set an alarm on your phone for you to remember these things. You have to take your medication on time or else you're going to feel like crap," she fusses at him. Epiphany shakes two large blue pills out of the bottle and then leaves the bedroom. She returns with a room temperature glass of water and hands him the pills. "I guess you can go ahead and take these now since we're about to eat. Your mother said you wouldn't eat all day."

C.J. shrugs his shoulders and then throws back the water with a wince.

"Baby, I know how hard this is for you. If you are dealing with half the stress that I am, I can only imagine that you feel like giving up, but you can't. Me and Najah need you to get better."

C.J. doesn't let the concern show on his face. He glances at the substantial amount of brown medicine bottles, trying to remember whatever it is that Epiphany thinks he knows.

"I talked to the doctors. They said that they don't think the fall you took last week has affected the cancer. They believe a few more rounds of chemotherapy should put you back into remission."

C.J. covers his mouth with his hands. The shock of the news is overwhelming him. He searches his mind, scrolling and scrolling down a long, blank page.

"How long?" he whispers.

"The doctors don't know everything C.J. We've been praying and we know you're not going anywhere anytime soon."

"No," he waves his hands. "How long have I had... brain cancer?" he inquires, finding a small clue peeking from beneath the large black blanket over his mind.

"Well, we don't know how long it was there, but they found it about three years ago during your NASA physical." The weight of her words fall heavy on C.J. causing even his body to sag from the pressure of them.

"You're doing so good C.J. I don't want you to get discouraged." She rubs his shoulder. "You're going to have bad days like this one, but it will get better. I promise you that. They say the tumor is shrinking so hopefully that will help your memory."

Tears come to C.J.'s eyes, as he realizes that his baldhead is not a fashion statement. He reaches for Epiphany and she hugs him longingly, feeling the sting in her eyes as well. She refuses to cry in front of him. She cries on her way to work after she drops off Najah and then takes the long way home to get her tears out before she picks her daughter up. Sometimes when the pain is too much, she hides in the coat closet and cries away from everyone. She doesn't want C.J. to see her break down when he needs her to be strong.

"I don't want you to fall again, so if you don't think you can make it downstairs, I can bring your plate up to you."

C.J. shakes his head. "No... I'm coming down. I want to eat with my family. The way I always have. The way I always will."

Epiphany smiles brightly at her husband. She is so proud of him. She takes his hands and helps him to stand. "Do you need me to go get Courtney to help you?" She asks cautiously, watching him wobble a bit on his feet.

"I got a lot of rest today. I feel fine." C.J. steadies himself and begins to take slow, confidant steps.

Once downstairs, they all take their seats for supper. Courtney, in his pressed shirt and slacks, sits at the head of the table. C.J. sits across from him at the other end. Camille sits to Courtney's left with Samantha at her side. Across from them sit Epiphany and six-year old Najah. Courtney gives the command for all to join hands. He bows his head and likewise, they all follow his example. He says the grace, humbly thanking the Lord Jesus for the meal which sits before them, for the lovely Black hands that prepared it, and for all of their many blessings.
"Amen," in unison.

Courtney carves. Camille serves. Each plate neatly arranged with chicken and whipped potatoes, smothered in yellow gravy and a side of cabbage mixed with collard greens, just the way Courtney likes them.

When mother passes out the biscuits, both Courtney and C.J. receive a double portion. They hold the thick, fluffy biscuits, using them to shovel their food onto the fork, as they eat from both hands.

For the seemingly insignificant accomplishment of a full belly, Camille awards to each of them a delicious piece of carrot cake with cream cheese frosting. A treat- for which Najah was almost passed over because she didn't eat all of her cabbage greens. Confronted with the pout on her angelic face, Camille folds and presents her with a thin, consolation slice of cake.

Darkness falls around the house. Najah sleeps at the end of the upstairs hallway in a small room that used to belong to Samantha. She is fast asleep before Epiphany can finish her bedtime story. Epiphany tucks Najah in tightly, snuggling the covers up under her chin, before clicking off the lamp beside her bed. She tiptoes down the hall, hoping not to disturb Courtney and Camille, who (according to the sounds coming from their room) are not yet asleep. Epiphany creeps into the bedroom opposite from the master and is surprised to find C.J. is still awake. His eyes lock on hers when she enters the doorway.

"Hey honey. You should be asleep." Her eyes are sad with deep concern. "You need all the rest you can get."

"Well, I am resting, but I've been asleep all day," C.J. replies lackadaisically. "I can't sleep anymore." The bitterness surfaces in his tone, as he turns his eyes back to the television. He lays, bathed in the blue glow of the screen, clenching his jaw to fight back tears. The shifting, flashing lights from the set cast long, dark shadows over his body. C.J. uncrosses his arms and rubs both hands over his head, overwhelmed with hopeless frustration and disparaging grief. "I don't want to sleep anymore. I don't want to sleep away what very well could be the last days of my life."

Epiphany rushes to his side, kneeling at the edge of the bed. "Don't talk like that C.J. It's not fair to me. I need you to..." Epiphany's voice trails off as she realizes that her words are falling on deaf ears. "Believe..." She whispers so faintly that she is not sure whether she actually said the word or only thought it.

"I'm just so tired, Ni." His eyes are moist and pained. "I believed once. They told me that I could get my life back. Now less than a year later, I'm right back here. Puking my guts out... too weak to take care of you and Najah or even just myself." His lips quiver, as he looks up at the ceiling, trying to stop the tears that are determined to fall. "We lost our house. We lost everything and it was all because of me."

"Baby, don't say that," she hisses with a deep threat in her voice. "All of those are just material possessions that we can't take with us anyway. None of it would have meant anything to me without you, C.J." She takes his face in her hands, staring eye to eye with him. "I would trade the whole world for one day with you C.J., even if I knew that one day was all I could have." She kisses his lips. "I love you."

"I love you too, sweetheart," C.J. sighs with closed eyes. "You always know just what I need to hear." He caresses her cheek.

"I only tell you the truth... what's in my heart."

"Bring my baby up here," he says, inching over for Epiphany to get into bed with him. "You know Ma says it's a boy."

"Well, I don't care. I just want the baby to be healthy," she puffs under the strain of the pressure on her chest when she lays back. Epiphany can't remember being this big with Najah at only five months, but she is already feeling like this will be a long, miserable pregnancy.

Epiphany lifts her teal oversized nightshirt and C.J. greets his child with a kiss, as he does every night. C.J. places his ear to her protruding belly button, listening for any sound that will signal activity from the fetus.

"I think the baby's sleeping," Epiphany whispers, covering his hands with hers.

"Well he needs to wake up for Daddy. I haven't had a chance to hang out with him all day." C.J. speaks the words into her belly. Epiphany giggles when the child within her begins to stir. C.J. is mesmerized, watching the tiny bump of an elbow, or a knee or maybe even a heel, poke to the surface under her beautiful, Black skin.

"There he is." C.J. claps with the enthusiasm of a young child. "You hear your Daddy, don't you? You know it's time to play." C.J. presses the mystery body part with his fingertip and the baby responds, poking the limb out in a new place. "My favorite game... hide and seek," C.J. beams, his smile so bright and radiant that Epiphany swoons for him. She rubs his head while he engages the unborn baby that wiggles within her. "I got you," C.J. mocks the baby, chasing the limb across her skin with his finger.

Suddenly small drops of blood drip on to Epiphany's stomach. C.J. is instantly distressed by it, as he presses his fingers to his nose.

"You alright?" Epiphany quickly sits forward in the bed.

"Yeah. It's nothing new." He takes the tissue that she hands him. "Just a reminder that my time is short." C.J. pinches his nose and holds his head back.

"I will call out of work and take you to the doctor first thing in the morning. I'm sure Camille won't mind driving Najah to school." Epiphany- the instant fixer, springs to action.

"No," C.J. commands, pressing his hand against her forearm. "I have an appointment scheduled this week. Anything that happens between now and then, they won't be able to stop anyway. The medicines and treatments just make me feel worse and they are only prolonging the inevitable." C.J. shakes his head.

"All the king's horses and all the king's men... right?"

Where there is love, there is no darkness

Burundi Proverb

CHAPTER NINE

I can remember the day I first saw C.J. the way one remembers their baptism or their first kiss.

*I thought he was so **beautiful**. He was tall, dark and handsome with a stone-face like chiseled obsidian, full, thick lips and deep, thoughtful eyes. I noticed early on that, as intelligent as he was, he struggled with a few of the concepts in our Chemistry class– mainly balancing chemical equations. That just seemed to throw him off every time. I sat at the front of the class in the middle seat directly across from the teacher. Daily, C.J. would slink past me down the aisle to the last seat on my row at the very back of the class and stare dismally at the board for an hour and fifteen minutes until the bell rang.*

After I saw his disappointment following the first test, I approached him and offered to help in any way I could- an offer that he initially declined. But the next day, when he returned to school after showing the test to his father, he promptly took me up on the offer, asking if we could start to study together that very afternoon in the library after school. C.J. didn't really need a lot of help. Once it clicked for him, he pretty much had it from then on. Still, he insisted that we continue doing our homework together each afternoon... just to make sure.

After a few weeks, we started to see each other on the weekends as well. Although I lived across town from him, we would meet at Eastridge Mall and have ice cream while watching the ice skaters glide around in elaborate patterns on the rink below the food court.

When C.J.'s grades improved so drastically, his parents asked who was responsible and invited me to dinner at their home. That was the beginning of our transition from a friendship into a more serious relationship. Mr. and Mrs. Turnage felt that I was a good influence on C.J. and as Camille put it– "such a pretty, young thing".

By the end of tenth grade, Courtney and Camille rewarded C.J. for making straight A's by giving him a car. C.J. didn't play sports that year. Instead, he unknowingly earned his car by helping his father to restore a 1980 Black Pontiac GTO. C.J. was satisfied just to learn about auto mechanics and spend quality time with his dad, but when Mr. Turnage surprised him by putting the keys in his hand, C.J. beamed, overwhelmed with pride. C.J. got to drive his car during the last week of the school year. He offered to take me home that Friday, so I obliged him, but we went to his house instead of mine. It was there, on that afternoon, that we lost our virginity to each other in his bedroom, while Courtney and Camille were away at one of Samantha's dance recitals.

I was so nervous, but C.J. took charge, kissing my trembling lips until he was sure that I was comfortable. He was gentle and kept asking me if I was okay every few seconds. His penis was so big, I was sure that he would split me in two, but I was surprised by how good it felt after just a few painfully awkward minutes. Our dark bodies moved with an instant chemistry, as if we were born to be together.

We went at it for hours, excited by the new discovery of our beautiful, naked Black bodies and the pleasure that we brought to each other with them. C.J.- aware of the lateness of the hour and the blood stains on his sheets, which would have to be cleaned before his parents got back, suggested that he take me on home.

When C.J. dropped me off at my door in Dalton Village, it took an hour for us to say goodbye. We kissed each other until our lips chapped from the friction. We didn't want to be parted even for the night, but I reluctantly crawled out of the passenger seat when the crackheads began to surround his car, peering into the steamy windows. C.J. watched me up the steps until I disappeared inside my door. Even then, he waited outside my building a few minutes more, as if he just might come on in.

In the days that followed, we were pretty much inseparable. We were on summer break from school, so after C.J. got done working at the garage with his father, the evenings were ours to spend together. We used every occasion to steal away in C.J.'s car and work on our Chemistry in his back seat. After about a month, Mr. and Mrs. Turnage caught on to what was going on between C.J. and me. One evening, after watching us make goo-goo eyes at each other and play footsies under their table, they pulled us into the living room for a little after-dinner conversation.

I was surprised by how forward Camille was with us. "C.J. and Epiphany, we know that the two of you have been having sex..."

Our eyes dropped but hers didn't. She didn't waiver or mince her words for the delicateness of our young ears.

"... We're not upset with you. What you are feeling for each other is perfectly natural, but you have to be responsible. Both of you are good children and we don't want you to do anything that will ruin your future." Camille reassured us with stern, but sympathetic eyes.

"Son," Courtney addressed C.J. in a man-to-man tone. "You and I have talked about many things, so I hope that you have been paying attention to me. I want you to always respect yourself and your female companion the same way that you have seen me do with your mother. If you are crossing this line with Epiphany, I hope that your intentions with her are honorable."

"They are, Dad," he replied with a solemn, sober expression. He swallowed hard and stood before his father with squared shoulders. "I know that we are still very young and we do intend to finish our education, but I want to be with her." C.J. put his arm around my shoulders and pulled me tightly to him. I was still very embarrassed and refused to lift my eyes up from the beige carpet. My face and chest burned with such intense heat. I probably would have run out of the room to douse myself with water, had it not been for C.J.'s arm around me.

"Are the two of you using protection?" Camille asked bluntly, her concerned eyes meeting Courtney's.

"Yes ma'am," C.J. answered promptly with a nod of his head. "Every time."

Both Mr. and Mrs. Turnage let out a tiny sigh of relief.

"Alright then," Courtney growled with a slight resignation. "We can't run your lives for you, but we can tell you what's right. This is a very grown up thing that the two of you have chosen to enter into, but your

mother and I are definitely in no position to judge you, only to teach and guide you by our own example."

"The two of you need to protect your hearts with the same diligence that you protect your bodies. Love can be a deceptive thing when you are young, but we trust you to make the right decisions concerning each other so long as you keep your priorities in order. If this relationship begins to affect either one of you in a destructive manner, Courtney and I will step in and the two of you will have to stop seeing each other." Camille explained her ultimatum with an extended finger. "Epiphany, do you want me to talk to your mother?" she gently asked me.

I wasn't really sure if her question was a threat or a genuine inquiry. I did know that I didn't want my mother to know anything about that talk. Not that she would care about the sex. Despite my constant insistence to the contrary, she already thought I started having intercourse years earlier when I began to fill out a C-cup bra. But she would be upset to know that C.J.'s parents got involved because that would make her look like a bad mother for not knowing.

"No ma'am," I mumbled. "I will talk to her myself." I was near tears when I spoke, my bottom lip trembling with the words.

Camille lifted my chin and compelled my eyes to meet hers. When they did I felt it, like an instant connection. She bonded with me in the smile that she offered before taking me into her arms.

"Don't be ashamed, Epiphany," she whispered in my ear. "I don't think ill of you. You're a beautiful girl and C.J. is lucky to have you. Just stay on track so that you can be a jewel in his crown and not an anchor around his feet... Okay, darling?" She pressed away the tear in my eye and kissed my cheek.

"Yes ma'am." I nodded.

In the years that followed, I got really close with C.J. and his entire family. I even began to live in the Turnage household during my senior year. C.J. and I both earned excellent grades. He had a 3.83 GPA and I had a 3.75 GPA. We were homework tag team champions. His parents felt comfortable letting us have our freedom because they saw that we were better together than apart from each other. They supported our

relationship because the alternative was for C.J. to be a ladies' man,
which meant him being with girls they didn't know or approve of and
whose head may not have been as level as mine. Hell, even with me as his
girlfriend, it didn't stop females from turning into groupies around C.J.
and pressing their fleshliest body parts up on him as often as possible.
There were several girls at our high school who were not ashamed to make
it known that they intended to challenge me for my position. Still C.J.
remained faithful to me and I think that made his father especially proud of
him. Since C.J. was devoted to me and we "kept the babies in heaven,"
they let us room together. I thought it was funny how that they made us
keep the bedroom door open at all times, as if they didn't know what we
were up to every time the opportunity presented itself.

Still our senior year was the most wonderful time of our lives. C.J. and
I graduated with honors. We each had so many cords and stoles that there
wasn't room enough on our gowns for all of them. His parents were so
proud of us. We were almost model teenagers when compared with our
counterparts. C.J. was the junior choir director at our church. He was so
commanding when he stood before the large body of his peers, leading and
directing their every breath with just a flip of his hand. C.J. dressed so
impeccably on church Sundays, wearing his white dress shirt and striped
tie under a fitted black vest that hugged his narrow waist. I used to feel like
such a heathen, crossing my legs in the pew to keep my cool while I
watched his long, sculpted arms extend in anticipation of the next
movement in the organ music.

His parents were pleased but saddened when C.J., still bent on his
NASA astronautics aspirations, decided to go to college at Florida State
University out of all the schools to which he received acceptance. My most
promising offer came from Chapel Hill, but since I didn't have two parents
with good credit like C.J., I followed him to Florida and went to FAMU on
an academic scholarship.

Our first night in college was the first time in over a year that we had
slept separately from each other. And since we were in separate programs,
C.J. in Astrophysics and I in Business Administration, we weren't much
help to each other academically either. That made the rift between us even

103

wider. Soon we were barely spending any time together at all; a fact which bothered C.J. much more than me. One day, he came to pick me up from campus after majorette practice. When C.J. saw me talking to one of the football players, a purely innocent conversation, he flipped completely out. He and Bryson almost ended up in a fistfight for like no reason at all other than male machismo. Then later that same night, C.J. and I got into a brutal argument about the whole incident because I told him that he overreacted. C.J. put me out of his car and I didn't hear from him for two whole months.

Then out of nowhere, he showed up at my dorm room; apologizing and asking me to marry him. I had missed too many meals and spent too many late nights and early mornings crying over how he could just drop me like a potato sack when I hadn't even done anything wrong. So, I wasn't about to make it easy for him to come back into my life.

We started all over again from the beginning. I made it clear to C.J. not to take anything for granted with me and to appreciate the time I gave him because he was put back into competition against every other guy for my attention and affection. I even went out on a few dates with a couple of co-eds from my college just to make C.J.'s blood boil... and it worked! He would call me up after my dates with endless questions; wanting to know when we got back, where we went and what we did.

"I know he better not have touched you," C.J. would threaten through the phone. "You are my woman, Ni. I would kill a niggah over you. You don't want to see me go to jail, do you?" He would ask quietly.

Just when I thought I had finally put C.J. through enough torture and was about to let him taste my flower again, he reached his breaking point. He came into the campus library where I was studying with a few of my girlfriends.

"Ooo," they bellowed like young, ghetto kids insinuating a fight. "C.J. here to get you, girl."

When I turned around to see him striding angrily down the aisle towards me, I could tell by his stone-face that he was not in the mood for games. I quickly packed up my work, so by the time he reached my table, I was ready to go. He didn't say anything to anyone. His jaw was working diligently to contain his words. He grabbed my wrist and dragged me out like an unruly child being chastised by a parent in the grocery story. I was embarrassed, but strangely enough, I was also very turned on. My nipples hardened when C.J. gripped my shoulders tightly and firmly pressed my back against the passenger door of his car.

"I heard you went out with that slick-ass, light-skinned Kappa niggah again last night." C.J. pointed his finger in my face. I had never seen him so angry before, but it made me cream in my panties. "I'm not putting up with no more of this bullshit from you, Ni. I know I hurt you and that was fucked up, but you need to get the hell over it. You gone always be my girl, so I better not hear shit else about you and no other niggahs from here on out or else I swear I'll-"

Whatever C.J. had a mind to say was too much even for him, so he broke it off suddenly, balling his finger back into his fist. "Get your ass in the car," he commanded me with so much authority that I felt the blood pulsing in my clit. I sucked my teeth and rolled my eyes at him acting all stubborn. But when he opened the door, I got my ass in that car **quick fast**.

He took me back to his dorm room and promptly proceeded to dig my back out. We had the best angry make-up sex ever. It couldn't compare to any of the other experiences we ever had before. C.J. was so backed up. I had cut him off for months, so he made sure to punish me like a real **bad girl** for it. We took all of our frustrations out on each other and finally squashed our little break-up beef between our hot, sweaty naked bodies.

"I meant what I said to you, Ni," C.J. whispered to me in the darkness.

One of our favorite songs– "Tender Love" by Force MD's came over the radio, as he continued to talk. "I don't ever want to have to think about you with another man, so long as I live. I couldn't handle that." C.J. leaned over me, supported by his elbows. He brushed my short locks away from my face. Only his eyes were visible in the Blackness of the room. "I want this forever, so I gotta know that no other man besides me will ever experience your body." I stared into C.J.'s eyes. There was no vulnerability in them– only intensity. "Promise me that now or else it's over between us– right here tonight."

C.J.'s words cut through me like a knife. I have never been a fan of ultimatums. I never gave him any, so I felt that it was unfair of him to put me on the spot that way. Still, I knew that I never wanted any other man besides him, so I nodded assuredly and kissed lovingly on his lips.

"I promise C.J. You are the only man I ever have or ever will lay with," I cooed with a small, childlike voice, while I ran my hands over the tiny, soft waves at the back of his head.

C.J. watched me suspiciously for a minute, then he accepted my oath. He began again to suck on my neck and breasts. He rubbed his large, powerful thigh between mine to part them. Reassured by my reaffirmed allegiance to him, he proceeded to finish what he had evidently only just started...

The next day C.J. moved me into his dorm room. He said that he wanted me to stay there until the end of the semester, then we would move off campus together during the summer. C.J. wouldn't let me out of his sight after that; taking me to class in the morning and picking me up in the afternoon. It was just like high school all over again, which was both a good and bad thing. We still got it in– a few dope ass house parties and homecoming festivities, but still, I felt I missed out on some of the college experience. C.J. and I were tethered together like conjoined twins. I couldn't go anywhere, if he didn't come along with me. However, I figured it was as good as I could get. When I saw the way my friends were being ran all through by an endless stream of assholes, I knew I had a wonderful man in C.J.

C.J. was on a mission, so he finished undergrad in about three years by going year round. We got trifling, started loving the way it felt when we rode each other raw. We had been together, wrapping it up for years, so after C.J. finished undergrad and put a ring on it, I let him get it however and whenever he wanted it. C.J. was just starting his second year of graduate studies and I had only one graduate semester under my belt when I came into the bathroom while he was on the toilet and told him that I was pregnant.

It wasn't the best timing, but we were old and responsible enough to handle the challenge. C.J. and I made the decision that since he was further along in his education than I was, he would finish school and I would work. C.J. said that he could be done with his degree before the baby was born, but of course that still put me up in an office building working long hours, full almost to bursting, with a baby on board. C.J. kept his word and got his Master's degree the same June that Najah was born.

It was still pretty disappointing because Najah had a lot of complications at birth. She was a breach baby. She had problems with her hips and the doctors were concerned that she may not walk properly. Najah had lots of medical needs. C.J. went to work, but I still couldn't go back to school because for the first two years of Najah's life, I had to stay with her, taking her back and forth, back and forth to specialist after specialist for tests, brace fitting, brace removal, physical rehabilitation-you name it.

The sacrifices only continued. Just when I thought I could start school again on a part-time basis and had signed up for the classes, C.J. decided to move the family from Tallahassee down to Orlando to go work for NASA. So many times I wished that C.J. would just give up on the pilot program. They had rejected so many applications from him. Secretly, I had hoped that they would never accept him, but finally they did. I guess I was wrong to discourage him because if he had not gone, we may never have found out about the cancer. It was during a routine cat scan, part of the applicant screening physical that they noticed the large, dark mass in his head.

C.J. always told me that things happen the way they are supposed to and I guess he was right because after that, my whole life became about C.J. and Najah and what each of them needed to thrive. Najah was finally out of danger and progressing well, but C.J. was taking a very fast, steep decline of his own. It became too much for me to work and care for our daughter, once C.J. began chemotherapy.

Soon I was placed on an extended leave of absence at my job because my attendance was too sparse and unpredictable. Long before our home went into foreclosure, Camille begged me to bring C.J. back to North Carolina. I wanted to oblige her because I needed the help. Still, it was going to take so much effort and money that we didn't have to move. But once the house was gone, we had no other choice. Courtney and Camille took Samantha's college fund and moved us back. Luckily, Sam got a full scholarship or I know that C.J. wouldn't have been willing to go along with the plan.

Living back at home with The Turnages wasn't so bad. With Sam away at college, Najah could have her own room to romp around in. Camille was a life saver when it came to helping out with her son. When things got down to the worst and C.J. could barely get out of bed, she was a champion support system, cleaning up vomit, bandaging bed sores and changing sheets sometimes two and three times a day to keep up with any number of different fluids that would involuntarily leak from his body. I was glad to have more help than I did in Florida, but I soon became far lonelier than I had ever been in my life.

Without C.J. to be there for me, I found that I almost didn't know what to do with myself. Everything was about him; always and only about him. People would call or run into me at the grocery store and never even ask once during the whole conversation how I was doing. They only wanted progress reports on C.J.'s condition. I was breaking my back at work and up all night seeing to any one of his many needs, but no one even cared to ask how *I* was holding up. Some days the pressure of it all would get to me.

I had always imagined C.J. and me; old, gray and toothless, feeding each other applesauce in rocking chairs on our front porch. And all in one day, that dream was seemingly stolen from me. The thought of raising Najah on my own was more than I could bear. Sometimes I would disappear in the middle of the night, driving around aimlessly for hours trying to escape the agony of my circumstances– even if only for just a few hours.

One such night, I stopped into an IHOP to warm up with a cup of coffee. I sat at my table for an hour, just babysitting the mug and trying to become as numb as possible, so that I could finally return back to the house. I wrestled within myself, but lost the battle. When I couldn't hold it in anymore, the pain stinging in my chest like acid reflux, I allowed one tear to slip from my eye to relieve the pressure. It plopped down on the rim *of my cup. The drop burst the dam, a precedent to the downpour which followed quickly behind, so it didn't take long for my bawling to catch the attention of the only other patron in the restaurant.*

"Hey ma'am, are you alright?" He asked lowly, placing a cautious hand on my shoulder.

"I'm fine," I answered shortly, dabbing my cheeks with a napkin from the dispenser. I didn't even acknowledge him with a glance. Instead I looked away, ashamed by my public display of distress. I closed my eyes and pressed the napkin to my lips to muffle my sobs.

"Well, something has to be wrong," he persisted. "I can't imagine you crying like this over nothing."

*"Well there's nothing wrong with **me**," I emphasized, placing my hands to my chest. "Nothing at all wrong with me that should warrant anyone's attention whatsoever, so I thank you for your concern Mister, but I-"*

My words got caught in my mouth when I glanced up at him. I had to do a double-take. I didn't even realize for a minute that I was holding my breath, as I took him in with my eyes. The misery that overwhelmed me seconds earlier had to take a short break because for just a few seconds the sexy stranger was all I could see or think about.

He was undeniably gorgeous; not the type of man you would expect to find seated alone in an IHOP, buried behind a newspaper in the middle of the night like a pervert. He had a smooth, fair complexion- the color of animal crackers. He was so beautiful that he looked like he tasted sweet. He wore a crisp, celery-colored dress shirt with sharply-creased, fitted khaki pants and a brown leather belt. I thought his attire was strange for somewhere around midnight on a Wednesday, but what could I- the woman crying in her coffee- really have to say?

"Do you mind if I sit down?" he inquired delicately, already lowering himself into the booth seat across from me. He sat confidently with his forearms on the table, no slouch in his posture. His features were strong, but refined. His lips were thin, but shapely. He had large, expressive eyes that were a strikingly bright shade of brown. He was a little above average height and had a tight, slender build. His shiny, neatly-trimmed, lightly-

salted hair laid down in waves that would surely crest into large, rolling curls, if he didn't cut his hair so close.

"Actually, I'm just about to leave," I stammered on the words, trying to catch hold of them like butterflies in a net. I snapped out of my trance and began to push my arms into my crimson cashmere sweater.

"Me too. Do you need a ride?" The assertiveness in his offer caught my attention. I glared at him with an invisible heat that instantly made him uncomfortable. "It's just that you don't look like you're in any condition to drive. I just want to help you out any way I can."

"Why would you want to help me?" I asked suspiciously. "You don't even know me. I could be crying because I just murdered somebody for all you know."

"Yeah. That's true," he huffed with a slight sarcastic smile that made him almost irresistible to me in that moment. "Or you could also be crying because you just lost someone you love." He shrugged casually, sitting back against the seat and dropping his eyes to his lap. "I'm just doing what I would hope that someone would do for my mother or my sister or even my daughter." His eyes darted back up to my face. There was something so seductive about his gaze. It was me who dropped my eyes next, hoping that he couldn't see the fire that ignited in my face. "I'm just trying to be a decent man and give a damn when I see a lady in distress."

"Look," I began reluctantly. "... I'm married" is all I could say.

"I am too." He flashed a bright smile and presented his left hand, complete with an extravagant wedding band. "I don't want you to take me wrong. I'm not trying to put any moves on you, only doing what comes naturally to me." He pressed his hand to his chest for sincerity. "But if I overstepped my boundaries, I understand." He surrendered his palms to me.

"No," I sighed with resignation. "I'm just not used to people caring about how I feel these days."

"Well hey," he said cordially. "If it means anything to you– I care." His eyebrows knitted together, as though he had something pressing to say. "I'm an editor. I work for the Observer, so I've been proofreading the news long enough to know by now when someone has a provocative

*story." He leaned across the table towards me. "My name is Jerome
Pettigrew." He pulled a business card out of his wallet. He scribbled
another phone number on the back of it. "If you ever just need somebody
to talk to... for whatever reason, you can call me at that number. I can be
your uninvolved third party– no pressure... no expectations."
With that he stood up quickly from the table and walked gracefully away
like he had never sat down.*

*If I had just thrown the card away like I planned and promised myself
to, I don't guess I would be in the position that I am now. I didn't call
Jerome right away. In fact, I lost the card, but weeks later when I went to
change purses, I found it at the bottom of my bag. I'd had a pretty rough
week. C.J. was steadily improving and the doctors were talking of
remission. He was regaining his strength which should have been the best
news ever, but I found that it was more disenchanting than I imagined it
would be.*

*I mean, I had been The Rock– the veritable Superwoman laboring
along, with all of my might, to take care of my husband and child. I had
sacrificed and suffered so completely that I had nothing left over for
myself. I needed so desperately for someone to help build me back up, or
even just to notice me; but yet again, even when C.J. got better, people
were even more absorbed in his struggle and triumph. He was still center-
stage, constantly being celebrated for his courage and solicited for his
testimony. I was glad that my husband was recovering, but his light was
casting an even longer, darker, colder shadow over my life.*

*The first night I called Jerome, the conversation was cordial and brief.
He was polite and unobtrusive. He just let me talk and didn't pry. It didn't
take long to get comfortable with him– to feel relief in the slow, steady
sound of his breath on the other end of the line. He was sympathetic, but
not overly empathetic and I found that refreshing. It was good to have
someone to talk to who wouldn't try to eulogize me; speaking to me like I
was dying. Soon the conversations went from over the phone to in-person,
but always in public, at coffee houses and parks.*

*Jerome was respectful. Oddly enough, he didn't seem to have any
physical interest in me. He was almost brotherly in his interactions with*

me. He made me laugh with his effortless sense of humor. Jerome made me forget... to be afraid, or stressed, or even worried. My time with him slowly started to become the highlight of my week. Jerome was very handsome with an impeccable fashion sense and an engaging personality to match. I easily should have been infatuated with him, but the more I got to know him the less I was attracted to him. He was much older than me, in his early forties, so he always gave me great, uncle-like advice and urged me to take my concerns and desires to C.J.

Maybe I just had a prejudice in my mind. C.J. was the only man that I had ever been intimate with, but my girlfriends in college always told me that light-skinned men weren't good lovers. I'm ashamed to say that I found out the evil way that they were very wrong. I could say that it just happened and that I didn't mean for it to, but that would be a lie. I had opened up my mind and my heart to Jerome. It was only a matter of time before I opened up my legs to him too.

Spread my legs, is just what I did that warm day in the late spring, as I climbed onto the back of Jerome's big, black Honda motorcycle. I hugged my arms tightly around his waist and squeezed my knees into his thighs, as he quickly pulled away from the curb. I felt the wind, slipping under my skirt like a soft hand and the powerful rumble of the engine vibrated up my spine. I soon found my fingertips, lightly tracing the shape of Jerome's muscular pecks and abs, as we rode along. That afternoon he took me to an upscale raw food bar in South End. We picked out exotic fruits and had them blended into the most delicious smoothies. As I sipped on my straw and stared into his eyes, I knew that day would mark a change in our relationship. We were becoming intimate with each other on an emotional level, so the physical could only follow. The motorcycle ride had me open and tingling from head to toe. So by the time, we reached his house in Clanton Park, I was ready to do just about anything he wanted to do. Jerome said that his wife, Sharon, was out of town at a conference for the weekend and that we were only stopping in to pick up some things he needed for a basketball game later that evening.

I saw it coming and I probably could have stopped it, but I didn't want to. I needed someone to cherish me, to fill me up with a warm feeling inside. C.J. and I hadn't slept together in almost nine months by the first time that I laid down with Jerome. Jerome insisted however, all the way up to the last minute, that we not go through with it. But as I laid naked in his bed, my blood boiling like hot lava under the surface of my dark skin, I couldn't halt the train that was speeding towards ecstasy. Jerome's skin was so soft and fragrant as his neck pressed against my cheek. His supple lips were so warm when they sucked on mine. Jerome's sex was masterful. His expressive hands touched me in ways that I had never experienced in my life. My body felt as though it was charged with an electrical current. Each time his tongue touched my skin, it was like a tiny spark of lightning. He felt so good to me that it almost hurt. My body continued to ache and throb for him even after we were done.

I knew after that very first time that I was in big trouble. He had me hooked; to say that I was catching feelings for him was an understatement. I didn't call him for two weeks. I had to give myself time to straighten the whole affair out. I had done what I promised C.J. I never would. And I did it to him when he needed me the most, at the time that he least needed to have to worry about his marriage. I needed time, but Jerome needed me. At least that's what his half-dozen voicemails on my cell phone said.

I vowed that I wouldn't see him again— that I would break it off with Jerome before I destroyed my family over some meaningless sex. But before that month was over, I was in a lavish hotel room, arching my back and curling my toes with Jerome probing and mining deeply between my thighs for hours.

We were together three more times before he started talking crazy. He said that he was ready to leave his wife for me and he wanted me to divorce C.J. I told him that he was insane and that he should seek professional help. All the same, I had opened up an even bigger can of worms than I was aware of. The following month my period never came. I didn't know what to do because even though C.J. was getting back to himself, he and I still hadn't yet started back to making love.

I refused to tell Jerome anything. I never talked to him again after the second dark pink line appeared on the indicator strip. I figured that I would never be able to pass the baby off as C.J.'s child. I was going to have an abortion; but before I could get an appointment, Camille found the positive pregnancy test in the trash and confronted me about it. I begged her to keep it a secret. I told her that I needed to get an appointment with an OBGYN to confirm it and that I had been spotting, so I didn't want to get C.J.'s hopes up until I knew for certain.

That bought me just enough time to get C.J. into bed with me that very same night so that I could pretend to procrastinate on setting up my doctor's appointment and then make the announcement three weeks later. In hindsight, I guess I should have gone through with the abortion and just told Camille that I lost the baby. Hell, in hindsight, I never should have laid down with Jerome in the first place. That's what I'm supposed to say because that sounds unselfish, but the truth is– as I felt Jerome's child grow within in me, it was with him that I wanted to share the experience. Secretly, I longed for him, for the friendship that we shared. I still loved C.J. but the months of being pampered incessantly by his family and friends were taking a toll on our relationship. He was much better but to them he remained as helpless and needy as when he first began treatment. I was about fed up with the endless demands that he put on me. I needed my strong, independent husband back– the man that I looked to for strength and comfort, but my C.J. never resurfaced again even when his health returned.

After three months with no response from me, Jerome's obsessive phone calls finally stopped.

"The shattering blows on the Negro family have made it fragile, deprived and often psychopathic... Nothing is so much needed as a secure family life for a people to pull themselves out of poverty and backwardness."

- Dr. Martin Luther King Jr.

CHAPTER TEN

"I'll take care of it," Epiphany sighs into her cell phone.

"You don't have to stop what you're doing for that. I'm just going to lay down and rest for a few minutes then I'll pick C.J. up when he's done with his treatment." Epiphany trudges into the house so fatigued and despondent that she leaves the front door wide open while she shuffles through the threshold. She sits her briefcase on the hardwood floor in the foyer.

"**No**," she huffs in frustration, switching her phone on her cheek as she slips out of her long, beige, suede-leather trench coat. "I can handle that too. Najah's school is right around the corner." Epiphany kicks off her brown wedge heels, then bends to collect them with the hand holding her coat. "I feel fine, Camille. I told you that I can handle this." Epiphany pulls the coat closet door open and groans internally, rolling her eyes at her in-law's persistence.

Epiphany is exhausted from a night spent rubbing C.J.'s back while he heaved into the toilet. She spent half of the time retrieving water, apple juice, peppermint tea, ginger ale, crackers or any other item that could possibly help to settle his stomach. She woke early this morning, dropped off Najah and went to her job on a little less than four hours of sleep. Little C3- as C.J. calls the baby, was very active during the day and soon Epiphany found herself unable to even keep her eyes open at her desk. Her boss even offered to have someone drive her home, but Epiphany declined the offer and just took her leave of duty for the day. She only called Camille to let her know that she could pick C.J. up since she was off, but of course like everything that involved C.J., Camille refused to let it go at that.

"Just finish up with what you are doing there so you can be here to start dinner on time. I don't want you to have to go back out later..." Epiphany holds the phone away from her face and stomps out a tiny tantrum before saying, "Okay... alright, Camille. No, I'll pick up C.J. I gotta' go now. I got a call coming in... Yeah... uh hunh... okay... bye... oh, what.... um hum... well, bye." She presses the red button in the middle of Camille's sentence and then exhales long and slow.

Epiphany slams the phone down on the dining room table along with her keys. She rubs her hands over her face and then behind her neck, as she drops her head back. Her locks feel so heavy today. They are coiled tightly on top of her head, but when unfurled they extend down to her hips. She contemplates cutting them, only a few inches– maybe to the middle of her back, just to alleviate some of the stress on her slender neck. Then she thinks to herself that C.J. would have a fit about it, so she pushes the notion out of her mind. As she does, she instantly feels the fatigue weighing just as heavy on her body, as the hair does on her head. Epiphany wants to just lay down right there on the floor. She is so tired that the thought of walking upstairs makes her want to cry. She pulls off her gray leggings, then scratches her belly through the thick itchy fabric of her purple sweater dress. She turns around and closes her eyes, willing each foot to move forward in slow, cumbersome steps.

"You don't look so good," he whispers into her ear.

A yelp escapes Epiphany's mouth, as terror rips through her mind. She stares wide-eyed at Jerome, clenching the chest of her dress with tight fists, as she heaves out frantic breaths. Jerome appeared as though from thin air. She didn't even hear him come in. He stood in the foyer, glaring calmly at her like his presence there was normal.

"What are you... doing here?" she manages to puff out, as the adrenaline drains.

"I asked myself that same question," Jerome responds coolly, with a genuine fascination at the prospect. "I don't know really," he answers finally with a shrug.

"How did you find out where I live?" Her shocked amazement fails to drain with the adrenaline and she remains frozen with her jaw dropped open.

"Now that's an easy one," Jerome says with enthusiasm. "I was coming out of my building for lunch when I saw you crossing College Street in front of the Wachovia building. I tried to catch up with you on foot but I couldn't."

Epiphany's brows knit with concern. "So why would you follow me *here*?"

"I think you have the answer to that question," Jerome replies, glancing down at her large, round baby bump. "You should be about what..." He counts silently on his fingers. "Maybe six months along now?"

"No," Epiphany lies. It comes natural now. She can rattle off the fake gestational age of her baby with rehearsed ease. "Just reached my fifth month."

"You're pretty far out there, aren't you?"

"I don't like what you're trying to insinuate," Epiphany snaps like a lioness, defending her cub. "What do you want, Jerome?"

"The truth," he answers shortly.

"You need to leave." Epiphany shuffles to the front door and places her hand on the knob in anticipation of Jerome's departure. She doesn't look at him. She stares instead out of the door at his silver Cadillac Escalade parked two doors down on the street. She feels the stinging pain within her pelvis, which begins when she has been standing too long. She grips the bottom of her stomach and lifts slightly even though she knows that the gesture won't really relieve any of the pressure.

"I'm not leaving until you hear me out, so you might as well have a seat." Jerome steps over to her and gently places his hand at the small of her back. Epiphany flinches away from his touch, but reluctantly closes the door, peering out to ensure that no one has seen them.

"If I listen to you, will you go away?" Epiphany extends her finger in his face, so close to his nose that Jerome could swear that she is touching him.

"Promise," he breathes with an irresistible smile, as he crosses his heart, then raises his palm. He places his hand under Epiphany's elbow and leads her to a seat like he is transporting priceless treasure in his hands.

As soon as she sits down on the sofa in the living room, Jerome places a throw pillow behind her back. Epiphany shifts a bit to find the most comfortable position. She relaxes against the armrest, leaning more on her left hip. The stinging in her pelvis subsides a bit in that position.

Jerome kneels at her feet and doesn't say another word– only stares at her with eyes that say so much more than his words could ever express. His eyes speak of questions, longing and loneliness. Epiphany is overwhelmed by his silence and instantly feels uncomfortable.

"You only have five minutes, so you had better say what you came to say, so you can go." She craned her neck, peering through the doorway of the living room to check the front door. No one should be coming home anytime soon, but all the same- one can never be too cautious.

When her eyes returned to Jerome's, there was something different in them. The sadness was replaced by an emotion that she could not as easily decipher.

"Well, get on with it..." She heaves in frustration, but before she can complete the sentence, "I don't have all-" Jerome grips her neck tightly and kisses her, pressing his tongue deep into her mouth. Epiphany would have resisted him, if she could have. She is drawn in before she knows it and finds herself pulling him between her thighs, sliding his gray wool overcoat to the floor.

"We can't... We can't... no, no, no... We can't," she gasps between the kisses that she does not prevent. Epiphany's nipples enlarge and tingle as his lips travel down her neck. Pregnancy has turned her entire body into a giant ball of hypersensitive nerve endings that can ignite at even the slightest touch. Her vagina throbs and gushes with the fluids of motherhood which quickly saturated her underwear. The baby curls up into a tight knot within her, reacting to the stressful contractions of her uterus when the blood rushes into her sexual organs. The sudden tension in Epiphany's womb startles Jerome. He stops kissing her and looks down at the bump. He places his hands on her belly and can feel the child within her. His fingers graze over the tiny, rigid limbs. Jerome is noticeably affected. His breathing quickens with the excitement.

"I want you," he blurts out. "-and I want this baby."

120

Epiphany gasps out shocked breaths and mouths words that don't come out. Jerome grabs her face between his hands and kisses all over her cheeks.

"I need you in my life. I miss my friend... and my lover," he whispers passionately. "I need to feel you."

Epiphany tries, but cannot withstand his seduction. The heat of his breath on her neck melts her resolve. Her hands slide down the back of his toned, muscular arms. Jerome presses Epiphany back onto the sofa and parts her legs. He pushes her underwear aside and slips his tongue inside of her before she can stop him. Epiphany's walls clench so tightly that she feels an intense cramp, but the dull pinch does not diminish the ecstasy of Jerome's tongue. If his love was a color, it would be ultraviolet, so bright that it shines like a light into her darkness. Epiphany's eyes roll to the back of her head while Jerome places her thighs over his shoulders and proceeds to bring her all the pleasure that he can conjure.

Jerome had just dipped the plump, engorged flesh of his manhood into her hot springs, squishing around in the warm nectar, when the sound of key in the lock at the front door catches both of their attention.

Epiphany and Jerome jump to their feet, scrambling around on the floor for clothing and even bump into each other in the process. Epiphany pushes Jerome into the laundry room just as the front door slams closed.

"Hey," Epiphany yawns, breezing into the foyer. "What are you doing here, Camille?"

"This is my house," she snaps brazenly.

"I know." Epiphany smiles sheepishly. "I meant that I thought you were going to finish out your shift at the school. I told you I can pick up C.J."

"It's just cafeteria food. They don't need me. Anybody can serve it." Camille eyes Epiphany suspiciously, while she takes off her coat. "I was on my way here just as soon as you called to say you weren't feeling well."

"You didn't have to come back here on my account," Epiphany insists.

"I didn't come for *you*," she says with an uncharacteristic snarl on her face. "I came back so I could ride with you, in case you were too tired to drive. I don't want you killing my son because you're hard-headed."

Epiphany resigns, rubbing her face with her hands. Her mind scrambles to find some way to rid herself of Camille so she can get Jerome out of the house.

"Besides," Camille begins with a bizarre smirk. "I had to come back home anyway."

"Why is that?" Epiphany's eyes narrow with curiosity. Camille is acting strange. She wonders what has her so charged up.

"Well, I got a call from Delia Dobson while I was on my way here." Camille hangs her coat in the closet and brushes lint from her green sweater.

Epiphany's eyes search the air, as if the answer to her unasked question will appear in a thought cloud above Camille's head.

"She told me that a fancy SUV she's never seen in the neighborhood before parked out on our street and then a handsome, well-dressed man broke into my house." Camille straightens the white cuffs on her shirt like it is taking all of her focus and concentration to get them right. "You wouldn't happen to know anything about that since you've been here the entire time?" Camille crosses her arms and looks at Epiphany passively, as if she doesn't really expect any answer at all.

Epiphany's jaw drops open and she begins to gesture an explanation with her hands.

"I have to use the bathroom. I've been holding it in since I left the school," Camille says calmly, brushing past Epiphany to get to the staircase. "I'll be back down in a minute and maybe we can talk then." She marches quietly up the stairs.

As soon as Camille disappears inside of her bedroom, Epiphany takes the opportunity to shuffle a slightly disheveled Jerome through the kitchen and out of the back door. He kisses Epiphany's cheek and tells her the he loves her before she can manage to press him forcefully out of the house, slamming the glass door in his face.

Epiphany rushes back through the kitchen and the dining room into the foyer. She peeks out of the narrow side window beside the front door. No sooner than she sees Jerome slip back into his coat and climb into the driver's side of his Escalade, Camille appears at the top the stairs, peering down at her.

Camille takes each step, slowly and cautiously, watching the stairs like she thinks she might fall. When she reaches the foyer, she turns right and goes into the dining room. Camille pulls a chair away from the table and sits down. She rubs her hands over the smooth, simple cherry wood finish, as if to polish it; but Camille is not polishing the table, she is attempting to contain herself.

"So is that the man you have chosen to replace *my* C.J.?" She asks calmly, her eyes still watching her own reflection in the table.

"It's not like that," Epiphany groans lowly.

"I don't know what kind of man he is– but he is *very* handsome," Camille says courteously of the man that she just watched from her bedroom window, as he scurried out of her backyard like an exposed roach.

"Really Camille," Epiphany sighs benignly. "Jerome is just a friend from work. He saw me leave early and was concerned about me getting home safely. He just came to check up on me."

A tiny grin appears on Camille's face, exposing the slight dimple in her cheek. Epiphany is instantly nervous by her congeniality. "Do you think I'm stupid, Nany?" Camille uses her nickname for Epiphany like she does when they engage in candid girl talk. She continues before the young woman has a chance to answer. "If he was just a *friend*, then why did you hide him? Why not introduce your *friend* to me?" The corners of her mouth sag into a pronounced frown. "Why were you a mess when you came to meet me at the front door?"

Epiphany turns back into that embarrassed teenager that Camille cornered in the living room almost fourteen years ago. Her eyes search the hardwood floor for answers that will not come.

"Come over here and have a seat," Camille states sharply, motioning toward the chair across from her.

Epiphany steps hesitantly over to the table as though she fears that Camille will eat her. She reaches out a trembling hand and pulls the chair back to sit down. Camille's eyes lock on to hers with a serious intensity that chills Epiphany to the core of her being.

"I'm going to tell you what I know and what I don't know, then you are going to fill in all the blanks for me." Her lips are tense with the urgency of her declaration.

"I know that is not C.J.'s child that you're carrying," she states with an understated boldness, pointing a rigid finger at Epiphany. "If you are going to be treacherous, Nany, then you should at least show me the respect of being intelligent about it." She leans back in her chair. "When I first found out that you were pregnant, I couldn't understand what was taking you so long to tell C.J., so I did a little investigating. I had a discussion with C.J.'s doctor and he had some very interesting things to say," she hisses with amusement.

Epiphany realizes, as she listens to Camille talk, that she has been holding her emotions bottled up for a very long time. This conversation is the slow leak on an extremely over-inflated tire. "His physician said that it would be very improbable for C.J. to father a child, as he is temporarily infertile because of his chemotherapy treatments... and he has been for quite some time." Camille taps her finger on the table with the syllables of the words– *temporarily infertile*. Epiphany's hands involuntarily cover her mouth. She is overwhelmed by the confrontation.

That is Camille's way.

She is not a gossip. She never speaks about what she cannot prove, but if given concrete evidence of something- she is as steadfastly immovable as a mountain. Camille presents her case with the excellence of a proven trial attorney.

"Now here's what I don't know," she asks coyly, turning up her palm. "Why would you do this to our family?" Camille closes her lips and crosses her wrists with finality. She patiently awaits the answer with a genuinely unpretentious expression.

"I don't have any excuses for what I did," Epiphany whispers on the edge of tears.

"Well that's just fine," Camille replies with fragile control. "Because I didn't ask you for any excuses. The world is filled up with plenty of those... What I asked for is an explanation. I need to understand why you would betray my son... What kind of woman could disrespect herself and her marriage in the very place where she sleeps with her husband?" Camille's expression is sincerely confused.

"Camille... I don't know what-"

"Call me **Mrs**. **Turnage**," she interrupts, speaking with vehement disdain. Unsatisfied by Epiphany's pathetic groveling and unable to contain her rant any further, the anger bursts free from the tiny, stinging knot in the center of Camille's chest.

"It's obvious you lack self-discipline. You young girls come up with no home training and no decency about yourselves these days. May God have mercy on you fast asses who don't know anything about being real women and supporting a good, Black man when you get one."

She points at her chest with pride. "I raised a good man; the kind of man that any woman would be lucky to have. I approved of you and placed him in your hands and just look at how you repay me." Camille stands from the table, almost knocking over her chair. "You're so damn selfish, Epiphany. How could you disgrace yourself... just spit on what it means to be a strong, Black woman."

"I just got tired... I was just *so* tired."

Camille's eyes sharpen with anger. "Tired of what? Not being the center of attention... You got tired because you forgot who we are." She straightens her shirt with a dignified pat before continuing. "We built pyramids thousands and thousands of years ago that still stand, magnificent and unblemished after all this time. There ain't nothing they could find or create on this planet that should be able to break a Black woman down. Make you stoop so low as to cheat on your own beautiful, Black man– your very own flesh– when he needs you the most... to quit on him when he can't even stand by himself. This is the moment in his life that you were created to fulfill."

"Epiphany, I don't know if it's because you grew up without a daddy that you want to go searching all over the world for a love that you will

125

never find– trying to fill a hole that one man left with another man who doesn't even have a shovel. There ain't no dick out here so good, that you should give up your soul to go acting like a whore over it." She walks over to glare down on the young woman. "You're pathetic and I hate that I didn't see earlier that you don't have the stuff it takes to be a real woman."

As hurt as Epiphany is by what Camille just said, she knows that her mother-in-law is right. She sits, almost bathing in her own tears, as the woman continues to speak.

"I just can't understand what it is with your generation. I tell Samantha this same thing, but it's like y'all dick crazy or something- just wanna' try all the flavors." Camille flips her hand like she is waving off flies.

"Did you really think that the grass would be greener on the other side of the fence with that Jerome?"

Epiphany doesn't acknowledge the question with any response at all. She never really thought any of her actions through to their completion. She was just moving and reacting to overwhelming emotions. Epiphany fears even now that her words will be emotionally-motivated and therefore does not answer.

"Well I can tell you this-" Camille continues. "Not all men are the same, but all marriages are. Full of hard work and more sacrifices than any one person will ever feel that they should have to make for it... but you make them and you suffer... because in the end you win. If you quit or forfeit, then you will find that your next relationship will hinge on the very same compromises you refused to make in the last one. Marriages ain't perfect because people ain't perfect. If your marriage is ever to succeed, you have to love your man more than yourself. You have to give up on what you want and being right all the time to let your man be **The Man**. If a Black man can't have that in his own home, then where will he find it in a world that is bent on telling him that he ain't shit?" She pounds her fist on the table.

"Haven't you ever just been lonely?" Epiphany pleads, looking up at Camille with sad, moist eyes. "Do you even know what it feels like to be so lonely- so hollow inside, that you feel like you could die?"

Camille purses her lips, glaring disapprovingly at her daughter-in-law. "It only takes coming close to death one time to make you appreciate the life that you have. You don't know what it's like to feel dead inside. You should ask your husband about loneliness and death. He knows more about it than you do... Did you ever think about him and what he needed from you, while you were so busy getting what you thought you needed from Jerome?"

A dim light appears in Camille's eyes and her eyebrows lift. "You thought your loneliness was the worst feeling that you could feel, but tell me– how are you feeling now?"

Epiphany lowers her eyes and begins to sob into her hands.

"Was it worth it, now that your deeds in the dark came out into the light?"

Epiphany shakes her head, still unwilling to uncover her face. "So I guess you are going to tell all this to C.J."

A puzzled expression appears on Camille's face. "After all these years, I guess you still don't know me at all, Epiphany." Camille places her first two fingers on the table and appears pensive as she speaks. "Something like this would kill C.J. It would break him down. Even if he physically survives this news, his heart would die and he would be nothing but a shell of a man– no more good to this world." She looks her daughter-in-law in the eyes. "I won't let that happen to him. C.J. is my gift from God, and my beautiful Black gift to the world. I won't let you or any other woman ruin him. You will not relieve your conscience at C.J.'s expense. What he doesn't know can't hurt him, but finding this out could destroy him."

Camille lowers her eyes for the first time. "I don't know about you- but I don't want to be responsible for damaging any Black man, woman or child, for any reason. The damage you did has already been done, but maybe we can contain it before it destroys this entire family."

"Then what do you intend to do?" Epiphany inquires cautiously with suspicious eyes.

"I am a God-fearing woman," she replies plainly, taking her seat with regained composure. "So I believe that what God joins together, no man– not me, not you and definitely not Jerome– better tear it apart. You and my son are one flesh. You are the extension and very reflection of the most beautiful, Black man that I have ever known besides my own husband. For that reason only, I will not treat you the same trashy way that you have treated yourself because you forgot that you belong completely to C.J. I haven't said anything to anyone about this yet and I don't intend to." Her eyes soften with compassion. "But what I do intend to do– is teach you."

"Maybe you did not have the luxury of a proper education, so I will train you myself– just like I was taught– to be a strong, Black woman."

"I don't understand what you mean." Epiphany is floored by her words.

"You are going to use all that energy you put into acting like a whore to become the wife my son deserves. I'm going to teach you how to be a proper woman and you had better learn everything you can from me; because if you mess up even just once more, I will pack you up and kick you out of this house myself." She thumbs her chest. "I promised you all those years ago that I would step in before you and C.J. ruined each other's lives and now, I'm going to do just that."

Camille takes Epiphany's hand and leads her over to the staircase.

"My son would give up his life for you and Najah without any hesitation at all. If it came down to you or him, he would be honored to lay down his life to preserve yours. That is the man his father and I raised him to be. That is how he has managed to stay faithful to you. He put you and what you needed before himself and anything that he may have desired at that moment. Now you must learn to do the same. The vast black void of selfishness cannot thrive where the light of love is. You cannot be a rock. People are only human– just flesh and blood. But love– first for God, and then for your husband, for yourself and for your children– that is The Rock that you must cling to when life sends you a landslide. That rock will hold you up and sustain you when doing right is inconvenient and doing wrong feels right." Camille lifts Epiphany's chin sharply and compels the obedience of her eyes. "There will be no more talk about what you want or how you feel. From now on, you will use your idle mind and idle hands to diligently seek out ways that you can satisfy your husband... Call it old-fashioned if you want to- but marriages back in my day used to last. Now with new-school females' blood-thirst for success and gain, you are more unhappy and unable to please a man than ever."

Camille tugs at the hem of Epiphany's sweater dress to straighten the fabric over her belly. "Luckily for you this baby will be born in the spring. Let's pray he gets your complexion; but in the unfortunate event that he doesn't, we'll just have to keep him out in the sun all the time," Camille says with a faint laugh.

Camille hugs Epiphany, a gesture that surprises her so much she almost pulls away. The shock drains from her body as the warmth of Camille's embrace relaxes her. She is so thankful that the woman, who has been more of a mother to her than her own, didn't abandon her in a mistake. Sensing Epiphany's thoughts, Camille whispers in her ear–

"I'm not gone give up on you, so long as you're willing to learn and change. You're mine and I won't leave you." Her grip tightens around her daughter-in-law's shoulders. "How will the Black children learn if the mothers don't teach them? ... I am here to guide you. We can get through this. Together– you and me– we're going to keep this beautiful, Black family undivided and be an example to these children– Hell, to this whole generation because they need somebody to do it. Alright?"

"Okay." Epiphany offers a reassuring nod. "I'm ready." She dries her eyes with the back of her hand.

"Now, you go on upstairs and get cleaned up. Put on something pretty and a little make-up, so you are glowing when you see your husband." She pats Epiphany's back, ushering her to the steps. "That would make C.J. happy– which from here on out is your only concern." She smiles brightly. "Hurry up because we've got to go get some eggs for my cake this evening, before we pick up C.J. and Najah."

"Alright, I'll be right back down."

"You feel like walking?" Camille calls out enthusiastically. "We need time to talk and I need the exercise. You know I have to stay sexy for Courtney." She laughs, running her hands over her hips.

"Sure, that's fine," Epiphany replies, turning into the bedroom. "A walk would be good for the baby."

As they trek along the sidewalk to the grocery store, the winter day suddenly turns cooler than both Camille and Epiphany anticipated. The sun tucks itself behind a dense, gray cloud and refuses to light up the day any further. Although it is still early in the afternoon, an icy chill begins to whip in the air, as they approach the street corner and wait patiently for the pedestrian signal to change.

"Excuse me, ladies." A bearded, White man with short, dark-brown hair, a missing front tooth and unsettling, brown eyes steps forward. "I hate to interrupt your conversation, but could you spare some change? I haven't eaten in days," he says extending his dirty palm.

"What's your name, son?" Camille asks quietly, returning his menacingly cold stare with a warm, amiable smile.

"My name is Shelton, ma'am," the man answers cordially enough.

"Well, Shelton," Epiphany snaps with some urgency, gripping Camille's elbow. "We don't have any cash on us." Epiphany tugs at Camille's arm, noticing that the pedestrian signal has changed. She wants to leave the corner promptly. Something about the man's eyes unnerve her, making even the child in her womb tense with his mother's stress.

"Sorry, we can't help you out, young man," Camille replies empathetically, taking a step off the curb. "I will however remember you in my prayers tonight, Shelton."

"Well, I don't need your prayers, bitch," he states with a calm courteousness in his tone. "What I need is your money," Shelton declares, producing his pistol.

god face

Now, I'm principled against emancipating, in any case. Keep a negro under the care of a master, and he does well enough, and is respectable; but set them free, and they get lazy, and won't work, and take to drinking, and go all down to be mean, worthless fellows. I've seen it tried, hundreds of times. It's no favor to set them free.

- **Harriet Beecher Stowe, <u>Uncle Tom's Cabin</u>**

CHAPTER ELEVEN

"Come here, sweetheart," Jerome calls from the den.

Epiphany takes a large gulp of chamomile tea from her teal ceramic mug, then rises from the large, black leather chair in the third bedroom that has become her home office. She glides down the hall in her teal tank top, purple lounge pants and socked feet, then stands at the doorway of the second bedroom turned den.

"What's up?" She asks casually, pushing her glasses up on her nose.

"Listen to this," Jerome replies, turning up the volume on the mounted flat-screen television. He lays back and throws his feet up, crossing his ankles on the green, crushed-velvet sofa. He folds his arms across his chest. Even in a gray long, sleeved t-shirt with navy track suit pants, Epiphany still thinks that her husband is the most breathtaking man that she has ever seen. She hesitantly turns her eyes from him to focus on the newscast.

"... Police have finally found the body of the pregnant woman abducted in North Charlotte last week. We reported to you then that Sharon Dellivere disappeared while going for a walk in her Hidden Valley neighborhood..."

"I really don't want to hear about this right now," Epiphany whines apathetically. "I don't understand how you can watch the news these days with all the murders in this city."

"Well not watching the news doesn't change the fact that crime is on the rise." Jerome beckons with his hand for Epiphany to come and lay down with him. "It's my job to keep you safe and I can't do that if I am not educated about what's going on out in these streets." His focus returns to the television, as the story concludes. He sucks his teeth. "It's real tragic what happened to that young woman."

Epiphany slinks down on to the sofa in front of him and he wraps his arms around her waist. She melts into the warmth of his embrace, while he lightly kisses the back of her neck.

133

"I want you to start being more careful when you're coming and going," Jerome whispers into her ear. "I couldn't bear it if anything happened to you."

"I'll be fine, Jay. I'm not a defenseless child."

"I don't know about that. You've been extremely forgetful lately. I think your mind's going."

"What are you talking about?" Epiphany rolls over to face him.

"You left the door wide open last week," he begins, designating one of his fingers for each incident of negligence. "You forgot to set the alarm clock a couple of nights ago and you didn't pick up the dry-cleaning yesterday."

"Whatever." She waves him off. "I've just had a lot on my mind these days."

"Like what?" he inquires with a raised eyebrow.

"Just work and stuff."

"Okay, well tell me what you were just working on before I called you."

Epiphany opens her mouth to answer but finds as soon as she does that she does not have a response. She searches her mind for the events which belonged to the preceding minutes before she entered the den, but cannot find them anywhere.

"*Well-*" Jerome urges, watching her with expectant eyes.

"I can't remember," Epiphany finally admits in defeat.

"That's what I'm talking about, honey." Jerome pecks the tip of her nose. "I don't know what's been up with you lately, but you need to see a doctor. In the meantime, I'm worried about you. The streets are no place for an absentminded woman. You are not safe if you can't stay focused."

Epiphany glares at him with pursed lips. "Mr. Pettigrew, your powers of observation are not all that keen either."

"How do you mean?"

"You haven't said anything about my new haircut since you got home." Epiphany sulks, running her hand over the tapered hair at the back of her head.

"Oh yeah," he sighs, turning her chin to take the style in. "Why did you cut it?" he asks, not giving any opinion at all.

"Well, the relaxer broke it off again, so it was either walk around with a fuzzy head of split ends or save what I could," she replies with a frown. "Do you like it?" The apprehension shows in her expression when she poses the question.

"Baby, I love *you*. You could shave your head bald and I would still think you're sexy." He hopes that he has sufficiently dodged the question. Jerome has never liked short hair on a woman. When he met Epiphany she was wearing a long weave that he has always preferred, but will never admit to her.

"I'll tell you what I didn't forget about," Jerome threads his fingers between hers. "I remembered that your birthday is coming up. So what do you want this year?"

Epiphany hesitates for a moment, then responds with the simplest, most honest answer that she can. "I want a baby, Jerome." Her voice quivers with a hint of vulnerability.

Jerome's face instantly becomes stoic and solemn. "I told you that is not in the plan for us right now, Nany."

"If now is not the time, then when will it be. I'm turning thirty this year. You are forty-three. Don't you ever want to have children?"

"Do you want me to be honest?" His light brown eyes burn with intensity when they meet hers. She nods slightly. He sighs. "Well then my answer is no. I honestly don't want any children and I told you that when we first got together."

"Yeah, but you mean to tell me that after ten years, you aren't willing to at least consider it?"

"Do you really think you are going to change me, Nany?... That you can just make my mind up for me?" His questions pinch at her with the sting of his offense. "There's a lot of niggahs out here that will fold for a piece of pussy, but I am not one of them. You need to go find someone else, if you want a man that you can rule over. You may be daddy's little girl but you're not a little girl anymore and I'm not a pushover like your father."

Epiphany is astonished by how quickly he switched up on her. She is still gasping for breath when he gets up from the sofa.

"I'm sorry," Epiphany rises behind him and tries to hug him.

"Don't touch me," he hisses at her. "You think after ten years, I don't get tired of hearing this shit over and over again?" He presses his feet into his tennis shoes and leaves the room. Epiphany shuffles after him, biting her lip and racking her mind to find a way to appease his anger.

"You've got student loans higher than our mortgage and you want to talk about having children like it's a viable option," he rages, seemingly to himself, as he throws open the coat closet in the foyer.

"Please calm down baby," she begs, pulling at his jacket sleeve. "You're right. I know you are only thinking of what's best for us."

"Don't give me that." He pulls his arm away from her and points his finger in her face. "I know what you've been trying to do."

Epiphany's moist eyes appear baffled. She holds her breath at his accusation.

"You've been pulling this forgetful act, but I know you stopped taking your pills because I found a whole unopened pack underneath the sink."

"I wouldn't do that." She shakes her head. "I wouldn't betray you like that. If you say no, then we won't have any children. It's just that simple."

"You know what?" Jerome surrenders his palms, shrugging his shoulders up by his ears. "I'm out of here. I don't have to keep putting up with this." He places his hand on the doorknob, but Epiphany covers his hand with her own.

"Please don't leave," she whispers. A tear streams down her face. "You said the last time that you wouldn't do this to me again."

"I need some space, Nany. I just need some time," he breathes with closed eyes. "I can't handle all this pressure you keep putting on me."

"I'm sorry, Jay. I won't do it anymore. Just don't leave here tonight." Her hand slips from his hand to his forearm. "You can sleep in the den and I won't bother you."

"You're my wife- not my enemy. I don't want things to be like this between us."

"I don't either," she cries into his chest, pressing her face against his shirt.

Jerome suddenly sweeps her up into his arms. Epiphany is surprised when he carries her into their bedroom at the end of the hallway. He lays her down into their tall, king-sized, four-post, acacia wood bed. Jerome tears off his jacket and climbs into the bed with her.

Epiphany is still apprehensive. She cannot just change gears like he can. She is still disturbed that he wanted to leave again, but as she feels his big, fat erection pressing against her stomach and his kisses that find first her lips, then her neck and last her collarbone in the darkness, she finds her way to forgiveness in his seduction.

She pulls his shirt off and places tiny kisses on his chiseled chest. He unbuttons her jeans and lets his fingers rub over the outside of her panties. His fingertips feel the warm moistness beginning to collect between her legs and he is satisfied to proceed. He lifts her sweatshirt over her head, but before he can take her large, brown nipples into his mouth, she prevents him.

"Hold on, one second," she whispers, slipping off the edge of the bed. Jerome lays back against the pillows, frustrated because of her routinely frivolous interruptions. He huffs out a long breath when she returns, minutes later, completely naked except for a colorful head scarf covering her hair. "Alright, now I'm ready."

"Well, I'm not hard anymore," Jerome says nonchalantly, folding his arms behind his head.

"That's not a problem that I can't fix." She crawls on to the bed like a shapely, Black panther. She pulls down his pants and reaches into his boxers. She takes his flaccid manhood into her hands and slowly begins to stroke the silky dark purple flesh of it. She opens her mouth and takes him in. She sucks gently on the big, pink head, feeling his organ begin to stiffen inside of her palm. She enjoys the sensation of his penis between her lips and begins to caress it with her tongue.

"No hands," he says to her. She releases her grip and bobs her head on his organ. "Don't suck," he commands, taking her head between his hands. "Open up real wide," he directs, pushing his penis as deep into her throat as he can before she gags.

"Yeah, that feels good," he groans, feeling her throat clench and the warm saliva drip down the shaft of his penis. Epiphany is uncomfortable. She can't breathe when he's so deep in her mouth, but she stays the course, keeping it as open and wet for him as she can.

The veins in his penis begin to throb with expectancy. Jerome's body tenses and he gasps for breath. Before Epiphany can untangle her head from his hands, he cums down the back of her throat. Epiphany gags to the brink of vomiting as her eyes begin to water. Jerome holds her head forcefully down until his orgasm finishes with the last jerk of his hips.

"Damn it, Jerome," she bellows at him, smacking his hands and spitting out what she manages to keep from going down her throat. "That's so fucking disgusting." She wipes her mouth with the back of her hand.

"I'm sorry, baby," he says laughingly. "It just felt too good."

Epiphany doesn't see anything funny about what he just did to her. She feels even more humiliated than she did begging him to stay at the front door. Her eyes blaze with rage, as she stares at him in the dim splash of light from the hallway.

"Look, I apologize," Jerome coos into her ear, collecting her in his arms. "Don't be like that, Nany." He shakes her shoulder, as she produces a pout. "It really was an accident. I was looking forward to feeling you on my piece," he says seductively, rubbing along the inside of her thigh. "Just give me a few minutes to re-up and I'ma take care of you the way you too."

Epiphany breathes heavily. She just wants to push away from him, but she knows that will offend him. She may not get any more action for weeks, if she makes him feel bad about this. Sometimes she is so astonished by how hypersensitive and insecure a man as attractive as Jerome can be.

"Hey queen." He tips her chin. "Do you mind going to get me a glass of water, please?" He asks politely.

Epiphany rises slowly and marches angrily out of the room, stomping down the hallway to the kitchen. She takes a few minutes to compose herself in the quiet calm of the space away from Jerome, who irritates her to the core some days. She flips on the light and takes a glass from the top shelf of the cabinet. Epiphany presses it against the arm in the door of the refrigerator. Once she fills the glass with ice and water, she trots back down the hall to Jerome.

She sits down on the edge of the bed and offers him the glass.

"Ooo," he winces, sucking his teeth. "You know I don't take any ice in my water," he states matter-of-factly. "The cold hurts my teeth. Can you please go back and get me what I asked for– which was a glass of *water*."

Epiphany bites her lip, and internally bites her tongue, rising without a word to go back to the kitchen. Watching the water stream into the glass, she imagines that it is her urine. She even holds the glass between her thighs after filling it. She has a mind to just piss in it, but then decides against it. As she goes back down the hallway, she tries to remember the place in her heart that still loves Jerome– the place where his goodness makes all of his bullshit worth putting up with.

"Here you go, honey." She holds the glass over his shoulder, but Jerome doesn't respond. "Baby," she calls, tapping his shoulder.

He finally replies to her with the sound of his snore. In that moment, Epiphany could have just poured the water right on his head. She plops down on the bed, slamming the glass on the nightstand. She wants to cry, but she knows that if she cries she won't be able to stop. She will have to cry for days, like she did the last time she allowed herself to cry. The tears do fall- but without her permission, so she doesn't join in with their parade. Instead, she lays down in the bed with her husband. She slips her arm under his and hugs his torso. She consoles herself with the warmth of his body. She would rather be with him, than without him-

At least that is what she will choose to believe for now.

"Too many fathers are also missing. Too many fathers are MIA. Too many fathers are AWOL. Missing from too many lives and too many homes. They've abandoned their responsibilities, they're acting like boys instead of men, and the foundations of our family have suffered because of it. You know and I know this is true everywhere, but nowhere is it more true than in the African American community."

- Barack Obama

Chapter Twelve

I can remember the day I first saw Epiphany the way one remembers their baptism or their first kiss.

I didn't know– or care what her name was, but her ass caught my attention right away. It put me in a trance, as she walked across the quad in front of the Kappa Phi Alpha plot. Those round, plump cheeks were hypnotic to watch; swinging back and forth, left to right, up and down. I caught myself drooling over it- truly a thing of beauty.

Homecoming at Chapel Hill was always my favorite time of year. The time when I could go back and recruit a couple of fresh, young undergraduate pieces of tail to add to my collection. College girls are the best. They are legal and can usually be bought and paid for with nothing more than a decent meal. For all the money spent on educating them, they are still pretty ignorant. Usually, White girls are more of my flavor because they are unadulterated freaks in the bedroom; letting me nut off in their buttholes and do whatever I want to them. The flip side is that they are docile, lamb-like women who can be easily controlled and subdued. Still– they don't have bodacious back sides like the home girls, so occasionally I have to bone a dark chocolate drop just for general purposes.

Epiphany Jennings, I quickly found out was just a little bit different. I dug her because she played real hard to get. She let me take her out for dinner, but afterwards all I got was a kiss on the cheek for all my efforts. Neither my sex appeal nor the money I dropped on her compelled her to take off her panties for me, which was just plain strange and unusual.

We exchanged phone numbers and the following weekend she came to Charlotte to spend a few days with her family. She let me take her out again, so I was even more determined to secure her drawers. We had a long date. I drove her out to South End, wining and dining her at the most luxurious places that I thought would impress her. I succeeded in getting her open enough to come back to my apartment with me, but once we were there she wasn't as cooperative as I had hoped. She clammed up on me; acting like she didn't want the D as bad as I wanted to give it to her. But one glass of Merlot and a little Force MDs later, she finally let me undress her.

After putting forth a championship effort, the most she let me do was eat her out until she screamed like a banshee. I felt for sure that she would let me have it after that, but she vehemently insisted that we not go all the way. She jacked me, but that just felt like some junior high school shit to me. I couldn't believe that a grown ass woman would play such a juvenile game as coming to my place and lying naked in my bed, but then not let me hit them skins. I guess I could have just taken the pussy. Most women really want you to do that anyway, but I'm a lover not a fighter. I don't want a woman I have to convince to give it up. If she doesn't think that I am the ultimate male and that she is privileged to get sexed by me, then to hell with her.

Still, against my better judgment, I pursued Epiphany. I didn't want to go all hard in the paint and make her think that I was her boyfriend. But all the same, I never had a piece of ass that I couldn't get. The challenge of her was exhilarating.

Usually the darkies are the easiest to reel in, because they're not constantly chased by men like the redbones. As gorgeous as I am, I'm not sure how any woman could resist me, but especially not a darky. Occasionally I meet some women who have religion or morals about themselves, but usually some compliments and kindness can get them out of their panties just the same as all the rest.

It took longer than I expected to get into Epiphany's undies, but not for a lack of trying. She finally caved after six months, when I did it up big for her on her birthday. She was definitely the hardest case I've ever had, but I have to say that she was well worth the wait.

Who knew?

She was a virgin: a twenty-year-old virgin! In this day and time, that's like finding a mythical creature. Nope– it's probably easier to find a unicorn or a leprechaun than an American virgin over the age of sixteen. You would've thought I won the lottery, when she finally let me pop her cherry. I had actually never slept with a virgin in my life, so she was a first for me in more ways than one.

After that night, I had a little more respect for Epiphany than the other women that I was sexing at the time. She was really devoted to me. She obeyed everything that I told her to do, which is rare to find in a Black woman nowadays. She wasn't all bitter and ruined, toting around huge loads of emotional baggage like a lot of Black women that I've had the unfortunate displeasure of meeting. She was a sweet, blackberry– a shoe-in for Mrs. Jerome Pettigrew, after Ajae fucked around and got pregnant by me.

Up until that point Ajae was the front-runner. I met her years before Epiphany in a nightclub. She's a beautiful, green-eyed, sandy-blonde, ghetto-ass White girl. I guess she felt the need to validate herself for me because she kept throwing around some line about being half-Black; but she didn't have to. She wasn't fooling nobody with that story anyway. The only thing Black on Ajae were the suede Pumas she was wearing when I met her. I know a White girl when I see one- even her pubes are soft and blonde.

She drives me crazy with her sexy ass, but she is way too much of a fire starter for me. Ajae won't stay at home and never respects what I tell her to do. She dresses like a tramp, always wearing more skin than clothes, and she causes problems everywhere we go. If it's not females wanting to fight her, then it's men all up in her face. One time, I almost got into a fist fight with some guy in my basketball league over her.

My friends were always heavy on me to close the deal with her; but in the back of my mind, I knew they all wanted to fuck her- and would if the opportunity ever presented itself. But I could never have married a woman like that– somebody that would always have me looking over my shoulder to see if another man was gaining on me. Jimmy Soul said it best, "If you wanna' be happy for the rest of your life... get an ugly girl to marry you."

143

Not that Epiphany is ugly. She's actually bad as hell, with a body that won't quit. But she doesn't seem to know it, so that works out in my favor. I'm sure she thinks that she can't do any better than me and that I'm the best man she will ever get; so I don't have to try hard to keep her. Plus, I don't have to worry about bringing my boys around her. They look at her like their mom or their sister, someone they could never find themselves physically attracted to.

So I put my women into their respective positions. My dad had two families so I figured I could best him, by having three. I married Epiphany because she was the most obedient and the best cook, but I let Ajae and Sharon have my babies because I knew they would be cute. I wouldn't want to bring a child into the world that didn't have a chance to be as beautiful as me with golden skin like rays of sun and soft, curly good hair like me, Sharon and Ajae.

If I had a baby with Epiphany, it could end up all dark-skinned with nappy, resistant hair that could break combs in half. Our child would be ridiculed and I wouldn't know how to handle that. I would have to lie to them and tell them that they are beautiful when I know that ain't the truth.

I can't even relate to that life. There hasn't been anything that I could not have; nothing has been denied to me since I was born. I've always had women making a fuss over me since I was a baby. I have always had the best of everything. What I could not get on intelligence or talent, my looks have gained for me.

Presently, I work a job that I am under-qualified for. I find it laughable every day that they see fit to call me an editor. I can barely even write my own articles, let alone proofread someone else's. I would have failed freshman English, if I had not started sleeping with my much older, White female professor. I helped lay to rest her curiosity about Black dick and she gave me a passing grade. By the time I graduated, I had a whole slew of intelligent females without common sense to complete all of my assignments. Even now at the Observer, I have a twenty-something, high-yellah assistant named La'Donna who I bone occasionally and she keeps my work up for me. All I have to do is show up to the office on time, smile genially, crack a few jokes, shake some hands and then call it a day. The

White people love me and the Black people want to be me. The only time I even touch a piece of paper is to sign it, but now that La'Donna ordered that rubber signature stamp, she can take care of that too.

I guess the way I'm am handling things is very selfish, but I don't care. If these women are silly enough to go along with it, I guess on some level they deserve it. If it wasn't me doing it to them, it would be some other asshole. I might as well be the one to reap the benefits of their ignorance. If I didn't keep Ajae's illiterate ass up, she'd probably be up on a pole right now and what kind of life is that for my kids?

Epiphany is my favorite though, because she is so resourceful. She does the most with the least. She is smart as a whip. She makes a shitload of money, so I can pay the mortgage each month and blow the whole rest of my check on whatever I want. She keeps a hot delicious dinner on the table for the nights that I actually show up at home and she does it all with a menial amount of my attention and affection. Besides, she's my best kept secret. I'd never let my boys know this– but she's the best I've ever had. Her cookie is good enough to make a grown man cry.

It can all get a little hectic though because I have to live a triple life. Occasionally, I get a little forgetful. Me and Ajae stay so high that sometimes I get my lies crossed up, but I dope up Epiphany's chamomile tea with sedatives, so most days she doesn't know if she's coming or going let alone where I am. Another down side is that I don't always get to see my gorgeous kids as much as I'd like to– especially that Jackson, he is a spit-fire, handsome as the devil with his mother's green eyes and my thick, wavy hair. He's getting prepared for college, so he needs me around more to show him how to rope in the groupies. I usually try to take off for what I tell Epiphany is a conference at work and spend a whole week with them about four times a year. Now that Sharon's met with her unfortunate demise at the end of a gun barrel, things should be a little easier to manage.

Beautiful, lily-White Sharon Dellivere should have been more careful to pay attention to my instructions. I told her from the start never to lie to me, steal from me, or cheat on me. She always wanted to act like she was so sophisticated and high-class. She wanted to be my wife, so she wouldn't be living in sin; but in the end she proved to be just as much trash as the rest of these lying hoes– just another treacherous snake like mostly all women. She got impatient with my situation. She got all hot in the ass and decided to let another niggah nut off in her, and then tried to put the baby on me. She should've known me better than that. The only thing I watch closer than my women is my money. I knew about her and C.J. – the mechanic. I was willing to let them have each other, but then she started making threats to tell my wife about us, if I cut her off. I had no choice but to make her ass disappear and that's just what I did.

Ajae agreed to bring Immaculate, my five-year old daughter by Sharon in to live with her and my teenagers–Jackson and Ashana. Now things are working out even better for me because all of my children are being raised in the same home like true brothers and sisters. I can see them all in one visit, which means more time and money for Ajae.

I can't complain though– My life is good.

"You can protect your liberties in this world only by protecting the other man's freedom. You can be free only if I am free."

Clarence S. Darrow (1857-1938), American lawyer

CHAPTER THIRTEEN

"Leave me alone, Jerome," Epiphany groans, digging her elbow into his ribcage. "I have to work in the morning. It's too late for all this."

Epiphany, still half-asleep, rolls over on to her stomach and throws her arm across the pillow. Jerome was away at another one of his conferences this past week. Epiphany doesn't know what they do at these company functions, but Jerome rarely returns when he says he will. Either he comes home days earlier than expected with a nasty, irritable attitude or–

"Come on, baby," he whispers on her cheek, running his hands along the sides of her body. The overpowering smell of strong alcohol on his breath reaches her nostrils. "Open it up for me. Daddy's home." Epiphany rolls her eyes at the notion of his fatherhood, then swats his hands away.

When Jerome finally does come back, days later than expected, in the middle of the night like this, he is usually so inebriated that he can't even make his way to the bedroom. Epiphany usually finds him passed out on the floor and covers him with a blanket. But tonight is obviously an exception to that general rule.

"I told you that I'm not having sex with you when you're drunk no more." Epiphany closes her eyes, trying to remain calm, as he climbs on top of her back. "You're too rough, Jay," she sighs angrily, as the pressure of his weight drops down on her.

"Stop fighting with me, Nany." He uses his knees to part her thighs and pulls her nightshirt up around her waist, exposing her firm, succulent buttocks. "Mmm," Jerome moans, rubbing his manhood between her cheeks.

"I haven't seen my wife in over a week. This is my pussy and I'm taking it tonight." He shifts his legs until they are free from his pants. It takes Jerome several tries to find what he is looking for. Epiphany gasps when he shoves his semi-erect penis into her femininity. Jerome instantly begins thrusting inside of her like a dog in heat. He growls out like a savage beast, then brutally bites down into her shoulder.

"Owww!" Epiphany screams. She twists to see him, but he presses her shoulders down firmly on the mattress.

"Hell yeah," he mumbles, smacking her ass so hard that Epiphany tenses from the sting. "I'ma beat this pussy up tonight." Jerome already drips with sweat, the alcohol pouring from his pores.

"That's it," Epiphany huffs. Her walls burn from the friction of his rough gyrations inside of her. "Stop Jerome!"

She tries to wriggle free of his grip, but Jerome lays down flat against her back, using his body weight to restrict her resistance. He places his hands on her elbows. Epiphany cannot guess what he is trying to accomplish in that position, but unfortunately for her– she soon finds out.

The next sensation she experiences is the ripping pain of Jerome's member entering her anus. Epiphany bellows an intense, ear piercing shriek, when she feels him enter her exit way. Epiphany's cries quiet to a whimper and she presses her face into the pillow, biting down hard on it to distract from the pillage of her body.

"Shhh," Jerome issues forcefully into her ear. "It only takes a minute to get used to this. Stop tensing and just relax. I promise you gone love it."

Epiphany's stomach turns. The searing agony of him, jabbing his manhood deeper and deeper into her makes her nauseous.

"Please..." she begs so sincerely. "Please stop. Don't do this to me, Jerome." Her tears mixed with saliva saturate the pillowcase. She gasps out her distress in sobs between his thrusts.

Epiphany strains against him until she becomes exhausted, both from pain and exertion. She closes her eyes. The agony of her heart breaking is more excruciating than the stinging fire ablaze in her rear end. She finally becomes numb, forcing herself not to feel what he is doing to her. She lays for what feels like hours– but only actually amounted to just a few minutes before the warm, fluid of Jerome's ejaculation fills her, signaling the end of the horrific torture. Jerome relaxes and slumps down beside her in their bed.

There in the dark– Epiphany listens to Jerome's breathing. She imagines for just a moment that the long, heavy breaths have ceased. But when the terrifying reality that those breaths would continue to come dawned on her, she burst into tears again.

"You really need to chill the fuck out with that shit, Nany." Jerome turns his back to her. "It's not that big of a deal. It's about time we spice up our sex life with something different."

"Oh is that what you call spicy, Jerome?" Epiphany whines– the bitterness evident in her tone.

"Damn right," Jerome answers matter-of-factly, glancing over his shoulder at her. "Do you how many women would love for me to give them what you just got? ... You just need to be glad that I'm bringing all this big, Black dick home to you instead of putting it on them."

Epiphany tries to sit up, but finds that she can't. Jerome's rape stole all of her strength. When she finally manages to roll over, she winces and then groans lowly, feeling perhaps the most debilitating injury that she has ever experienced in her life. Her entire pelvis throbs, swollen and engorged.

"That's strange," Epiphany grunts, pressing up to a seated position with all of the energy that she can muster. "You call that adding some spice, but I call what you just did– some *gay shit*." Epiphany spits the words at him, hoping to damage his ego as badly as the hot, stabbing spasms that course through her bottom.

"What the hell did you just say to me?"

"You heard me," Epiphany whips her neck, then pushes as best she can to throw her legs off the edge of the bed. She realizes as she twists in a cold, sticky puddle on the comforter that more than just cum is on it. She becomes enraged at him. "I figured that you were out in the street fucking stray bitches, but I had no idea that you were up in the mirror for hours, getting all pretty to go out and attract other men, you faggot-ass bastard."

Epiphany wasn't facing Jerome, so she never saw his hand. Only felt it strike the side of her face. His backhand was devastating, causing her to lose equilibrium for a second. She shakes off the dizziness and then with all the power in her, raises her hand and smacks the taste out of Jerome's mouth. Jerome is taken aback for a minute. He clutches his cheek in shock as he stares, angry and astonished, at Epiphany. He can only see her silhouette in the darkness, but he lunges at her. Jerome grabs her face and launches her off the bed. Epiphany crashes against the wall, before crumpling to the floor.

"Don't you ever touch my face again!" He yells at her, before striding into the bathroom. "Black bitch," he mumbles to himself, as he flips on the light switch and frantically searches his face. He studies his reflection carefully, turning right to left, left to right again. There is a slight, reddish tint to the left side of his face, but nothing that should leave a mark.

Epiphany assesses her injuries in his absence. She is most concerned about the bruised tailbone she more than likely suffered from the long fall from the bed. She slithers the short distance on the floor to her nightstand. Epiphany shuffles her underwear around in the drawer to find the small, unnoticeable groove. She flips open the false bottom in the drawer.

Jerome is too busy checking his face and obsessing over the light pink fingerprints on his cheek to care what Epiphany is doing in the corner of their bedroom. However, she captures his full attention when he hears the click of the gun, as she racks the slide. Jerome slowly turns to look in the direction of the sound. The Glock 9mm is only inches from his face, clearly visible, gleaming in the light from the bathroom.

Epiphany remains somewhat obscured by the shadows from the dark bedroom, but her eyes are clear and focused with an intention that frightens Jerome. The revelation of the fact that he has spent so many years sleeping in a bed beside her, unaware that only inches away she kept a firearm, was enough to scare him straight.

"Baby," Jerome whispers softly. His body so tense that the short, sharp breaths he draws in wheeze within his chest. He surrenders his palms in a gesture of obeisance to her.

"Jerome." Epiphany acknowledges him with a tiny nod. She closes her left eye and squares her sites on his chin. "I'm going to give you exactly one minute on my mark to get your clothes on and leave this house."

Jerome's bottom lip trembles. He wants to plead with her, but he is sure that even the movement of his lips could be enough of a trigger to make her pull her trigger.

"Go," she blares suddenly, moving aside so he can dart out of the bathroom. She stalks him with the barrel of the gun, careful to keep at least some body part of his within the sights at all times.

"30 seconds," she barks assertively. He frantically pushes his foot into the wrong pants leg. Jerome pulls the pants on backward, panicking when Epiphany begins to count backwards from fifteen. Jerome grabs his shirt and decides to use his dwindling seconds to slip into some shoes and grab his wallet. The front door swings open at three. Jerome goes shirtless and shivering out into the icy chill of a black, starless winter night to avoid the consequences of being inside the house when Epiphany gets down to one. Jerome doesn't believe that she would really burn him down, but betting that her threat is unfounded in her obviously fragile emotional state are some three-to-one odds that he's not willing to take.

Jerome's eyes, brimming with confused sadness, meet hers in the second it takes him to disappear behind the front door. Epiphany exhales long, feeling both relief and dread fight for the dominance of her limbs. The gun feels heavier in her hand than it did seconds before. So heavy, in fact, that she cannot hold it up any longer. Her hands drop at her sides. Her body trembles violently and she collapses to the floor. She curls into a tight, convulsing ball, wailing at the top of her lungs.

It's not the aggression and anguish brought on by the rape that she is determined to expel; it is her love for Jerome that she wills herself to release in the form of saltwater tears spewing from her eyes. She heaves in hiccup-like sobs so deep that they produce a gag in her gut. She rolls from side to side on the floor, needing to free herself, needing to detox off the fatal drug that is her husband– Jerome.

Epiphany hugs her knees to her chest. She feels like a fool after so many years. He is the only man that has ever had the intimate knowledge of her mind, her body and her soul. She was so completely his. The agony of the thought that their marriage is over turns her inside out. Epiphany feels an emotion like her heart is being scraped out with a bitter cold ice cream scoop. She twists her huge twenty-four carat gold wedding bands from her finger; both the one Jerome placed on her finger at their wedding day and the three carat diamond anniversary band he gave her one month ago to commemorate their ten years together. She heaves them at the wall with all of the strength of her anger, then presses her blazing, fiery cheek against the cool hardwood floor.

"Jerome," she whimpers his name hopelessly, smacking her palms against the floor.

god face

Light is meaningful only in relation to darkness, and truth presupposes error. It is these mingled opposites which people our life, which make it pungent, intoxicating. We only exist in terms of this conflict, in the zone where black and white clash.

- **Louis Aragon**

CHAPTER FOURTEEN

On the third day, Epiphany finally rose out of her bed.

She received a phone call from her supervisor that morning because it was very unusual for her to miss three consecutive days of work. In her seven years with the Financial Accounting Branch at United National Bank, other than scheduled vacation leave, Epiphany never missed a Friday. Her phone rang incessantly that morning. After the supervisor phoned, a barrage of calls from Epiphany's assistant as well as other colleagues ensued about issues that needed prompt attention. The constant interruption of life going on as scheduled was enough to finally rouse her from a deep, catatonic depression.

She shuffles slowly, her hind parts still tender, into a shower– her first in days. The soft, warm water, seemingly more fragrant mist than droplets, invigorates her. Epiphany feels the rapid spray begin to caress her skin in a reassuring massage. For some strange reason, she begins to feel an invisible sensation like an affectionate hug confirming that she is still loved. The force is spiritual and it consumes her within its rapture. She begins to weep in deep guttural sighs. The weight of her pain begins to press on her shoulders and she feels that she just may faint under the pressure of it. Instead, she washes her tears away, ducking her head under the rushing current of water. The tears and the shower cleanse more than just her body, but also her soul. Epiphany's sobs turn to laughter, as she rubs the water away from her face.

Following her shower, she dresses slowly, ignoring the ringtone of her cell phone, which initiated seconds after her home phone went to voicemail. She is no longer moved by anyone else's urgency. Epiphany towel dries, then slips into the flowing comfort of a long, tangerine colored Egyptian linen dress that she brought on vacation with Jerome, but then never wore outside of the house. It is more of a spring outfit, with the elaborately colorful designs on the bib, but she doesn't care. The fabric feels good brushing against her skin, as she drifts down the hallway and into the kitchen.

It is well after lunch time. Although Epiphany laid in bed for two days without even so much as a passing desire to consume any food at all, she finds herself ravished with an untamable hunger now that she has entered the kitchen. She searches the shelves, almost frantically, for something quick, and then settles on a bowl of raisin bran cereal. She pours a portion heavy enough to satisfy, but not so much as to upset her stomach after the fast.

Epiphany glances around the celery colored kitchen while she pours the milk. She always hated that color. It reminds her of the color of her puke during a stomach virus one winter. But they painted almost all the rooms in the house that color because, strangely enough, it is Jerome's favorite. Epiphany taps the spoon against her bottom lip and begins to conceptualize what color schemes she will use to redecorate the house. As she finishes the cereal, she decides on a bold, but understated gold champagne paint that she saw in a catalogue. She suggested it when they first bought the house, but Jerome overrode her decision, picking the celery instead.

She smiles to herself, tracing the ceiling with her eyes and letting her mind wander with the possibilities. Then she contemplates on further embellishing and expressing herself by adding a tan/beige paisley border around the top of the walls. As her heart and stomach settle, her thoughts turn to consider all the prospects of which she never previously allowed herself to even conceive.

Conceive?

The word enters her meditation. It just appears, as if from thin air and then wafts around in her heart like a spirit resurrected from the dead. Epiphany puts her bowl on the counter and her hands drift involuntarily to her womb. She cups her hands over the tiny pouch of not quite middle-aged spread under her belly button, as if it is already full with life. It might as well be because Epiphany is aroused by the fantasy of it. She bites down on her bottom lip to contain a smile that threatens to take over her entire face. A giggle escapes her lips when she begins to visualize her body swollen with the expectancy of a child and finally sharing her life with a man who desires the same.

Epiphany dreads the years she spent as a hostage in an obviously dead end situation with Jerome, but gratefulness- in the form of appreciation and relief, flood her limbs releasing the anger and resentment. She bends her body forward and presses her fists to her forehead, thankful that it is over now after ten years instead of twenty. Hell– at ten years instead of eleven. The weight, like heavy bricks, falls from her frame, as she realizes that she doesn't have to spend another day in what had become a prison sentence. She seems to stand just a little bit taller when she rises back up from taking her final bow for an award-winning performance in a Broadway production that will not be reprised.

She does a little spin, then sways to the tune of some internal, inaudible music. She sways across the kitchen and opens the pantry door. She takes out the box of green tea, instead of chamomile. She wants to be energized for this day.

As she sips from her teal ceramic mug, she allows her imagination to entertain her. She thinks of finally being able to go out with her girlfriends and stay out as long as she wants without fearing any repercussions. Her mind immediately zooms from there to her high school crush, C.J., whom she ran into just a few weeks prior. They played a quick hot-potato-like game of catch up in the aisle at the grocery store. He offered her his business card along with a discount on any services that she might need. He was polite and respectful, but something about the intensity in his slender eyes and the way his hand lingered on hers when he reached out the card told her that not all of the services he wanted to offer were mechanical.

She smiles, holding the cup to her lips and imagining that its warmth is that of C.J.'s thick, dark lips on hers. Before she can begin to imagine how beautiful of a child she could have with him, Epiphany quickly catches herself and halts that train of thought in the station. She gathers herself, patting her hair to ensure that it is dry before she goes out into the unseasonably warm, but still dead-of-winter day.

She presses her arms into her soft, full-collar, red cashmere sweater jacket and places huge, brown shades over her eyes. Epiphany steps out into the piercing, bright sunlight, looking a tacky, mismatched, nappy-headed (but happy) mess.

By the time Monday morning rolled around, Epiphany was ready to face the world. Armed with a new resolve to live victoriously, she breezes through the doors, across the floor, between the aisles and into her office as if carried in on a cloud. She is the main attraction. All eyes are on her for the first time since she sports a new look, so radically different from her normal appearance that her co-workers can't help but stare.

Epiphany made her weekend very productive and it shows in the glow of her dark cinnamon-colored skin. Neal, her assistant, instantly makes his opinion known; following her into her office, as close as a tall, white shadow.

"Honey chile, I think you look *marvelous*," he hisses with a swipe of his hand like he is swatting flies away from her.

"Thank you, Neal," Epiphany answers with cold, mechanical diplomacy. "What's the order of business for today?" she asks flatly, pulling two files from her inbox.

"*Well*," Neal drawls, as if he is about to gab about the juiciest office gossip. "You missed a lot being out so many days last week, so I did my best to keep you caught up, but you know can't nobody do this job like you."

Epiphany rolls her eyes internally, knowing that Neal wants her position. So much so, he is even willing to stoop so low as to feign kissing her ass, just to get close enough to her back to stab it. She knows he probably figures it should be his job and that he is entitled to it because he is White and dresses better than she does. Epiphany figures that Neal should know by now that it takes more than a pretty face and sucking up to get the top positions in this world.

An opinion that she will hold firmly from now until next month when Neal becomes her new supervisor.

As Neal begins to rattle off her itinerary, she realizes that he hasn't touched much of anything she delegated to him during her absence. *I see you bitch-* such a passive-aggressive saboteur, she thinks to herself, knowing that it is going to take a tiny miracle to keep her cases from going overdue without his help. She's going to look like the negligent Fiscal Manager while Neal gets to look like a fat, over-grown Baby Jesus in a tan sweater vest when he comes to save her from the same work that he should have already done.

"But we'll rope this bucking bronco together," he sighs heavily, flipping curly, auburn hair, that is way too long to be considered professional on a man, behind his ears. "Don't you worry about a thing, sugar." He pats her hand, before picking up half of the folders that he just brought into her office. "I've got your back." He winks mischievously before starting out of her office.

"Oh excuse me," Neal breathes, stopping just short of running headfirst into Jerome's chest. Instead of brushing past him, Neal takes a few steps backward into Epiphany's office. Epiphany doesn't notice that Jerome stands at the doorway of her office. She had already buried her face in a file, to keep from cursing while Neal was still talking.

"Mrs. Pettigrew," Jerome pipes softly, stepping inside the space of her office, made a little too crowded because of Neal's presence.

Epiphany freezes in mid-pen stroke. The sound of Jerome's voice makes her skin crawl. She lifts her eyes to meet his, but refuses to let Neal see the disdain she has for her husband in her expression.

"Oh hey, darling," she squeals facetiously, with a tight, sarcastic smile that passes for seductive coyness because she offers it with her cheek pressed against her shoulder. She doesn't want to give Neal any Intel about her life that he can feed to the workplace gossip piranhas.

Epiphany glares at her husband with astonishment which resembles admiration. He out did himself with this move. Epiphany has never known Jerome to be the brightest crayon in the box, but coming to her office was ingenious. Here, he can get a civilized audience with her. Even more, he is dressed casually, in a ribbed crimson turtleneck with nice expensive dark denim jeans, but irresistible with the collar flipped up on his light brown leather jacket. Epiphany knew that he probably took a whole meticulous hour making his cream colored scarf look as though he nonchalantly draped it around his neck.

"Happy Birthday, my love." His words brim with a passionate desperation too intense for the casual salutation. He reveals a large bouquet of probably two dozen or more dark, red roses from behind his back. "These are for you."

"Awww," Neal groans with moist eyes like he is watching the ending scenes of Jerry McGuire. "This is just too sweet."

Evidently Jerome's presence makes a movie-like scene because several eyes across the floor, most of which belong to females, are focused on the glass wall of Epiphany's office. She even sees one of the interns cross her legs and fan her chest, as a gesture to the woman across from her.

Jerome turns his eyes to Neal, as if to say an inaudible *goodbye*. Jerome subdues the intensity of his gaze by presenting it with a courteous smile. Neal blushes, his pale skin turning bright pink, when Jerome looks at him.

"I'll just go put these flowers in some water for you," he stammers, grabbing quickly for the bouquet. He scoops up all of the remaining folders on Epiphany's desk with the very limited space left in his arms. "I'll go ahead and take care of these too, since you'll probably be very busy today." He grins naughtily.

Neal does his best to use his foot to close the office door, but Jerome assists making sure that it is completely secure. Jerome turns around and pulls the cord for the blinds, releasing them to cover the entire window panel.

"I'm so sorry." His back is still faces Epiphany. He drops his eyes in shame before turning around.

"I'm very busy. What do you want, Jerome?" She returns her eyes to the papers on her desk.

"Another chance."

162

"Too bad you didn't need a loan because I probably could have helped you out with that." She picks up her pen and begins to push it around on the paper. "Have a nice day."

Jerome feels her words like a cold ice pick puncturing his chest. He never thought this day would come, so he never prepared for how terrible it would feel.

"You look beautiful," Jerome confesses honestly. "I love what you've done with your hair," he says of her low, close-shaven haircut.

Two days ago, Epiphany sat down in a barber's chair and told the tall, older, Black man to "take it all off."

"How low do you want to go?" the barber inquired cautiously.

"How low can you go?" She replied and did not stop him until only a fine layer of hair, just enough to cover her scalp remained. Epiphany returned home that day and colored the fuzz on her head a vibrant shade of blonde. She brushed it the following morning until it laid down in shiny waves on her head, and then smiled with satisfaction at her reflection in the mirror.

Jerome watches her carefully, trying his best to gauge her response but she only offers him a cold, blank expression. She really does look so much more beautiful to him today than she ever has. He is not sure if it is because of her makeover or because he may be losing her, but he feels a passion for her that he never has before. It is different from the beginning when he was chasing her panties and more significant than any emotion that he has ever felt towards any woman.

Could this be... love? Jerome asks himself internally. The prospect of the answer overwhelms him and he takes a seat in one of the chairs facing her desk.

"I really will have to ask you to leave now," Epiphany sighs, losing her patience with him.

Jerome doesn't even budge in this seat. He doesn't even acknowledge Epiphany's statement. He pulls the scarf from around his neck and watches his hands while he winds it around them. Epiphany isn't even sure that he is still present-minded until he says–

"Since the night I left our house, I have come here and waited every day for you to show up at the office." He lifts his eyes to meet hers. She feels a flash of heat in her face. He is still so gorgeous to her. "Today you are finally here." He continues simply, "And I am not leaving." His jaw clenches, working just as hard to contain his anger as his brain is laboring to choose the most persuasive words. "The only way I will leave this office is if you are coming with me."

"I can't go anywhere with you Jerome... even *if* I wanted to. I am behind on my work." Saying the word *behind* made her cognizant of the slight pinching sensation. She shifted in her leather seat to remedy the discomfort.

"Just let me take you out for your birthday and then I will leave you alone," Jerome states with resignation.

"My birthday was yesterday, so that really isn't necessary."

"Come on." Jerome stands and offers his hand to Epiphany. She disregards him and goes back to reading a sheet of paper on her desk. Jerome takes advantage of her inattentiveness and grabs her elbow tightly. He pulls her forcefully from her seat, but before she can resist him, he throws her office door open, knowing that she won't cause a scene in front of her co-workers.

"Alright," she snaps through tightened lips. "Just let me get my coat." She reaches over to the mounted hooks on her wall.

It is rare for Jerome to ride his motorcycle in the winter, but it is parked across the street when they exit the building. He must have gone back to the house to get it when Epiphany went to work. He is so careful when he puts his helmet on her head, and then buttons the top buttons of her coat up to her chin before zipping up his own. When she wraps her arms around him, he pulls them even tighter needing to feel her body pressed against his.

At brunch, Jerome barely says anything to Epiphany at all. Only stares across the table at her, as if dissecting her with his eyes. He is definitely conducting an inspection of his wife. It is as if she has been abducted by aliens and replaced with a pod person. Nothing about her is the same. Everything- from her appearance to her demeanor, even her mannerisms have changed. The haircut fits her so well. With no hair to obscure or distract from her face, Jerome finds her features so alluring.

She sits with dignified composure, poised and sophisticated. She isn't wearing her glasses. Her back is straight which does amazing things for her breasts, drawing more than a little attention from both Jerome and the waiter. Jerome almost wants to cover her up with his jacket.

Jerome can't believe it. Epiphany is a knockout. He couldn't even imagine letting her out of the house or bringing his boys around her now. Epiphany is usually so modest and homely. Jerome has never seen her dress this way. Her three-piece navy and turquoise pinstripe pants suit gathers under her bust, tailored tight to her slender waist, then contours to trace her full, round hips. She picked a turquoise cotton V-neck, instead her usual crew neck or high collar shirts. The top dips down behind her vest, revealing the smooth, silky brown skin of her chest. Jerome holds the menu in front of his face, but his eyes follow the narrow, part between his wife's breasts. He finds himself wanting to place his tongue in the dark space between them. Jerome feels his organ stiffen between his thighs as he fantasizes about his wife like he doesn't already know what lies beneath her clothes. He even wonders if her pussy will feel different now that she is evidently such a different woman. Her newness arouses him, but he knows he has to put in some serious work before he will get the opportunity find out.

The waiter, who is showing their table way more attention than his others, returns to the table, snapping Jerome out of his fantasy. Jerome puffs up his chest like the Alpha-male and even orders for Epiphany to keep the young, White man's attention on him and away from his wife.

"What do you hope to accomplish with this?" Epiphany cuts straight to the chase once the waiter leaves.

"I love you, Nany," Jerome states desperately. Epiphany finds herself rolling her eyes before she knew that she would. "I've been waking up without you for a week now and I realize that is not how I want my life to be."

"Yeah," Epiphany interrupts. "About that... Just where have you been waking up these days?"

"That's not important. You obviously don't care or else you wouldn't have put me out of my own house in the middle of the night," he responds with considerable irritation. Epiphany raises one eyebrow, checking the way he just threw the blame on her like stolen goods. "The point here is that I haven't been at home with my wife... which is where I really want to be more than anywhere else."

"Where have you been sleeping, Jerome?" She asks more directly, lowering her lids.

"I've been staying with some friends."

"Which ones?"

"Different ones," he blurts angrily. "Most of my boys are married with children. They can't board no grown ass man."

"Hmm," Epiphany huffs in disbelief.

"Look, you're getting off the subject." He rubs his hand over his mouth in frustration. "Baby, I want to come home. I miss you like crazy."

"And you would really come back after I pulled a gun on you?" Epiphany's question is more of a delighted statement.

"Yeah that was some wild shit," Jerome retorts with a sly smile. "But I understand why you did it." He rubs his palms together. "You needed to make your point and I get it now. I've been way out-of-line, but you reeled me back in. I promise things will be different- like night and day, if you just take me back."

The dull, nagging pain in her anus flares with a vague throb when she considers the prospect of reconciliation with Jerome. She shifts in her seat to quell the faint ache.

"Well Jerome," Epiphany takes a large sip of lemon water. "I need a little time, but I do want you to come back home." A slow smile begins to spread across his face. "I'm going to spend the weekend with some friends in Atlanta, so that should give you enough time to clear all of your things out of the house before I return." Jerome's smile fades like a dimmer light switch. "Make sure to lock up and leave your keys on the dining room table before you go." She casually sips her water. Before she can put her glass back on the table, the waiter returns swiftly.

"Let me fill that up for you ma'am," he says courteously, pouring only about an ounce of water into her three-quarters full glass. The waiter smiles and gets his eyeful.

"Hey man," Jerome says calmly to the waiter. "Don't come back to this table until you got some food in your hands." Jerome cups his hands together on top of the table, and then glares directly at the man to signify that his tolerance level has been reached.

"Thank you," Epiphany offers amicably to the waiter's back when he turns to leave.

"Look Nany, this is not funny. I'm coming home with you today and we are going to sort this whole thing out over a big cup of chamomile tea." He lays the bedroom eyes on her. "I'm gonna' massage your feet and give you my full attention because that's what you deserve from me. Let me cater to you tonight," he whispers, reaching across the table to take her hand.

"I don't think you understand," Epiphany responds ambivalently. "What you did to me was unforgiveable." She lowers her eyes and takes her hand back from him, placing it onto her lap. It is the first time in the conversation that she appears vulnerable.

"Honestly," Jerome begs, pleading with his hands. "I only did what I did because I thought you would enjoy it. I just wanted to do something different– something that we have never done before."

"Or..." Epiphany sits forward in her chair. "Maybe you were too drunk to know which one of your bitches you were fucking and did some shit with me that you usually reserve for her... or *him*." Epiphany adds quietly.

"That's low, Nany," Jerome broods, simmering with a heat that threatens to boil over.

"Our sex went from being hours long to barely even five minutes, from a daily activity to hardly even once a month." Her eyes narrow with the accusation. "Do you really expect me to believe that you haven't been cheating?"

167

Jerome drops his head back, then licks his lips before looking back at her. "To say that I have never cheated on you at one time or another during our relationship would be to say that I am not a man," Jerome replies dejectedly, as if he is condemning the acts that he is actually presenting a very weak defense for. "I have made many mistakes in this marriage, but the most devastating one was taking you for granted." He says solemnly. "I swear before God, if you just take me back– I will change."

"You already swore before God... that you would honor and cherish me," Epiphany retorts with sarcasm. "And we see how that's been working out. So why should I give you more years of my life to ruin?"

"Because I love you," he whispers earnestly. "Please give me another chance."

Epiphany studies her husband's handsome face. His eyes are glossy with a slight moistness and his cheeks are pink. She doesn't know just how serious he is. He can't find the all the words to express his sincerity to her. He truly and desperately wants to come home with her and make her feel secure in him again.

"No," Epiphany answers shortly, as a waitress comes to place their food down onto the table. Jerome holds his comment until the female leaves.

"Why, Nany?" he whines like a child in tantrum. "I really think you are blowing one little mistake way out of proportion."

"That's why I won't take you back," she snaps at him, squeezing the fork in her hand. "You really think that it was okay to do what you did. It's just a part of what you always do to me. If you still think that was okay, you'll do it again."

"What do you mean?"

"You don't treat me like a person. You treat me like your trained pet, but not even that good because you expect *me* to take care of *you*. I'm supposed to bring home the bacon, fry it in a pan, but then serve it all to you on a silver platter." Her eyes blaze with rage even though her tone is low and even. "There's **never** any consideration for my feelings, my desires, or my needs and that night was just further evidence of what the very terminal disease of *your* selfishness is doing to *our* marriage."

Jerome, still in his own defense, offers, "C'mon. That's not the same. Anal sex is something that lots of heterosexual couples do. I've been told by women... *in my past*-" he emphasizes, "That it feels really good."

"Okay, I'll tell you what," Epiphany says callously. "Since it feels so good, how about I get a strap-on and do it to you? I mean, it ain't no fun if the homies can't have none, right?"

Jerome's face shrinks up at her suggestion. He looks as though he might vomit. "That's disgusting, Nany," he cups his hand over his mouth and pushes his plate away.

"What so different, Jerome?" She whips her neck with amusement. "How come you can feel that way, but I can't?"

"Because I'm a man."

"And I'm a woman," Epiphany responds quickly. "But that doesn't give you the right– married or not, to take from me what I am not willing to give you." She places her palms down on the edge of the table. "Look, if this was something that you really wanted to try, I would have been willing to experiment with it and you know that, but you should have done it the right way. You didn't even give me the respect of asking me."

"I'm sorry. I was drunk-"

Epiphany holds up her finger to stop him. Her eyes are still on the table. "You really hurt me, Jerome, and not just my feelings either." Her chest begins to heave. "I had a giant welt on my face last week, and still have purple bruises all over my body. I can't even take a dump without wanting to scream from the agony." Her eyes moisten. "You treated my body like a trash can. You raped and abused me– your very own wife. You put your hands on me to cause me harm and I cannot tolerate that."

"You don't have to," Jerome swoops in on the edge of her words. "You are right, I didn't give you your woman's worth, but I will never hurt you like that again." He reaches out and snatches her hand up before she can move it. "Please baby. I was wrong, but just tell me how to fix it. Just tell me what you need from me and I'll do it. I don't care how big or small, I'll do anything you want me to." Jerome grovels, kissing her hand.

Epiphany can't help but laugh lightly. She has never seen him look so pitiful. Jerome smiles brightly, enchanted by her laughter. He scoots his chair closer to his wife. He leans over to kiss her and she doesn't prevent him. His lips produce a warm simmer in her body. He takes her face between his hands and devours her lips.

"I love you, Nany," he whispers in her ear. "I want to give you my child." She pulls back and stares at him with bewilderment. He nods with a smile spreading across his lips. "I'm ready," he offers enthusiastically.

"You really want to do this?" Epiphany asks suspiciously. "All of a sudden, just like that after all these years?"

"I just want to make you happy," he replies kissing her fingertips. "Honestly, for the first time in our relationship that's the most important thing to me." He shakes his head. "I've been selfish all of my life. I didn't even know what it meant to love and need someone else until just right now." His bright, brown eyes burn with passion as they delve deep into hers. "I've been so fucking miserable without you. I've had enough. I'm ready to straightened up and treat you right." Epiphany still looks unconvinced. "C'mon. Let me make it up to you." Jerome pleads longingly. "John Henry misses you too," he whispers in her ear as he pulls her hand down under the tablecloth and places it on his rock hard erection. "You look so sexy today. Let me take you home so we can work on this baby."

Epiphany's head rolls to the side when he kisses her neck. She feels her femininity throb with the expectation of Jerome's love. She is embarrassed by such a passionate public display of affection and upset with herself for succumbing to his seduction, but all the same... Jerome is all she has ever known.

She is so completely his.

god face

"I was brought to Missouri when I was six months old, along with my mama, who was a slave owned by a man named Shaw, who had allotted her to a man named Graves. When a slave was allotted, somebody made a down payment and gave a mortgage for the rest. A chattel mortgage. Times don't change, just the merchandise."

- Sarah Graves, Nodaway County, Mo.

CHAPTER FIFTEEN

In the quiet pitch black darkness of a winter's six am, Epiphany stirs before the alarm.

She begins to shift under Jerome's heavy arm, which is draped over her body. She wakes him and his arm tightens around her waist. He pulls her close to him.

"Don't go," he whispers, kissing her cheek. "Stay here with me."

"I've got to get ready for work," she replies lowly. Epiphany throws back the covers, but when she feels the icy early morning chill, she recovers herself and snuggles back into the soft, warmth of Jerome's naked body. "Maybe just a few more minutes."

"You might as well tell them you're not coming in today." He sucks on her neck. "I have too much work for you to do here at home," he says, letting her feel his arousal.

He rolls over on top of her and rests his head on her chest. She runs her hands through the curls that he has allowed to grow out over the past few weeks, at her request. He listens to her heart beat and his love for her grows with each thump. Her thighs are warm as they encircle his waist.

"Nany," Jerome calls softly, lifting his head to gaze at her. "Can I talk to you?"

"You already are, honey," she replies playfully.

"No, I mean *really* talk to you." He traces her collarbone with his fingertips. "I've been doing some soul searching, so now I want to share with you what I've found." Epiphany nods silently, studying the profile of his face in the darkness. "I'm going to be as honest as I know how, but I don't want you to take anything I say personally."

Jerome props up on his elbows, and sighs heavily. "I can honestly admit that when I married you, I was just looking out for myself." He rubs his forehead. "I knew you were a good woman and that you would take care of me. I knew I couldn't keep you with me if didn't marry you, so that was pretty much my whole motivation." He clears his throat and his brows knit together with contrition. "I was never really in love with you."

"I'd better get ready for work," she inserts calmly into the silence.

"Let me finish." Jerome presses her shoulders back down. "I don't know how or even when it happened, but somewhere along the way, I fell so completely in love with you. I have watched you over the years– your tirelessness, your sacrifices, and your unconditional love for me; somehow you got me. You just won me over. I cannot imagine my life without you and now I don't want to." He kisses her lips. Jerome is gripped by a sudden, surprising surge of passion for his wife. He exhales long, as he sucks on her lips. Epiphany presses against his chest.

"Am I supposed to take this as a compliment?"

"No, I'm ashamed to admit that to you, but I just want to be honest." His eyes are sincere. "I want to have an intimacy with you that I have never had with any woman and that starts with telling you the truth." He pecks the tip of her nose. "Just know that I love you. I hope it's better late than never."

Epiphany wraps her arms around his neck and pulls him into a deep kiss. His admission is disturbing but she doesn't want to shut him down. If his words mark the beginning of a new start for them, then she is willing to take the trip.

Jerome can't resist her anymore. He presses his love inside of the early morning warmth of her femininity. She feels so good to him that he cannot contain the long, low moan that escapes his lips. Her body feels like his very own personal Eden; a springtime garden in bloom right there in his hands. He caresses her soft, brown skin. His back weakens, as tingly waves of pleasure travel along his spine. Epiphany loves the pressure of his weight between her thighs. She holds his body tight against hers, wanting to feel every inch of his long, thick manhood, probing inside of her. She is shocked when she feels her climax coming so soon. Jerome's honesty got her open, making their sex explosive. She grips his buttocks tightly and lets him carry her to ecstasy. His strokes are long and hard. They begin to howl out together, their hearts racing in unison. Epiphany feels her orgasm burst inside of her. She bites down on her bottom lip to contain her smile.

She is so satisfied that she almost wants to stick her thumb in her mouth and roll back over to sleep.

"Damn baby," Jerome sighs against her neck. A slight twitch runs through his limbs when he pulls out. "That was the one."

"What are you talking about?" Epiphany giggles.

"That was our baby right there. It's a boy too. That's how you make a boy."

"What would you know about baby-making?" She inquires with focused curiosity.

"More than you think," he offers sarcastically. "Just take my word on this one. You're pregnant."

The thought of pregnancy washes away the suspicion his comment raised in her. Epiphany smiles in the dim orange radiance of the sunlight that creeps into their bedroom. Her deep brown complexion begins to glow, as the sunrays kiss her skin. Jerome joins in with the celebration, pecking soft kisses on her neck and shoulders.

"Come on." Jerome rises from the bed. "We're not going into work today. Let's have breakfast and go for a walk."

"I really have to go in today. It's Friday."

"They don't need you as bad as I do," he offers, kissing the palm of her hand. "Besides they're gonna' have to find a way to part with you when you go out on maternity leave." He rubs her stomach.

Epiphany laughs. She doesn't believe that she is pregnant but just the idea of it fills her with happiness. "Alright," she whispers seductively. "What are you prepared to do to keep me here?"

"Anything you want me to," he breathes solemnly, pressing his forehead against hers. "Everything you want me to." He adds a bright smile. Jerome reaches over to the nightstand and picks up the two rings that he found days ago on the floor by the baseboards near the front door.

"Can I put these back where they belong, Mrs. Pettigrew?"

"We all live in a house on fire, no fire department to call; no way out, just the upstairs window to look out of while the fire burns the house down with us trapped, locked in it"

-Tennessee Williams

Chapter Sixteen

The early spring afternoons are just a little warmer and longer than their winter counterparts.

Jerome and Epiphany walk slowly, hand-in-hand, blanketed by the long, shifting shadows of early evening. He leans over and lightly pecks her lips before they watch the orange-purple sun sink behind the tall trees. Jerome smiles brightly at his wife when he sweeps her up and carries her across the threshold like a newly married groom with his blushing bride.

"Put me down," she complains, smacking his shoulder. Her irritation turns to affection as he places her feet down on the floor. She wraps her arms around his waist.

"See, I told," Jerome says lowly, speaking of his prediction one month earlier.

"Whatever." Epiphany rolls her eyes. "I know the pregnancy test was positive, but I still have to follow up with a doctor. Besides you can't pinpoint conception down to the day like that."

"Give credit where credit is due," Jerome replies confidently. "Your man knows how to make a baby. If I did it right, you may even be having twins." He nips at her neck with his teeth.

Jerome lets his hands wander all over her body which already feels more supple under his palms with the news of her pregnancy.

"Can this be true?" Epiphany sighs into Jerome's ear. "I keep feeling like I'm dreaming and I could just wake up any minute."

"Oww," she bellows, as he pinches down hard on her left forearm.

"Believe it, baby." Jerome places a finger under her chin and lifts her lips to his. "This is very real."

Epiphany lowers back down from her tiptoes, smiling with satisfaction. She begins to step away from her husband.

"Where are you going?" he asks aggressively, clutching her wrist before she is out of his reach.

"I'm going to run some bath water," she replies with a seductive pout.

"No let me handle that," he offers quickly. "Since you can't have champagne anymore, why don't you go and pour us two flutes of ginger ale." He kisses the back of her hand.

Epiphany steps out of her tennis shoes and floats down the hallway into the kitchen. Tonight she is in a euphoric state, high and love-drunk off Jerome's romance. He surprised her by cooking a very simple, but delicious, spaghetti dinner and then escorted her on a long, talkative walk around their neighborhood. He was catering to her like it was a paid position with health benefits. Epiphany bites down on her bottom lip, as she hears the water begin to pool into the tub. She feels a deep tingle in her femininity when she thinks about her husband's love. Lately his fervor and stamina have returned. Some nights, he pleasures Epiphany over and over until she has to beg him to stop. She closes her eyes and begins to fantasize. In the secrecy of the kitchen, she rubs her erect, throbbing nipples getting her body warmed up for Jerome. She hadn't even begun to pour the ginger ale, when she hears a knock at the front door.

"Jerome!" she calls out to him. She shouts once more, but realizes that he probably can't hear her over the rush of the faucet.

Epiphany shuffles back to the front door with her feet snuggled in multicolored toe socks. She tightens the drawstring on her gray sweat pants before pulling the door open a few inches. She is surprised to see a short, shapely White woman standing on the other side of her door in a denim outfit.

"Can I speak with Jerome?" she asks directly. Her green eyes focused with an undeterred intensity. "*Please*," she adds with a courteous tone that is forced through tightened lips.

"Sure," Epiphany states graciously, opening the door wide for the woman. She steps through the threshold, then glances around the foyer as if she is casing the house.

"Who can I say is here to see him?" Epiphany inquires hesitantly, eyeing the petite woman suspiciously.

"Look I didn't come here to start anything, so I don't want to be rude, but you need to mind your business and just go get Jerome for me."

Epiphany gasps in shock at the female's boldness. She instantly becomes defensive. "Jerome is my husband and therefore my business. Whatever business you have with him, is my business too." Epiphany responds sharply.

"Look, bitch," Ajae snaps back with a wag of her head. "I am the mother of two of Jerome's children. What I have to discuss with him ain't got shit to do with you."

"Nany, which bath beads do you want– vanilla or black cherry?" Jerome stops abruptly in his tracks when he rounds the corner into the foyer. He looks like a deer caught in headlights, as he glances from Epiphany to Ajae... from Ajae back to Epiphany. He is frozen in place, holding his breath in a suspended state of animation.

"What the fuck is your problem, Jerome?" Ajae begins in on him like Epiphany is not even standing between them. "How you gone try to drop off the face of the earth, ignoring my calls like I don't have your three children– one of which, may I add, ain't even mine."

"Ajae, you should have waited for me to contact you, and not come barging all up at my house." He heaves the words angrily at her.

In the heat of the argument that ensues, neither Jerome nor Ajae seem to notice that Epiphany has slipped from the room. It's not until she returns that Jerome even realizes that she was gone. The hairs stand up on the back of his neck when he remembers her gun whose hiding place he has yet to discover. He turns slowly to discover that Epiphany is pressing her feet back into her tennis shoes, her face shiny and glistening with petroleum jelly. Her determined expression does not give her intentions away, but before Jerome can ask what she is doing, Epiphany lunges at Ajae.

She slams the woman into the front door and then delivers a slap to her face with the strength of a punch.

"Whoa, whoa!" Jerome jumps in quickly wrapping his arm around Epiphany's waist and pulling her off Ajae, who she has been dropped to the floor from a set of ghetto girl punches to the face.

Ajae jumps back to her feet and grabs for Epiphany's hair only to be disappointed by the lack of it. Jerome pushes Ajae forcefully back with his forearm. "Stop Ajae!" he shouts. "She's pregnant."

Ajae is stunned. She stops short, her fists still clenched, and her chest heaving. Epiphany takes advantage of the pause and pushes away from Jerome. She charges Ajae again. This time scratching her in the face.

"What the fuck is yo' problem?" Ajae screams at her, as she clutches her cheek. "You need to be mad at yo' trifling husband– not me."

"This is not about him," she hisses. "You can take his sorry ass back with you." Epiphany spits at Ajae's feet.

"Why are you attacking me then?" Ajae asks with genuine curiosity, pressing her fingers against her red, stinging cheek.

"Because of the disrespect. You forgot to wipe your feet on the mat when you came in my house, bitch." Epiphany replies acridly with pursed lips.

She lifts her hand and Ajae cringes against the door, but Epiphany turns the hand on Jerome instead and begins to wail on him with determined fists. She beats on his back, as he turns away from her curling his shoulders to withstand the blows.

It is Ajae who intervenes this time, trying her best to pin Epiphany's arms by her sides.

"Think of your baby," she breathes into the woman's ear, exerting herself to restrain Epiphany. "He's not worth it. Deep down inside you know that."

Epiphany rages against the small woman, lifting her off of her feet, still Ajae has her from behind in a tight grip with interlaced fingers. Epiphany relents for a moment, lulling Ajae into the false sense that she has calmed down.

Just when Epiphany would have attacked Jerome again, there is a second knock at the front door. The knock is assertive and authoritative. Epiphany looks at Jerome. Jerome looks at Ajae. Ajae looks at Epiphany. Then, in unison, they look over at the door.

"Is this the residence of Jerome Pettigrew?" A tall, stocky brown-skinned officer stands on the porch when the door swings open on three bruised and exasperated people.

"I'm Jerome Pettigrew," he replies with his forearm resting against the doorframe. "Officer, I assure you that everything is fine here," he offers mildly, standing back to let him have a full view of the two women. They anxiously nod their affirmation while the officer's eyes scan over them.

"We are not here about a domestic disturbance," the White officer chimes in. "We have another matter that we need to bring you in for questioning about."

"What's going on?" Jerome is considerably irritated, crossing his arms over his chest.

"Maybe we should just talk about it down at the station." The Black officer beckons with his hand for him to come.

"I'm not going anywhere until I know what this is about," Jerome states with narrowed eyes.

"We need to talk to you about your relationship with Sharon Dellivere," the White cop offers eagerly with an almost menacing stare. "Now you can *come* down to the station with us or we can *take* you down to the station." The officer lifts up on his duty belt, then rests his right wrist on the hilt of his gun.

Jerome doesn't reveal any emotion in his expression, but Ajae does. She bites down on her lip, her eyes darting around with a nervous anxiousness. Epiphany searches for answers to the questions that have begun to flood her mind.

"Alright," Jerome sighs benignly. "Let me get my jacket."

Black and white is abstract; color is not. Looking at a black and white photograph, you are already looking at a strange world.

- Joel Sternfeld

CHAPTER SEVENTEEN

"Alright, Mr. Pettigrew," the deeply tanned, Italian detective begins.

"I'm Sgt. Catilano and this is Detective Simmons," he says of the young petite, light-skinned female who takes the seat next to him. He offers a weathered, freckled hand that Jerome glances at with disdain.

"I really don't appreciate you people holding me like this and not allowing me to make any phone calls." Jerome's brows knit together as he crosses his arms across his chest, leaning back in the metal chair.

"Well Mr. Pettigrew," the sergeant exhales with hesitation. "We have some much more pressing issues than that to discuss with you right now." He rubs his thick, black moustache, and then glares up at Jerome. "I'll begin by telling you what we already know and then I'll tell you what we don't know. Then we will give you the opportunity to fill in all the blank spaces for us. Alright?"

Jerome offers a slight nod.

"We know that you were having a relationship with Ms. Dellivere," Sgt. Catilano spits out the words like hot soup in his mouth. "We know that you were supporting her financially and that you had one child with her and one on the way when she disappeared."

"It seems like you know a lot about me, Sgt. Catilano," Jerome responds sardonically. He flashes a smile and casts his eyes on the female detective. She masks any emotional response, but the drop of her eyes to her tablet gives her away. Jerome notices her chest heaving slightly beneath her just-a-little-too-snug baby blue cotton, button-down collar shirt. "You have me at an unfortunate disadvantage."

"What is unfortunate, Mr. Pettigrew, is that we have the body of a pregnant, White woman with no idea why anyone would want to murder her," the sergeant huffs with narrowed eyes. The crow's feet peek out at the corners, showing that the sergeant is older than he appears. "That's

183

what we don't know here. We don't have a motive. This is why we come to you, Mr. Pettigrew. Do you have any idea who would want to harm the mother of your child?"

"It's true that I *had* a relationship with Sharon," Jerome begins, licking his lips and cupping his hands on top of the table. "But as you also probably know, I am married. Sharon and I are not actually that close. I know very little about her personal life outside of the time that we spent together."

"So you're telling us that you don't know who would want to kill her?" The soft-spoken female chimes in, making adequate but not lingering eye contact.

"That's exactly what I'm saying," Jerome answers in an even tone. "I don't know any of her friends or family, her hangouts or habits. Like I said, outside of the time I spent with her I didn't know anything about Sharon at all."

"Okay." Sgt. Catilano exhales, wringing his hands. "You seem awfully calm and collected for someone who just found out that a woman carrying his child was murdered."

"I don't mean to seem so callous," Jerome responds sincerely. "But Sharon and I were moving in different directions before her death. I have been reconciling with my wife and from what I understand she was in a relationship with another man." Jerome shrugs, then casually leans back in his chair again. "You might want to ask him these questions– not me."

Sgt. Catilano snaps his fingers and a slow smile spreads across his lips. "You see," he says with delight. "I think I really like you, Mr. Pettigrew." He nods his head with a gleam in his eyes. "I knew you would be honest with us. So then, you did know that Sharon was stepping out on you?"

"Sharon wasn't stepping out on me." Jerome hurls the words like an accusation. "I told you– Sharon and I were pretty much through. I didn't have any ties on her and she didn't have any on me. I was actually glad that she had someone new in her life."

"Really?" Sgt. Catilano offers with sarcastic astonishment, raising his eyebrow. "I can't imagine that a man like you would be okay with a woman choosing another man."

184

"Alright," Jerome blurts, losing patience with the interrogation. "If you have any further questions, don't bother wasting my time. From now on, call my attorney." Jerome rises to stand up from the table.

"Yeah about that," Sgt. Catilano wheezes, rubbing his palms together. "We are not going to be able to let you go right now." The man produces a satisfied smile.

"I have rights," Jerome declares with dignified integrity. "You can't just keep me here when I haven't done anything wrong."

"Well that's just it, Mr. Pettigrew." The sergeant crosses his arms across his chest, allowing his forearms to rest on his protruding belly. "We actually have a lot of probable cause to believe that you murdered Sharon. Even as we speak, specialized teams are searching your homes, vehicles and office, confiscating anything that could be of use to this investigation."

"How can you do that?" Jerome whispers in angry desperation.

"With a few of these," Sgt. Catilano muses, waving blue sheets of paper in Jerome's face. "These warrants cover everything from your clothes, property and personal belongings to the blood running through your veins."

Jerome drops down dejectedly into the chair. He buries his head in his hands. "I swear, I didn't kill that girl," he whispers through his fingers.

"Well, I promise you this, Mr. Pettigrew," the female detective adds softly. "We will do a very thorough investigation to find out the truth." Her eyes stare directly into his. "If you didn't murder Sharon, then you don't have anything to worry about."

"In the meantime," the sergeant interrupts. "Get comfortable. You're gonna' be here for a while. We'll get you processed into the system and then someone will be around to take your DNA."

Being deeply loved by someone gives you strength, while loving someone deeply gives you courage.

- Lao Tzu

CHAPTER EIGHTEEN

"Hey man. How are you holding up?... I mean under the circumstances."

"I would say I feel blue, but with all this orange around here that doesn't exactly describe my mood." Jerome shrugs and lets his hands drop into the lap of his jail jumpsuit. "So what news you got for me today, Cairo?"

"Alright, Jerome," the young, pecan-colored man begins with apprehension, smoothing his lightweight, navy sweater with his palms. "I've got some good news, some really good news, some not so good news, some bad news and some awful news." His expression remains blank. "Which do you want first?"

"Which do I want first?" Jerome turns the question back on his attorney and fraternity brother, Cairo Baldwin.

"Hmmm," he groans taking a glance down at the paperwork on the steel counter. "Okay," he offers the sly half-smile that always won him the females over Jerome. "The really good news is that I shouldn't have any problem getting these charges thrown out. You're going to walk free and clear on Murder One, which is next to impossible; but since you really didn't do it, we have nothing to worry about."

"How can you be so sure?" Jerome says with nervousness. He adjusts himself in the seat, causing his leg irons to clink. "I don't want to get my hopes up and then be crushed in the courtroom."

"Nah, trust me when I say this is as sure as that three pointer you sunk at the buzzer against Virginia Tech our junior year. It's a certain victory, dude," Cairo replies with his usual, but casual swagger.

"So what's the good news?"

"The good news is that Ajae will testify as an alibi witness. They put a whole lot of pressure on her- told her that they would take the kids away if she was lying, but she held you down. She told the investigators that the two of you were together the entire night Sharon disappeared. She gave them her story and told them come hell or high water she was sticking to it." Cairo flips Jerome a thumbs up. "I also got them to throw out the GSR results on your clothes. The owner of the range you frequent, corroborated the story that you come in at least twice a week for target practice. They couldn't link your DNA to any that was found in the case. They ruled you out as the unknown male contribution on Sharon's bed sheets which- might I say- is excellent news for you, my friend." Cairo beams, throwing up a mock hi-five to his friend on the other side of the bars in the attorney room.

"I told you I wasn't fucking around with Sharon no more. Double dipping has never been my style. Once she let that other niggah put a baby up in her we were finished."

"Now, the DNA did link you to the eighteen-week fetus that Sharon was carrying," Cairo states in a solemn tone. "You didn't know that was your baby, Romeo?"

The silence between them becomes as thick and tangible as the iron bars. Jerome's eyes sadden, dimming his already bleak countenance. "No, I honestly didn't know it was my baby. I didn't even think it could be."

"Well now you know." Cairo hands a piece of green paper through the opening to Jerome. "The DNA doesn't lie. It wasn't your semen they found in her bed, but that was your baby growing inside of her."

Jerome shakes his head in disbelief. He tries his best to contain the emotions that fight and strain to burst forth. His face is a pale pink color when his eyes return to Cairo.

"You alright?" Cairo's voice brims with genuine concern.

"Yeah man, I'm fine. Just upset about the baby." Jerome sits forward in his chair. "You know that I didn't do this. You believe me right?"

"I believe what you tell me. You are my line brother. They made our big asses sleep in the same twin bed together during rush," Cairo retorts laughingly. "Big Brother Kappa-tal Punishment made us wear each other's underwear. I would hope after all that there isn't anything we can't share."

Jerome smiles slightly at the memory. His smile fades as the gravity of his current situation weighs back down on him.

"Okay, you ready for the not so good news?" Cairo asks in preparation. Jerome offers a nod, figuring that the news of his child's death cannot be trumped by anything else said in that room.

"The prosecution is delaying the indictment hearing a second time," Cairo sighs heavily. "They asked for another continuance."

"That's not fair," Jerome bellows out, catching the attention of the tall, brawny, blond guard who eyes him suspiciously through the glass divider. "I've already spent two months in here. I can't take it anymore. I was counting down the days and now you tell me I still have to wait even longer."

"I know, I know," Cairo mumbles apologetically. "If there was anything else I could do about this I would do it. They know they don't have enough to indict, but they got a Black man who put babies in a White woman. In their minds you committed a crime even if you didn't kill her." Cairo's eyes show the intensity of his words. "This is not exactly all bad though because if they could indict you, they would have done it by now. This is just their way of punishing you for fucking with White girls. I told you about this a long time ago, man."

"Now is not the time," Jerome breathes dismissively. "It wouldn't be so bad if Nany would just post my bail."

"Actually- that's the bad news. Her lawyer contacted me last week. She is filing a petition for divorce."

"Can't say I didn't see that coming," Jerome exhales, dropping his head into his hands. "I call and write to Epiphany almost every day, but she won't answer me at all." His voice trembles. "I love her, man. I honestly love her. She's the only woman I think I've ever really loved and now that I see it- all the fucked up shit I did is finally catching up with me."

"I tried to talk to her on your behalf." Cairo shrugs. "But it was like negotiating with a brick wall. She wouldn't budge. She refused to mortgage the house for your bail and she absolutely refuses to reconsider the divorce."

"How did she look?" Jerome asks eagerly with wide, childlike eyes.

"Beautiful."

"How is the baby?"

"That's the awful news," Cairo responds, lowering his eyes. "I know how you are about your kids so this may be very hard for you to take but... she terminated the pregnancy."

Jerome cannot contain the stunned expression that spreads across his face. "She wanted that baby so bad. How could she just..." The words take his breath away and his voice trails off.

"She said she didn't want to the baby to grow up without either of its parents."

"What does that mean?"

"She wouldn't tell me. She said that you should know," Cairo replies with more questions than answers in his eyes.

Jerome slinks down into his chair, looking as though the weight of the entire world has been delicately placed down on his two feeble shoulders.

"Look Jay, my time is almost up, but just know that I am doing as much damage control as I can for you, both personally and professionally. I will do everything in my power to help you. Just call me if you need anything. I'm praying for you, man."

Jerome offers a slight, dejected nod. Cairo places the paperwork inside of his briefcase and then stands to leave.

"Keep your head up, homey," Cairo sighs deeply.

"Easier said than done." Jerome motions for the guard. He rubs his wrists, preparing to be handcuffed and escorted back to his dormitory. He watches his best friend and brother disappear through the door on his side of the divider. His heart sinks, as Cairo takes with him all sense of normalcy. The walls, that continue to close in on him daily; the bars which remind him that his freedom has been confiscated and the barbed-wire fences to separate him from a world which– at present– believes he is unfit to walk the streets- is all that's left to Jerome now.

He shuffles down the hallway in a half-trot. The leg irons pinch his ankles. Still- he has some small solace. The chaffing is not as bad now that Ajae sent him some funds to buy socks and thermal undershirts from the Inmate Commissary. She has really stuck by him during the most distressing time of his life. He could almost fall in love with her for that, if his heart didn't still belong so completely to Epiphany. Although Ajae writes to him and willing accepts his phone calls, his mind is filled with constant thoughts and images of Epiphany- his sweet, chocolate Nany.

It is her that he fantasizes about while stroking his manhood in the late night seclusion of his cell. In vivid imaginations, he can almost feel her body on top of him, her thighs squeezing against his waist. But sometimes the sadness of her rejection is too painful for him and he cannot finish. Occasionally when Ajae does come to mind, he dismisses the thought. Deep inside he believes that she only hangs in so tight to keep him from turning snitch on her, since it was her gun, her finger and her cold heart that took Sharon out of the world.

Ajae doesn't love him. He knows now that she isn't capable of love, doesn't even know what the word means. Try as he might to forget what she did, Jerome can't. Seeing the look in her eyes when she pulled that trigger, showed him just how black Ajae's soul really is. He had always guessed it, but never had the evidence until that night. In some ways, Jerome did feel somewhat responsible. After all, he was the one who told Ajae that he would never see Sharon again; but he had no way of knowing that she would end a life to keep that from happening. Still- he couldn't go against Ajae now. It would be his tarnished, Black word against her unblemished, White word. Best case scenario– the prosecutors would make them co-conspirators and offer Ajae the better deal to help fry him, which she would do because he outed her. So Jerome remained silent in the light of the false accusation, knowing he has a better chance of beating the charges with Ajae on his side.

Jerome snaps back to reality when he hears the mechanical doors to his dormitory slide open.

"Do you want rec today, Pettigrew?" The guard asks gruffly with his usual, undisguised disinterest.

Jerome glances over at the steel door that waits to lock him inside and decides for the first time that he will take his recreation time on the bricked-in yard, which is more of a bigger cell than it is a yard. The guard escorts him through the glass door on the left instead of into the dormitory.

Jerome is instantly glad for his decision. He feels a breeze, dank with the scent of decades of sweat, mold and only God knows what else– but still a welcome change from his cell. It blows, cool and free over his skin before escaping through the metal mesh opening at the top of the recreation yard. Jerome longs just for a moment to be that wind... to be that free again... and to escape.

"You got thirty minutes, Pettigrew," the officer barks as he removes the handcuffs and shackles. It is then that Jerome notices the two other men, one White and one Black, standing far across the way in the corner of the yard, under long, striated shadows cast by the sunrays that manage to shine into the hovel.

The guard closes the door, locking all three men outside, displaying that they are still prisoners, even during their *recreation time.*

"Hey mane," the baby-faced, Black guy whispers. "You wanna' smoke?" He displays a full, snow-white smile with the offer.

"How did you get cigarettes in here?" Jerome's eyes dart from side-to-side with paranoia, then focus back on the short dark-skinned man with a smooth, baldhead.

"First- I ain't smoking no cigarettes," he says slyly, presenting a tightly rolled, marijuana joint from behind his back. "Second, if I told you how I got it in here, you probably won't wanna' smoke it." He inhales deep, then exhales slowly. "You look like you on edge, mane. This right here is just what you need. Don't ask so many questions, just enjoy ya' self."

Jerome obliges more out of peer pressure than any real desire to get high. He pinches the end of the tiny roach and pulls a drag off of what he can before he feels the heat on his fingers. The man seems satisfied and set at ease when Jerome hands the joint back. He crosses his arms over his broad chest and leans back against the wall. He watches Jerome with heightened curiosity.

"My name is Moses," the Black man offers with unabashed pride. He extends his hand for a pound with Jerome.

"I'm Romeo," Jerome replies with his nick name, as they press their knuckles together.

"Yeah," Moses says between puffs. "I can see people calling you that." He nods a bit scanning Jerome's face. "They tell me you in here for murder. How a pretty niggah like you end up doing such a hard crime?"

Jerome is caught off guard by the man's knowledge of him. He feels at a sudden disadvantage, but tries his best not to let it show in his demeanor.

"Yeah well, that's a long story, man."

"Call me, Moses," the man interrupts with some urgency.

"Okay, Moses." Jerome states diplomatically. "This is all a big misunderstanding. I will be out of here soon."

"Mmm hmm." Moses squints his dark eyes and strokes the remarkably smooth skin of his chin. "That's what everybody in lock-up says, but I'll take your word for it."

Jerome hopes that the line of questioning is finished. He doesn't want to share any more intimate details with Moses. His eyes cut to the White man still standing despondently in the corner. Jerome quickly realizes that he will more than likely not offer any distraction. The White man, with long, unkempt shoulder length brown hair, looks like a homeless vagrant- and what's more- completely absent from the place where they stand.

"Who's he?" Jerome inquires with a point of his finger, still essaying to use the man as a deflector.

"Oh that's Shelton," Moses responds dismissively . "He ain't wrapped too tight. He's a murderer just like you though." Moses still finds a way to circle back to Jerome in conversation.

"I'm not a murderer," Jerome replies vehemently. "I didn't kill anybody."

"Of course you didn't, *Romeo*." Moses shrugs. "I just meant that y'all got the same charges." He holds his palms up in front of his shoulders. "That's all."

"So what you in for then?" Jerome heaves the question at Moses like a heavy medicine ball.

"Oh me?" He points to his chest. "I'm in here for pushing weight out on the streets and lots of it at that." He shifts his oversized orange jumpsuit up on his shoulder with arrogant cockiness. "I did what they accused me of, so it's all good. I'm sure I'll get more time than five murders would if you stretched their sentences out back to back. If you were guilty, both you and Shelton would get out before me. I'll die behind bars and I've accepted that."

He extends the last dying ember over to Jerome, who refuses it with a wave of his hand.

"Well, you be easy, Romeo." Moses eyes him closely while twisting the tiny nub between his fingers until it disintegrates. "I'll check you out later." Moses glides gracefully on his short, muscular legs over to the glass door and taps to alert the officer that he is ready to leave the recreation yard.

Jerome turns his focus to the tall, slender White man, who hasn't budged an inch since he came out onto the yard.

"What's good with you, Shelton?" Jerome makes a half-hearted attempt at contact with the man. Shelton, who is leaning with his head and foot propped up against the wall, doesn't acknowledge Jerome. He continues to stare at the net-less, basketball hoop on the concrete wall across the yard. Jerome writes the White man off. He just figures that Shelton is as loopy as Moses described. The silence on the court begins to stifle him, as it grows and stretches in the dense air between them.

Jerome begins to pace for a minute, until he feels a sudden awareness. His senses perk up with the sensation. He feels eyes on him and turns to see Moses standing with some other taller, toffee-complexioned inmate watching him through the glass door. They seem completely engrossed in serious conversation broken up only by a few sideways glances at him. Jerome can't help but feel like prey being stalked by predators. Moses shoots Jerome a casual thumbs-up with an amiable grin before he and the other inmate are escorted around the corner by the guards. Still his absence doesn't resolve Jerome's discomfort.

Jerome's flesh continues to crawl. Even the hairs on the back of his neck stand at attention with apprehension. Jerome glances back over his shoulder to find that Shelton is watching him also. Shelton's eyes once glazed over are now focused exclusively on Jerome. His eyes lock into Shelton's intense, cold stare. His dark, brown eyes exude a hatred that chills Jerome to the bone.

"You'd better watch your back real close," Shelton grumbles his cryptic threat almost inaudibly as he steps away from the bricked wall. Shelton strides slowly to the door, never taking his eyes off Jerome until he reaches it. The guard comes to the door, ready to collect them both because it is almost time for lunch.

Jerome and Shelton are escorted back to their separate pods within the same maximum security housing unit. Jerome glances over when the officer keys the large, mechanical sliding door. Shelton gestures to him, pointing a V made with the first two fingers of his right hand towards his eyes as if to inaudibly indicate- "I'm watching."

Yeah- that dude is definitely a lunatic, Jerome thinks to himself as he shuffles into his dormitory.

"What goes around, goes around, goes around,
Comes all the way back around."

- Justin Timberlake

CHAPTER NINETEEN

"What's up, Romeo?"

Moses greets Jerome graciously, as he comes sauntering out on to the recreation yard on an already blistering hot summer morning. "Check," he says, pushing the basketball over to Jerome.

Jerome palms the ball easily, gripping it with his long fingers. He dribbles it, smooth and effortlessly from hand to hand, as if the motion is involuntary.

"Oh, so you a baller?" Moses asks with astonishment, tapping the shoulder of the same tall, brown-skinned brother with long cornrows from the other day.

"I hooped a little in school," Jerome replies with a grunt, as he heaves the ball at the basket. The ball glides through the goal without so much as a brush against the rim.

"Alright," Moses exclaims with an eager giddiness. "I see you got some skills and I can put 'em to use. I'ma definitely need you on my squad going up against all these big-ass, John Henry niggahs in here."

The tall guy lets out a faint laugh. Jerome looks from Moses to the man then back again, as if to compel an introduction.

Moses obliges Jerome's gesture. "This here is my man Stacks." Jerome studies the man's robust stature and figures that **Stacks** must refer to weight piles.

"As in throws up stacks?" Jerome inquires with a raised eyebrow.

"As in... blows stacks," the man rumbles in a low, thunder-like growl

"I told you," Moses sighs, pulling a joint from his jumpsuit pocket, "We're paper pushers... business men. Maybe if you play your cards right, then we'll set you up fresh on the outside. You can move some product for us... you know help us keep our baby mamas living nice... since you getting out soon and all," Moses suggests with a hint of mocking sarcasm

197

in his tone. His eyes gleam with an orange glow, when he sparks up his lighter.

"I'm not really into that kind of thing," Jerome breathes faintly, then drifts away from the two men in a light jog. He maneuvers the ball, letting the drill take him away. Jerome imagines for just a moment the he is back in the Carmichael Auditorium, running warm-ups before the big game.

In no time, Jerome works up a light sweat. He unbuttons the top of his orange jumpsuit and ties the sleeves around his waist to keep it from falling down. His white t-shirt underneath sticks to his moist skin.

"Well," Moses says with a playful twinkle in his eyes. "You are quite impressive." He scans Jerome from head to toe. "I wouldn't think you were a day over thirty-five if your gray didn't give you away."

"It's premature," Jerome responds, not completely sure why he feels compelled to explain. "I've had gray hair since I was twenty-five. Just gets a little grayer every year. I stopped trying to hide it a long time ago." Jerome launches the ball, missing his first shot of fifteen, as it hits the rim then bounces high into the air.

"I find you extremely fascinating." Moses narrows his eyes with an intensity that instantly makes Jerome feel uncomfortable. Under the scrutiny of Moses' roving stare, Jerome realizes that something is very unsettling about Moses's interest in him. Jerome suddenly feels like chattel being thoroughly inspected on a slave block.

"They tell me you got a banging ass female that comes down here every week to visit you," Moses offers, trying to ease the tension that he just watched seep into Jerome's muscles. "A white girl?"

"That's not my girl," Jerome declares of Ajae, but offers nothing more. Both men watch Jerome more closely. His offense caught their attention. Jerome quickly realizes the predicament he put himself in and says candidly, "What I mean is—" Jerome turns his palms up. "I'm married to a sister. My wife would be the one locked up for murder, if she ever found out." Jerome lets out a genial laugh that draws the other two men in with him. "Know what I'm saying, man?"

"I know what you mean," Stacks bellows in his booming, baritone voice.

"That's your story and you're sticking to it," Moses chuckles heartily, smacking and then sliding his palm across Jerome's hand. He is struck with a sudden surprise. "Man, your skin is really soft," Moses comments with amazement. "What kind of moisturizer do you use?" He allows his hand to caress Jerome's forearm. Jerome jerks his arm away instinctively, feeling as though he could jump out of his own skin to get away from Moses in that moment.

"Time," the guard calls to them from the doorway. Jerome is flooded with relief at the presentation of the C/O. The adrenaline that began to rush through his limbs drains when Jerome watches Moses and Stacks walk in front of him towards the door.

Moses glances over his shoulder before exiting and calls out, "Later, Romeo," with just a pinch of coyness that makes Jerome regret that he ever told him his nickname.

Jerome's eyebrows remain knitted together until he watches them disappear behind the mechanical door.

"All in all, I have no regrets. The sun still shines, the sun still sets. The heart forgives, the heart forgets. One more kiss, even though it's come to this. I'll close my eyes and make a wish... hoping you'll remember."

-Anonymous

CHAPTER TWENTY

I can still remember the first day I ever saw Jerome.

I ain't no homosexual by any stretch of the measure, but he was a beautiful man. The kind of man who can just as easily catch the attention of other men as he could women. He came waltzing out onto the jail rec yard like he owned it. He was so confident, trying to hide his nervousness with hubris, but he was naïve. I could tell immediately that he didn't belong there. Jail is the wrong place to bring attention to yourself. Take me, for instance. I try my best to blend right into the background, almost disappear when in a crowd of inmates like I'm not even there at all. As pale and White as the institution walls, I should stick out like a life raft floating in the sea of Black and Hispanic inmates that surround me– but I don't.

I just blend in with them, almost as if I am just as Black as them. That's what I was doing that day when it happened. Just practicing the art of nonexistence. Most of the inmates think I'm crazy, so they just leave me to myself. They go on about their business- whatever it is– and disregard me like I am a fixture: a table or a chair in the room. I've been like a fly on the wall. Seen so many things all because of the assumptions that people make about me.

Like the day them other niggers raped Jerome. I was there but they acted like I wasn't. I tried to warn him weeks before it happened, but I guess I had been acting crazy for so long that, for the first time, my reputation actually worked against me. He walked right into the trap, like a mosquito flying into the glowing, blue light of self-destruction.

Jerome had gotten some good news from his lawyer. The judge was putting pressure on the prosecution to indict or he was going to let Jerome walk. According to Jerome's rec-yard rant, things were looking up and if everything worked out, he would be released within the week. He was floating on such a cloud that he didn't notice the vultures beginning to circle him. It took me a minute to become aware of what was going on. By the time I became conscious to the fact that it wasn't the average jail house beat down, they'd already ripped Jerome a new one- literally.

They, Moses and Stacks, tore off his jumpsuit and took turns violating him. They mocked him and tormented him, tossing him back and forth like a rag doll. The scene was as hopelessly tragic as watching a half-dead possum be pulled apart by two rabid pit bulls.

"Let me get some of that," Moses hissed, pressing mercilessly against Jerome. They held him down, bent over with his face pressed against the ground and his arms spread apart to keep him from gathering his strength. He tried to fight them off, but he didn't have a chance. Maybe he could've taken out one, but the pair of them was a deadly combination. I had seen them run the dormitory, intimidating the other coons with their brawn, but Jerome didn't necessarily deserve that; no man does- nigger or not.

At one point, he bit into the hand Moses held over his mouth to muffle his screams. Moses smashed his face against the concrete almost knocking Jerome unconscious. That blow would be the one to leave a permanent, deep purple bruise around Jerome's left eye that hours of surgery could not completely repair.

"Stop squirming, bitch!" Stacks yelled at him as he pushed Moses aside. "It won't hurt so bad if you just relax. I promise you will love it after a while," he grunted between thrusts.

I couldn't take it anymore. I tried to turn my face to the wall, but my stomach was turning flips inside of me. I don't usually intervene in the niggers' business. They are as ignorant and violent as jungle beasts to me; but I couldn't consider myself superior to them, or even humane at all, if I allowed that to go on right in front of me. If it were possible that I could hate anything more than a nigger, it would have to be a flaming homosexual and there they both were wrapped up in one disgusting package right before my eyeballs.

The blow to his face took all of the fight out of Jerome and he laid there on the floor of the recreation yard looking like a fish that had lost its battle to breathe. He eyes locked onto mine, making me present in the room; although I didn't want to be. He stared at me, a lifeless glare that was too defeated to even beckon for help. His eyes just watched me, looking so focused that they bore into and finally pierced right through me, then suddenly once again- I was invisible on the yard.

I wished in my quiet corner that they would just stop… just finish already. Stacks did. He released his lode and then slumped over to the side. But the torture didn't end there because Moses took over yet again with renewed zeal. Jerome was as limp as an overcooked spaghetti noodle. He didn't move or struggle anymore. That seemed to make Moses take even more time with him. It was just disturbing how he caressed him the way a man would do with a woman. I kept praying that an officer would come soon and deliver Jerome; but Perez was on duty that day, and he is known by the inmates to be the most inattentive of all the officers.

There was no end in sight. Jerome's eyes, steady and unblinking, remained on me. My spirit began to scream out within me– **Do something**! My mind sprang into action, but my body wouldn't cooperate. I knew that if I tried to intervene they would either beat me down for getting involved or bend me over beside Jerome and give me a dose of what he was getting. Panic gripped my heart, making icy, adrenaline-saturated blood begin to flood my veins.

"You that fucking yellah nigger that killed my brother!" I bellowed, rushing towards Jerome. I grabbed him up off the ground and dragged him away from them. "You nigger, coon-ass murderer. I oughta-" I commenced to choking him, wrapping my arm around his throat. He didn't resist me. He didn't even try to free himself. He just sagged in my arms like a heavy rucksack. Somewhere deep inside of the shell of a man that I gripped, maybe Jerome hoped that I would strangle the life right out of him- but I had no intention of killing Jerome. I was simply creating a diversion and holding him pressed against my chest, but he didn't seem to care at all. I shook him with my forearm tight to his throat, but he could not be roused. He was in a catatonic state of shock. I screamed curses at him– calling him every name for anything other than a child of God.

My plan worked. My sudden attack on Jerome stunned Moses and Stacks. They stood quickly and collected themselves. My eyes darted from each one of them as I held Jerome in front of me; more as a defense than a *threat- but they didn't know that. They looked helpless. I knew then that they were more afraid of me, than I was of them. They didn't even try to help Jerome on their own. They ran to go and get Perez instead. Their taps on the glass finally woke the officer from his sleep and he came to open the recreation yard.*

A whole lot of chaos later, I wound up pepper-sprayed, tased, handcuffed and thrown into solitary. No one was interested in my side of the story because- of course, I am the "crazy guy". My name was dragged through the mud and all over a damn nigger. After the rape, Jerome was catatonic and unable to speak for weeks. It took about forty stitches and maybe a few staples to sew him back up. Them baboons said that I was the one who sodomized Jerome- which made me out to be both a nigger lover and a faggot.

I'm sure that once I get out of solitary confinement, my Aryan brothers will want to have me killed for what I have done to our reputation. But I am far more disappointed in myself than they could ever be of me. It would be very commendable of me to believe that I had done something noble by "rescuing" Jerome, but I can't subscribe to that. Truth be told, I wish I had a strong enough constitution to just let those hyenas devour themselves the way they are bound to do when left to their own devices. If you deliver one duckling nigger from the mouth of an alligator nigger, then rest assured he will turn around and be consumed by a falcon nigger, if he doesn't ruin himself first. That's just the nature of coons. They are the most self-destructive race on the planet. That is why I can't respect or even tolerate them.

My father was right. I'm glad he raised me up to know the ways of the world, before I was ever exposed to them. I used to wonder why he disliked Blacks and coloreds, but now I understand. They are easy to hate because they first hate themselves. I even distinguish them African-Americans from the ignorant Blacks. At least the Africans got some culture and they seem to value education and entrepreneurship; not like these jungle monkeys they spawn over here in the United States. Black Americans are a waste of space and oxygen if you ask me.

My daddy, Donovan Jasper Coggins, was a pretty wise man. He grew up in the South, down in Georgia. He was a member of the illustrious Ku Klux Klan. It's not as bad as it sounds. The organization has gotten a bad reputation from the misleading propaganda of nigger lovers. My father didn't hate Blacks. He just believed that in order to protect the integrity of the White race from the infectious Blackness of the niggers' self-hatred, the races needed to remain separate. He was all for Blacks having equal rights, he just didn't want their rights (primarily to destroy themselves) to impede on the rights and safety of Whites.

My father grew up as what some may call poor, White trash. After my grandfather died, he was raised up with his four brothers and two sisters by my grandmother in a low-income housing project. My father recounted to me, time and time again, stories of intimidation and violence, theft, extortion and moral debauchery- the likes of which I could never have imagined at the time. He would lament to no end about the woes he and my family suffered at the hands of those jungle monkeys. My father didn't develop his disdain for coons out of fear or ignorance. He knew all too well, through firsthand accounts, just what carnage and desolation those spooks were capable of.

"Shelton," my father would address me while we worked on the family pickup truck. "It ain't no profit in gettin' mixed up wit' niggers. They ain't good for nothin' but bringin' people to ruin. I useta' watch 'em... sittin' out on their porches all day long 'til way after the sun went down. They wouldn't do nothin', not even move a muscle. They'd just sit there, talkin' and gossipin', whoopin' and hollerin' all loud. When they weren't laughin', they was fightin'–always fightin' 'bout somethin'. All the time competin' and fightin'. Fightin' over property that didn't belong to none of 'em. Fightin' over possessions. Stealin' from one another and then sellin' it right back to the same people they stole it from. Couldn't none of 'em get ahead because they were all too selfish and too jealous of each other, couldn't never work together for nothing." He'd shake his head and wipe sweat from his brow. "They wouldn't work.. wouldn't even watch over their own children. Just let 'em run around like wild animals out in the *street from sun up to sun down. You couldn't even tell which ones belonged to who. Half of 'em had the same daddies but didn't nobody know where they were. Most of the fathers were in jail or headed there. I ain't never seen nothin' like it in all my life," my daddy would drawl on. "If you ever wanna' have somethin' and be somebody in this world, you have to stay just as far away from them niggers as you possibly can. I know this coon-loving government done gave them criminals access to just about everythin' that the White man done tried to preserve, but you can still manage to carve out just a little piece of the American pie for yo'self so long as you keep yo'self undefiled."*

"Don't let them bleedin' heart progressives brainwash you," he would command with intensity. "Don't let 'em try to convince you that acceptin' them baboons is the way to peace. Cause I assure you that it is not. Niggers will always destroy. Aggression and violence is all those people know. Them same soft-hearted, nigger-loving White men built 'em beautiful brick housing, and planted flowers for 'em, even put up parks for their children. They let 'em live in the place for free. Within a few years, the niggers ran it down- turned it into slums. They broke out the windows and covered 'em with trash bags. They tagged the walls with graffiti, claimin' allegiance to the same groups that made their communities live in fear. Instead of takin' the few steps it took to go inside the house, the nigger men just pissed on the sides of the walls in plain sight."

My father's eyes would narrow and he'd produce a determined pout. "No, that just won't do. I took this mill job and moved us up north to Philadelphia because I wanted my family to have a better life. I work hard to keep y'all up in this White neighborhood, so that you could grow up without fear. This is all the protection that we got– to stay separate and keep our race pure. You see son, that's what the niggers want," his voice would rise, as he threw up his hands. "That's what all that civil rights, integration bull-snot was about. They want to infiltrate the White race, intermix with us and create a new race of brown people. Then they can dominate the White race and enslave people like you and me 'cause they're still bitter about slavery. Everything that our forefathers fought for will be lost and America will be plunged into darkness. Niggers are simpleminded– just a cruel, compassionless people. You only need to look at how they treat each other to know what kind of leaders they would make. This country will never survive if the Black man is allowed to take control."

My father gripped the back of my neck and commanded my eyes to meet his. "We got to keep our White race pure and stay separate from them niggers."

I loved my father and I would have done anything to make him happy. I saw the way he worked so hard and sacrificed so much for me and my two younger sisters. My mother passed away in childbirth with my youngest sister when I was five. My father was all I had and his love meant the world to me. As soon as I was old enough to take a job and help him out, I started working after school at a local pizza joint. Things were going fine in the Coggins' house until my senior year of high school.

I was dating a gorgeous, blonde cheerleader named Ajae Burgess. We went to a private school. Our high school catered to a special program for the academically gifted and therefore was predominantly comprised of White students. I was never all that vocal about my White supremacist views, but I didn't feel that I had to be. I surrounded myself with strong-minded, proud White friends. They were a good support to me and we spurred each other on to excellence in our endeavors just the way that my father always said it would be if I kept clear of nigger influence. Ajae was somewhat feisty and outspoken, even negative at times. I guess I should have known that she was different from the rest of us, but I didn't want to see it. She was beautiful and seductive. She had me hooked from the day I gave my virginity to her. When I ran my fingers through her soft, silky blonde hair and looked into her green eyes all I could imagine was pure, White blood flowing through her veins.

As I said before, there were very few black students at the school. So few you could count on your hands how many attended. Most of those affirmative action kids were there on scholarships just to keep the nigger-lovers happy. Some of the alumni would sponsor a few ghetto children and send them to our prestigious school to "give them a chance" at an exceptional education that may not have been afforded to them because of socio-economic circumstances beyond their control. The audacity of those White traitors is astounding to me at times. They build up the Blacks and immigrants to take educational and professional opportunities away from hard-working White Americans. Then, when they fall short of expectations, the progressives turn back to blaming their environment and upbringing for their lack of success, instead of admitting to the truth- that investing in the Negro is a waste of time, money and energy. The niggers and immigrants receive a string of never ending handouts and never evolve beyond the degradation of their race. They profit off the exploitation of each other. One only needs to examine their media to see how they objectify and insult one another. Even the few coons who do manage to transcend the normal plight of their people will soon separate themselves in order to preserve their success. They may give back to their community, but you will never catch them living or intermingling there because they know (as do most Whites) that consorting with niggers will bring them to ruin.

Those Black students infested our school like vermin. Luckily our high school had a uniform dress code so they couldn't wear their baggy hip-hop clothes and expose all their body parts like the pimps and hoes that they glorify in their music. After a while, they got so comfortable they started to forget that they were just visitors in our high school and started treating it like it was their own. They even started a Minorities organization on campus that was open to any and every one- except White males, as if that was fair. The high school would never have sponsored a club that only catered to Whites (I know because I tried running that past the student advisory board). Then I saw their plan unfold, just what my father always talked about. Those Black students got everybody from the Jews to the Asians and even the White girls on their side by telling them that they were an oppressed minority being held back by the tyranny of White men. Next thing you know, all of the nigger boys at the school had White girlfriends; a sight that drove me to rage every time I witnessed them together.

One day within the security of a group of my White friends and confidants, I gave voice to my frustrations. Without warning, Ajae- my own girlfriend cold-cocked me right in the face. I should have known at *that point that she had that damn jungle monkey blood in her by her capacity for violence. She knocked out my front tooth and almost scratched my eyes out before I could get free from her. Whether I knew then or not that she was half-baboon, the truth was revealed when our parents were summoned to a conference before our expulsion.*

Ajae's mother was a darky. I mean a real tar baby. I couldn't believe it. There was just no way in my mind. How could she be her mother when Ajae was so clearly white? My first thought was maybe she was adopted, but Mrs. Burgess made it clear in no uncertain terms that Ajae was her biological child. My father went ballistic following the conference. He called me every name that could be derived for a child forsaken by God. He accosted me for bringing that nigger bitch into his home. My father had been approving of my relationship with Ajae until that day; but somehow he blamed me for the biggest act of disobedience that any one of his children could commit. He treated me as though I knew she was Black and had willfully disgraced our family with her. I begged my father's forgiveness and pledge undying allegiance to him and our separatist lifestyle, but all to no avail. He disowned me- just threw me out of our home with only the clothes I could carry in one duffle bag.

I was already eighteen so there wasn't anything that could be done to force my father to allow me back into his home. I lived in a shelter and manage to finish a GED program, but I sat idly by and watched as every one of those Black students got full scholarships to well-esteemed colleges, while my White friends had to take out huge loans to pay for their education. My anger was fueled and pooled against niggers. I held them responsible for the loss of everything that I held dear to me. I didn't even have to worry about college or anything else for that matter. My father had cut me off completely and refused to even answer letters or phone calls from me.

Soon I found myself headed down south. My grandmother in Georgia agreed to let me come and live with her. I wasn't excited about the prospect because (despite its history) the south is much less segregated than the north, so she lived in a neighborhood with lots of Blacks, but I didn't have much of a choice... or so I thought.

I got held up and robbed by some vagrants at the bus depot in Charlotte, before I could purchase my transfer. I had never been so afraid in my life. Those niggers attacked me like a disorganized band of wild animals. Never had I been exposed to people so devoid of civilization. I feared those gorillas would take my life, but luckily all they took was my money. I was stranded in a city that I had never even heard of.

I made a phone call from the police station and my grandmother assured me that she would send some money and buy me a new ticket down to Georgia. Then, as if I was conceived out of bad luck and birthed under a blood moon, my grandmother passed in her sleep that very same night.

I was referred to a shelter after a few days passed. I tried to call my father but he wouldn't even come to the phone and he forbade my sisters to speak to me. I was desperate and destitute. I hadn't eaten in days. I had no clothes and nowhere to sleep. The men's shelter was not so bad when I considered the alternative... or so I thought.

The staff seemed despondently jaded, but all and all, most of the men in the shelter were so depressed and/or drug-addicted that they didn't even care who was coming and going. I was there a few weeks when a predatory gang of niggers organized and began to terrorize the dormitory. As usual they seemed more set on intimidating and harassing their own kind, so I thought I was safe. I had just secured a job and was hoping to move out of the shelter soon. However, just like locusts, when the baboons got done shaking down their own kind for everything they could possibly extort from them, they decided to move on to the other ethnic groups. They tried preying on the wetbacks, but them Mexicans stick together and they outnumbered the niggers; a fact which kept them protected from being ransacked by them thieving jiggaboos.

I was never very athletic in school. I have always been a very tall, bird-framed young man. My father raised me up to compete with my brain, not my brawn. My father told me that the true strength of a man lies in his ability to reason and not his physical prowess. It didn't take very long for the niggers to figure out that it was easier to pillage the White residents than any of the other ethnic groups. We didn't have the Mexicans numbers and we didn't have the niggers' brute aggression.

The bullying came to a head for me when this big gorilla-looking nigger all but threatened me for my watch. The watch was a gift from my father given to him by my grandfather. There was no way I was giving it up without a fight.

And fight is just what I did. I was holding my own until I slipped up and called the jerk a "nigger". Next thing I knew all those same Blacks, who previously couldn't stand each other, banded together like they were marching on Selma. I was hospitalized for almost three days following the beating.

Needless to say, I lost that job before I ever even had the chance to start. I'd had just about enough of niggers pushing me around and taking everything that was good away from me. I didn't go back to the shelter after they discharged me from the hospital. It was still summertime, so walking the streets wasn't quite so bad yet. It was then that I met Jackson.

Jackson was an addict, so he couldn't keep the stringent rules of the Men's Shelter. We started panhandling on the streets during the day. Occasionally we would get enough money to eat and to get a room for a couple of days. Other times we would spend the night in a little tent community of vagrants who slept beneath an overpass. It was astonishing to see that whole other way of life. My father had sheltered me from so much. I counted my blessings and prayed every day to one day be united with my family. In the meantime, Jackson and I became good friends and made our happiness while sharing as many laughs as we could. He needed me to monitor all of his money for him. If left to himself, he would smoke it all up and have nothing to eat for days. He didn't need a bed. He didn't need a meal. He didn't need a woman. Hell, he didn't even need a friend. All Jackson needed was an escape and any drug he could drink, inject, ingest or inhale would do the trick. He was hopeless in some ways I guess, but we were all we had in those days.

Jackson and I were vulnerable to our environment. I didn't feel safe on the streets of the city with so many unemployed Blacks walking around. So I started carrying a gun. I was able to procure one from an addict who all but gave it me so he could get enough money for his next high. I never considered myself a violent man. I hoped that I would never have to pull, let alone discharge the gun.

But as the dog days of summer dragged on into an unseasonably cool fall, my discontentment grew. I didn't even want to apply for employment because I had no interview clothes. Most days I wreaked because I had nowhere to shower. I could barely even get a job when I had a bath so I knew my chances of changing my situation would be slim to none. I grew weary of begging on the streets all day long and still not having enough to thrive above the most basic survival. Then one day, I finally found my element. I became acquainted with a group of Neo-Nazi skinheads. They took me into their fold when I shared with them my mutual disdain for the parasitic immigrants and negroes that are draining the American economy.

But the Aryan brothers were a lot different from the Klan members that I grew up with. They were not peaceable at all. They considered themselves to be soldiers preparing for an inevitable race war. They didn't believe that Blacks, Browns Muslims and Jews had to be separated from Whites. They believed that they should be eliminated from the planet. The guys I met were willing to set Jackson and me up in a house with some members of the brotherhood. But for some strange reason, Jackson was opposed to their help. I couldn't understand why. I secretly hoped that he wasn't a nigger lover. We never had the conversation, but what could he benefit from holding on to some politically-correct propaganda. It wasn't like a nigger had ever given him a place to live or tried to help him out. I couldn't let Jackson's prejudice keep me from having somewhere to sleep, so I moved in with the Aryans. I would still check on Jackson periodically and bring him whatever reinforcements I could, as fall began to turn bitterly cold.

I could tell you what happened that night, but it would only be a part of the whole story. Besides I don't even remember it clearly anymore. The details have been counted and recounted to me so many times in so many different ways that it's broken up into little puzzle pieces in my mind. I know that I had been around panhandling with Jackson because I needed

some extra money that I didn't want to have to depend on my Aryan
brothers for. Everything after that begins to move in slow motion every
time I think about it.

It was getting dark... Jackson and I were about to call it a fruitless day,
when he ran into a big, tall, slave-looking Negro who I could only take for
a friend of his because they walked off together. I guess I should have just
left it alone and went back to the place where I was staying, but I decided
instead to follow them. Jackson reasoned with the man for what seemed
like hours. When I couldn't take his groveling anymore, I approached the
pair of them. I was brimming to the top with animosity for Blacks. I had
reached my boiling point without even knowing it until I was face-to-face
with a man whom Jackson introduced but whose name didn't become
burned into my frontal lobe until after hearing it over several dozen times
at my indictment hearing- **Courtney Ulysses Turnage Jr.**

The way he reduced Jackson to begging and groveling at his big, Black
feet sent me over the edge. He was a young man, yet he had no respect for
this man who was White, as well as being his elder. I don't actually
remember pulling the gun out, but I do recall thinking that I would just
scare the boy with it.

It was stupid I guess, but I just wanted to put the fear into a nigger that
I had felt all my life. I wanted him to feel as powerless and afraid as I did.
For once I wanted to stand in front of a Black man and hone my
superiority over him; to feel that power in my hands. It was the best high I
ever experienced in my life. As I watched his lips begin to quiver with
panic, I reeled with pleasure- so much so that the discharge was
completely accidental. When Jackson began to struggle with me over the
gun, I pulled the trigger as a natural defense mechanism.

I can honestly say that I didn't intend to kill anybody that day, but for a
minute... just a short minute- as I watched the big, Black man lay on the
ground gasping for breath, I was proud of what I did. But then, when I saw
the blood, the dark purple blood, begin to gush out of the hole in his chest,
it captured all of my attention and drew me into its ebb, as it spread across
his shirt in a shifting pattern. It was then that he became human to me; no
longer the vicious, obstinate symbol of my oppression, as I had been

conditioned to believe. There he lay, bleeding just as he would if he were a White man. It was then that the transfer took place.

Courtney became the helpless, defenseless dying man and I became the monster. I became the inhuman, stoic image of his demise. I could hear the chanting voices of the Aryan brothers, who no doubt would have cheered victoriously for me had they been present. When I stared down at him, I saw myself reflected in the Black pools of his dilating pupils. What I saw in them terrified me beyond all reason. I heard my father's warning in my head.

"Beware their influence... Remain undefiled."

I realized then that I was not a morally and racially superior White man anymore. I had succumbed to the very same black plague of hatred and rage, which brands the degenerates that I detest. I took my life and threw it in a trash can, all so I could put a small, smoking hole in a Black man's chest. I had allowed myself to be infected with the angry, self-destructive disease of depravity. I had become the very thing I feared the most.

I had become... a nigger.

"Cross over children. All are welcome. All welcome. Go into the Light. There is peace and serenity in the Light."

- Tangina, "Poltergeist" (1982)

CHAPTER TWENTY-ONE

If Shelton thought that he would face hell when he was released from the solitary confinement unit, then he had no idea what torturous fate was truly awaiting him. Shelton had only been at the County Jail on a writ. His murder case was being reviewed for a possible appeal; but after the whole ordeal with Jerome, it was decided that he should be returned back to the Black Creek Correctional Facility.

That fact, in and of itself, didn't necessarily bother him. He had called Black Creek home for quite a few years and was actually glad to return to the normalcy of its more restrictive environment. County Jail had been like a barbarous jungle for Shelton.

He instantly noticed that he was not reassigned back to the same unit he was previously housed in before his transfer to County. Shelton was a little apprehensive because in prison one must have associates- a gang even, in order to be protected within the pecking order. He had forged a reputation (which he prayed remained intact) with the Aryan brothers in his dormitory. In this new environment, he couldn't be assured of any allies. The Neo-Nazis had a loose communication framework throughout all of the housing units, but Shelton needed to be in contact with his closest confidants to guarantee that the travesty with Jerome hadn't cost him his alliances.

Shelton realized as he was lead to his new cell that his concerns were only half of his predicament. He wanted to go running from the dormitory when he was introduced to his new bunk mate- a man that the guard announced as Kirkpatrick, but who re-introduced himself as "Pretty Nicky", no sooner than the guard disappeared.

"My real name is Dominic," he expounds, as if the explanation is necessary. "But don't nobody 'round here call me that." He beams with a slight twist in his neck. "What can I call you?"

217

Shelton is hesitant to even dignify his question with a response. "Don't call me nothing at all," he states, letting the disdain show on his face. "Just pretend I'm not even here."

"Ooo, what's done crawled up in yo' draws." Nicky snaps. "Look, there's been peace on this block and peace in this cell, so you need not think that I'm gone put up wit' no mess in here." Nicky delivers his address with mother-like intonation.

Shelton eyes him suspiciously, sickened by his feminine mannerisms. Dominic didn't have a slight, petite frame like most gays that Shelton met. His medium, athletic build would never have given any indication of his homosexual nature. He has a smooth, clean-shaven chestnut complexion with large bright, brown eyes and long intricately-braided cornrows. Nicky's fists rest on his hips, which are cocked to one side, and his head continues to swivel on his neck like a snake that is being charmed. Shelton turns his back away from him, fearing that he may turn into stone if he continues to look on Dominic Kirkpatrick.

"You ain't got to worry about me," Shelton insists, huffing out the words lowly. "I don't want no trouble with you and won't be here long enough to cause none."

"Whatever then," Nicky smirks.

Shelton fumbles his navy blue property bag around in his hands, dreading the question that he must pose to Nicky.

"Top or bottom?"

"Since I'm so gracious. I made up both beds with new sheets. You can pick whichever one you want and I'll adjust." His tone borders just between genuine and facetious, but his expression remains unchanged. "If you will excuse me then," Nicky begins courteously, glancing into the plastic mirror mounted on the wall. He quickly arranges his braids around his shoulders and pinches his cheeks. "I have a date, but you can just make yourself at home and I will see you later on." He breezes past Shelton with long, graceful gazelle-like strides, switching his hips from side to side in a walk that is so seductive, it draws Shelton's eyes against his will.

god face

"No man has ever been born a Negro hater, a Jew hater, or any other kind of hater. Nature refuses to be involved in such suicidal practices."

~ Harry Bridges

CHAPTER TWENTY-TWO

They came for me in the middle of the day, right after chow time.

It's such a small thing sometimes; just appreciating what you have at the time you have it. Being in the County Jail for so many months had caused me to forget what it felt like to sit in the sun. To feel the rays on my skin and know that I still belonged to the living, despite the fact that I had been exiled from the general public. Here at Black Creek, they actually have large, spacious, green yards- places where a man can still experience the privilege of being made to feel like he is free, even though he is still only just a rat in a cage.

People always talk about Karma, like she's a person you can know personally, and always in a negative connotation- like every time she shows up it's a bad scene. Karma is this revenge-seeking, super-bitch, Anti-Santa Claus who knows your bad deeds and spends her existence planning to pay you back for every single one. Well, I'd like to think of Karma as a loving mother, part-discipline, part-guidance; a careful hand molding you for your destiny. I believe Karma keeps just as detailed an account of all the good deeds you do as well... She just has too or there is no justice in her; no truth or righteousness in her commission... She is little more than a cantankerous street thug- a bomb-wielding jihadist terrorist, if there are no good acts for her to requite with the same veracity as the bad. What motivation or merit can there be for those who have been visited by Karma to change- to repent even, if all there is to her is revenge and dismay?

Karma, she changed my life- saved my life that day; in more ways than one...

The day is still pretty much a blur, but if anything good came out of it- it changed me... or at least it was the day that solidified the change that had already began in me...

I remember so little about that day. My understanding is that some of the Aryan brotherhood heard I was back at Black Creek and waited inside my cell to ambush me when I came in from recreation.

They pulled a makeshift pillowcase over my face and tied a belt around my neck. They pummeled my body mercilessly. I was beaten and punished by what felt like a million assailants but turned out to be only two... Just when the pain began to disappear and I felt myself slipping from the ledge of consciousness, I was dropped to the floor. I was totally oblivious to what force had caused the pillage to cease, but it began to create a whole new struggle in the room somewhere on the left side of my body.

I could hear the feet shuffling. Yelps and bellows came from somewhere far away in a great distance vaster than the cell could have been; but I was grateful for the space of time when the ringing in my ears and pulsing electric vibrations washed over my body, taking up residence where the fists had once been. The next sensation I vaguely recall was being grabbed and handled forcefully. My stomach dropped and my bladder released at the thought of being hit again. The hot urine ran down the pants leg of my brown jumpsuit. I prayed to pass out but instead the hands hoisted me up and began to carry me. I could feel the care and concern coming from the hands that held me. My body felt weightless and the relief of the moment overwhelmed me to the point of being overtaken by that peaceful black oblivion for which I had just previously prayed.

god face

"I miss your faces. They remind me of God."

- Cleveland Heep, "Lady in the Water" (2006)

CHAPTER TWENTY-THREE

Before the sun rose on the next day, Shelton could already tell that something had changed.

Not anything that could be seen or touched- but something on the inside of him had- shifted. At first, there was just an empty place; a hole left in his heart where the hatred had resided. He never knew until then that he had been hating with his whole heart. He was consumed- infected, infested with it; a hatred as deep, if not deeper, than love. The line between the two so thin, that it could be erased, removed even, and not disturb the conscious; not even be missed.

Somewhere a seed had been planted. Shelton could feel the shell breaking and tender green petals of repentance beginning to emerge. He closed his eyes to whisper a silent prayer, thankful for the opportunity to know something... anything other than hate in his heart and when he opened his eyes, it was the next morning. Shelton woke in the infirmary. Dominic sat at his bedside reading aloud, an article in a Black Hair magazine about how to get the perfect doobie wrap. After listening for some time, trying to figure out when the marijuana and rolling papers would come in, Shelton finally interrupted him.

"Hey, what are you doing here?"

"Well now," his face wrinkles up in frown. "Is that anyway to talk to someone who saved your life?" He widened his eyes and clutched the chest of his jumpsuit dramatically.

"I apologize... what I meant is why are you here?"

"I'm here to check up on you. You are still my cellmate after all," he answers matter-of-factly, returning his eyes to the magazine. Dominick is a sullen, straight-faced man who has grown accustomed to keeping his true feelings and emotions hidden. For all of his flamboyance, his stoic visage never betrays his heart. "They say you are supposed to read to people in comas to keep their brains stimulated."

"I am not in a coma."

"Yeah well *your* brain could still use some stimulation," Nicky hisses through pursed lips.

Shelton surveys Dominic's face. He sees a long, thin laceration over his left eye that will never fully heal back the way it was before even with the sloppy prison stitches. A few dark bruises on his face and a busted lip told the story that Dominic's voice wouldn't repeat.

Perceiving the question in Shelton's expression, Nicky answers "They would've killed you... You would have been murdered right there in that cell, if we hadn't helped you."

"The Aryans aren't my brothers anymore-"

"Look I already know what you are all about, so I don't need any explanations from you just because you're feeling guilty about your hate crimes now. It's blood-in-blood-out with those crazies, so don't think you can just change your mind about being down now."

"I just can't understand why someone like you would help someone like me," Shelton replies half-ashamed, half-astonished.

Nicky's eyes narrow but his face remains unchanged. "I'm not sure what you mean by someone like me, but all you need to know and understand is that I am **not** like you and that turned out to be a blessing in disguise." Dominic closes the pages of the magazine. His features become dark and stoic. "Everyone has made their own share of mistakes, so my job is to love- not judge, honey."

"But how can you love?"

"The same way you hate... With the same veracity and passion that you hate people you don't know or understand," he paused for effect. "How do you hate for no real reason?... Don't you know that both are just two sides of the same coin? Why do I have to know you or agree with you or understand you to love you? Can't I just as easily hate you for the very same reasons? People like you believe you are brave because you have the audacity to hate."

Shelton's eyes drop to the floor. The words are like raindrops on his heart. A hot sting burns his face and he instantly becomes angry.

Why had he never heard these words before?

How had he lived so many years and never been told this?

He became ashamed of all of those whom he had called *brothers*. He began to understand that he had never been surrounded by people who actually loved him. He had always determined that hate was stronger than love because hate didn't make you weak; it didn't make you vulnerable. Now, he realized that people bonded together by a mutual hate for others didn't necessarily *love* each other. *How could people bonded by hate possibly love one another, if they didn't even really know what love was?* He was pondering this thought and thinking of his father, when Dominic interrupts his meditation.

"It takes courage to love," he said benignly, as mildly as one might comment on the weather. "Hatred is cowardly because it preys on people's weaknesses instead of their strengths. Weak people love hatred. There is no power in hate because it takes ignorance and fear to thrive."

Shelton's face began to warm with embarrassment. He couldn't explore his feelings about what Dominic said too far because of the dull ache at the base of his head and the throbbing pain of the rushing blood coursing through his bruised face.

"It's a good thing that we'll never know what your *brothers* would have done to you had Roderico and I not intervened."

The weight of the words and the exhaustion of healing overtake Shelton's mind and body, sending him into a light, fretful sleep like a ship drifting on dark, choppy waters.

And He said, you cannot see my face: for there shall no man see Me, and live.

- God, Exodus 33:20

CHAPTER TWENTY-FOUR

"This is the last picture I have of my son, C.J." Courtney says in a quiet voice that quivers with the immensity of his restraint.

"He was nineteen years old in this photo; but if he were here today, he would be thirty-five." His eyes moisten with giant tears which form, but only hover on the rim of his lower lids.

The six stern faces- four White females and two White males- which comprise the Parole board, stare out at Courtney Sr. with expressionless, unblinking countenances.

"My son, C.J. wanted to be an astronaut and I believe that he damn well could have done it... but maybe not though." Courtney shrugs his broad shoulders and scratches his almost completely gray beard. "Maybe he would have been a mechanic like me. He may well even have been an athlete; but whatever he would have been, I would have been proud of my son." A lone tear streams down the man's weary face. "I loved my son very much. His mother could not bear to come and face the man who took our C.J. away from us, but to be absent from this hearing was a luxury I could not afford. I had to come today, because I need this board to understand how much grief our family is continuing to suffer because of Shelton Coggins's actions." He points to the grim-faced man seated to his left in chains and shackles. "I need you to know that he should never be set free." Courtney sliced the air with his hand before bringing it back to rest at his side.

An uncomfortable commotion begins in the small room, as a few of the board members adjust in their chairs. "My son didn't get a second chance at life; so therefore, I don't think Shelton Coggins should either. You have made long lists of all the good deeds he has done to prove that he is rehabilitated." Mr. Turnage offers a faint sarcastic grunt. "But C.J.'s accomplishments, even in his short nineteen years of life, would eclipse that list twice and he never killed anybody. C.J. did what was right, just because it was the right thing to do- not because his freedom was riding on it. People say that C.J. didn't deserve to die, but I say Shelton Coggins doesn't deserve to live," Courtney issues, his voice dropping to a sinister, baritone hiss. "But that wasn't my decision. A jury decided that he could keep his life. Still- if there is any mercy... any justice in your hearts, please don't let him have his freedom back too," Courtney begs. An expression of sheer helplessness covers his face, erasing all traces of the reserved, self-assured countenance which preceded it.

"Sometimes I have nightmares," Courtney confesses meekly. "I see his face," he whispers through a sob, as he glares over at Shelton. "It's me he shoots down in cold blood. I'm the target in the sights of his gun. He squeezes the trigger and mows me down like a stray dog in the street. I can feel the gunshot and even the blood leaking out of my chest. Sometimes the vision is so real- so clear that I wake up gasping for breath and soaking in sweat."

The clarity returns to his eyes and he utters calmly and presently. "Shelton Coggins is not a man. He's a murderous monster. He's an animal. I'm not even sure if he can be considered a child of God. To loose this **bane**- this **scourge** on the population, would be a grave mistake. An anathema like Shelton Coggins needs to be eradicated and eliminated from society."

Courtney Turnage concludes his soliloquy with the most compelling and persuasive words he could find. He spent the entire week prior to the hearing, searching the dictionary for just the right words to convey his emotions. Words he hoped the Parole Board would hear and be dissuaded from releasing the man who executed his defenseless son for no other reason than being born in Black skin.

Precious Lord... Take my hand

Earlier that morning, Courtney prepared himself for the day that would most likely be his last on earth. He took meticulous care to dress impeccably.

Lead me on...

His hair and beard were neatly cut and he took time to trim the stray hairs which protruded from his nose and ears. Courtney put on a crisp, white undershirt and clean, white briefs. He slid his arms into a gray dress shirt that had been pressed to perfection and his legs into tan slacks, which donned creases so sharp, he could have sliced cheese on them.

Let me stand

Courtney chose a mustard colored sweater and a navy sports jacket, which he painstakingly groomed with a lint brush to ensure that not even microscopic lint or fuzz would be found on his clothes. He cleaned and clipped his fingernails, buffing them to a smooth, glossy white finish, and then checked his teeth for any stray food particles. Courtney Sr. stood tall in the bathroom mirror and stared at a face that had belonged to his ancestors, his father and his son. A face he had hoped would continue on eternally, but would now end with him.

Precious Lord, linger near...

Courtney knelt down at his bedside, bowed his head and clasped his large, Black hands in prayer.

Hear my cry, hear my call

When he rose to stand up from the floor, his right knee (which had a metal replacement) refused to comply; so he took extra care gaining his balance. His first few steps were unsteady. The knee- for all of its pins and aluminum alloy could not replace the original. It would always be inferior and resist the natural range of motion that the knee was created to fulfill.

Hold my hand, lest I fall

231

Courtney carefully double-stepped his way down the staircase, walked through the foyer towards the den, and then across the room to the closet at the back. He reached up on the top shelf to retrieve a box. The contents of which, he purchased several months ago, but never intended to use. Today, however, on the last day of his life, he opened that box.

Courtney's mind returns to the hearing and to the matter at hand, when he hears Shelton's voice filtering through the room.

"Mr. Turnage is right," he begins. "I don't deserve to be set free. Sixteen years inside these walls is not even as long as Courtney Jr. was alive. I was given twenty-five years to life and I intend to fulfill that sentence," Shelton utters with finality. His hands are cuffed together and chained to his waist, so it takes several attempts to push the long brown and gray hair behind his ear. His thin, wiry face seems much too small for his large, thoughtful brown eyes. He stands before the Parole Board looking more like a martyr- like Jesus incarnate, than a murderer. His shoulders stooped under the weight of an invisible boulder the approximate size and shape of the world.

"I have come to realize that only a monster, only someone devoid of human compassion, can take a life the way that I did. I don't think there's anything that I could ever do to balance that scale again." Shelton's eyebrows knit with contrition. He has lost another tooth, this one is on the right side of the one he lost in high school. He wears the permanent scar that begins above his left ear and then treks a ragged path across his left cheek to his upper lip; just a friendly keepsake from the Aryans. Still- there is something so alluring about him; an internal smile, a meekness that has softened his countenance. No longer the menacing glare, he donned in the years his heart was filled with malice. He lifts his eyes to look at the Parole Board, comprised completely of his *peers*. Each lily, White face staring back at him. The light in his once black, now golden brown, eyes isn't a reflection from the fluorescent bulbs in the room, instead it radiates from inside of his spirit. He has finally found the love. He has found the *life*. Shelton is not wandering anymore... He is not lost. He is free. Inside or

232

outside of the walls, Shelton has been made free and nothing the Parole Board says will change that.

Precious Lord...

Earlier that morning, before the sun rose, Shelton knelt down on the concrete floor, bowed his head and clasped his hands together on his bunk.

Take my hand...

He prayed to the same God as Courtney Sr. The same God, whose forgiveness he entreated Jerome to seek in his final days. Shelton bowed his head this day, same as he had done three years ago when he held Jerome's hands, covered with dark purple legions. Shelton taught Jerome the Lord's prayer in the chapel at Black Creek shortly before they sent him to the AIDS ward in the county hospital. Shelton had kissed those same hands and cried tears of joy with his condemned friend, when he too received that life. The life, which assured him as he watched them wheel Jerome out on the gurney, that he would see his friend again one day.

Lead me on...

Shelton had attended four parole hearings; each with the same result. He had come there that afternoon, with no expectations. Truth be told, it was within those walls that Shelton received his pardon from an existence, which would have consumed him and left nothing but a smoking Black hole; a life that was smothering him more and more each day. Now his life would matter- it would count. If he had never come there, Shelton was certain that he would have been an uncelebrated stain; a villain and an assassin in the great span of time. His life would have been ashes scattered on the ocean, a dandelion blown by the wind. But Shelton could never be lost now, never so insignificant that he would need to hide behind a gun ever again.

Hear my cry, hear my call

Shelton had found the life.

The Parole Board whispers lowly, tapping their pens and passing papers. Their eyes dart from Shelton to Courtney and then back down to the table, as they discuss the matter in hushed voices. The large, White man with dark eyes and a thick black moustache stands up from the table.

"Shelton Coggins, please rise."

Shelton labors to get up from his seat. His leg irons and waist chains clink loudly.

"Ladies and gentleman of the Parole Board, what say you in the matter of Shelton Owen Coggins?"

The first to speak is a middle-aged, blonde female who avoids Courtney's eyes. "Parole," she answers softly, folding large masculine hands with press-on nails on the table. The board members each take their turn offering a verdict.

"Parole," says the young redhead hiding the needle marks on her wrists under the cuffs of her pink floral sweater.

"Deny" replies the thin, fair White man with the telltale bulbous nose and flushed, rosy skin of an alcoholic.

"Parole," answers the older, round White female with blue-gray hair and a gravelly smoker's voice which doesn't yet denote the cancer in her left lung.

"Deny," peeps the squirrely raven-haired woman with thick, black-rimmed glasses that only partially obscure the dark blue bruise and untreated hyphema in her right eye.

"Parole," says the man with the dark steady eyes, who proudly flies a Confederate flag from his truck and has invisible gunshot residue on his hands. "This board finds just cause that Shelton Coggins should be released- under supervision, from the custody of the North Carolina Department of Corrections-"

Guide my feet

Courtney stands up from his seat... this time his knee doesn't fail.

Hold my hand

Courtney retrieves the small .38 special from the place behind his knee where he had secured it. It feels so much heavier than it should in his hand, as he lifts it to aim. When he catches Shelton in his sights, Courtney prays that he doesn't miss.

When the darkness appears

The loud rattling of Shelton's shackles, as he shakes the hands of each Parole board member, is distraction enough. No hears the sound of the hammer cocking back. It is the first shot, followed quickly by the second- which finally rouses the room. Both shots hit their intended target, peeling back the skin and splitting the flesh of Shelton's face wide open. His head bobs and swivels, as he falls to the ground, leaving little doubt that his life has escaped from his body through the two tiny, Black holes near his temple.

Lead me home...

Courtney turns the gun on himself, pressing the barrel underneath his chin.

"Don't do it!" The large, White man barks the command pulling his taser from its holster.

"Don't do it, baby." Camille appears in the room in front of him. "He ain't worth it," she coos tenderly. Courtney blinks incredulously, knowing that his wife cannot possibly be there. She is younger than she should be. Her hair is styled in a neat pristine bun and she wears a turquoise dress with a pink, checkered apron. "Don't do it. Put the gun down, C.J."

"What," Courtney replies astonished.

"C.J. put the gun down... **now**!" Camille shrieks with tears in her eyes.

"I'm not C.J." Courtney says, then looks down at his hands to see that they are younger. The flesh of his hands is supple and smooth. Camille begins to transform in front of his eyes. Her hair becomes matted and missing in patches. The skin on her gaunt face become ashen and her dull eyes are sunken. Camille's emaciated frame shivers where she stands.

"Mama," C.J. yelps involuntarily. His voice sounding boyish. A faint drum begins to pound in C.J.'s ears, blending with his own heartbeat. The ancestors arrive with tears in their eyes. Seemingly hundreds of scared, sullen faces, each murmuring faint, indistinct petitions and prayers.

"Run!" Camille shouts over the rush of mighty winds that fill the room.

"What?" C.J. bellows.

"Run son, run!"

"Put down the gun!" the officer yells at him.

"Hunh," C.J. spins around. The officer's service weapon is already drawn on him. The eyes are locked on the target in a menacing glare. The shiny, gold badge gleams in glow of the streetlight. The nameplate underneath states in neat, stoic letters- **S. Coggins**. C.J.'s limbs are frozen, although his body is pumping out hot, prickly sweat.

"Put your gun down, now!" The officer growls more assertively, aiming his sights center mass at the young boy's slender chest.

"What gun?" C.J. says raising his hands from the empty pockets of his navy hoodie. "I don't have a—"

Pow

Lead me... home

god face

god face

ABOUT THE AUTHOR

Devian Nikei is a native of Charlotte, North Carolina. This actress, singer/songwriter, choreographer and entertainer is also an author. She has written the critically-acclaimed book, Safety in Lovers (2011) and fan favorite novel, Just in Case (2015) on her own publishing company Nikei Novels. Her love of writing and literature began on the campus of Fayetteville State University where she wrote competitively earning various awards, accommodations and acknowledgements. She is currently writing and pursuing a B.S in Psychology in her hometown.

Subscribe to her website: www.deviancebydevian.com for upcoming events or email her at contactdevian@deviancebydevian.com Be sure to read other titles by this author.